AS YOU ARE

TAILS X HORNS BOOK 3

SOPHIE O'DARE
LYN FORESTER

AS YOU ARE © copyright 2021 Sophie O'Dare

All rights reserved. No part of this publication may be reproduced, distributed, or transmitted in any form or by any means, including photocopying, recording, or other electronic or mechanical methods, without the prior written permission of the writer, except in the case of brief quotations embodied in critical reviews and certain other noncommercial uses permitted by copyright law.

This is a work of fiction. Names, characters, businesses, places, events and incidents are either the products of the author's imagination or used in a fictitious manner. Any resemblance to actual persons, living or dead, or actual events is purely coincidental.

Cover Design Copyright © 2021 L&L Literary Services, LLC

Book Design Copyright © 2021 L&L Literary Services, LLC

www.llliteraryservices.com

Copy Editing by L&L Literary Services, LLC

Printed in the United States of America.

ISBN: 978-1-953437-55-6

First Printing, 2021

ALSO BY

Lyn Forester writes under multiple pen names. To find what you're specifically searching for, visit her website at:

www.LynForester.com

Series under Sophie O'Dare

MM pairings

Tails x Horns

Marked by His Alpha

Series under Lyn Forester

MF, MMF, and MFMM+ pairings

Fate's Will

Poison World

Poisoned Houses

Tales of Port Lapton

Series under Lili Black (co-authored with LA Kirk)

MF, MFM, and MFMM+ pairings

Accidentally Dead

Children of the Shifting Gods

Manberry Witches

Museum of Magic, Mayhem, and Wonder

Spearwood Academy

To everyone who has questioned, or continues to question, to everyone who looks around and wonders why you don't feel things the same way as everyone else. To those who have chosen labels and those who are still unsure. Our world is ever-changing, ever-broadening. Know you're not alone.

TAILS X HORNS UNIVERSE

The three stages of growth in the Tails x Horns Universe.

- **Age 0-6: The genderless:** At birth, children have no gender. They are small and soft, with large eyes and pointed chins.
- **Age 7-17: The pre-transition:** When a child turns seven, they go through their first transformation. Their small, soft bodies have a rapid growth and a gender presents itself. This is the form they hold until they turn eighteen and is referred to as the pre-transition phase.

- **Age 18-Forward: The transition:** At age eighteen, each person goes through a final transition into adulthood, where they grow either a tail or horns. This is a volatile time for everyone, where desires and aggression become more pronounced. For the next two years, they continue education at the high school level while they gain control of their new bodies and decide what they will do as adults, either continuing on to university or setting out into the working world.

The difference between Tails and Horns.

- **Tails:** Usually the more timid of the two groups, they lean more toward vegetarian diets and find it difficult to pack on muscle. Their tails are sensitive, and they have extra ridges on the palate of their mouth that can be stimulated by one of their horned counterparts. The palate is also how they find their mate, and once a mate is found, no one else can stimulate their palate.

- **Horns**: Usually the more aggressive of the two groups, they lean toward carnivore diets and are larger than their tailed counterparts. They are driven to dominate and seek out their mates. In addition to horns, they also have black nails that can become claw-like if not taken care of and a black tongue with short barbs on it that are used to identify their mate.

How mating works:

- **Fate**: Fate has an active role in the Tails x Horns universe, and for every Tailed person, there is a Horned fated to be with them. But not every horned and tailed find their mate. Pairings often happen between the un-Fated, though pairings between two tailed or two horned is still frowned on as going against Fate.
- **Mating**: Mates bonds are identified through kissing, where the barbs on a horned person's tongue fits perfectly into the palate on a tailed person's mouth.

When this happens, their souls briefly merge, and it sometimes comes with a period of adjustment when they can feel each other's emotions, though this doesn't always happen and is more common with younger pairs.
- **Children**: When two males or two females mate, their options for children are adoption or surrogates.

AVOID BEING PUNCHED

The clatter of feet out in the hall fades as students flee the school. With a little over two weeks left before Yule break, the Town Center has daily activities set up to distract kids while parents plan their family celebrations.

I should pick up decorations on the way home soon. Rin is now old enough to start noticing that stuff and ask why we haven't picked out our Yule log yet. Never mind that we can't use the old fireplace in our house. The combination pre-k and daycare Rin attends started decorating pinecones and painting suns on paper last week.

I glance out my office window at the quickly emptying parking lot. Interspersed through the concrete lanes, raised medians with trees make an attempt to soften the hardscape. This far into December, though, piles of gray snow cover the dead grass, and bare branches scrape at the gray sky.

Already, the sun dips toward the horizon, and I pull the collar of my padded blazer closer. This time of year is always hard, made doubly so by coming to work in the dark and leaving after the sun sets. It begs for warm blankets and cocoa while curled up on the couch with my child, not sitting in a chilled office filled with files and books.

Shoulders drooping, my attention shifts from the bleak winter view outside to the even bleaker stack of files on the edge of my desk. Only a few green flags poke out amidst the reds, denoting students destined to rise or fall in class standing.

I dread this time of year. While some parents will be proud to see their kids move up in the curriculum, it doesn't make up for the anger and disappointment waiting for those who will be dropped to the lower classes. I understand the logic behind making this decision before the two-week break. It gives time for emotions to cool and kids to mentally prepare themselves for facing new classmates when they return after the New Year celebration. But I can't help but feel I'm ruining the holidays for a handful of people.

With a deep breath, I grab the stack of files and push up from my desk. Taro and Ryuu, the transition counselors, will be waiting in the conference room. When students hit their eighteenth birthday and go through their final transition into their adult forms, growing either horns or a tail, it comes with a barrage of emotional changes along with the physical ones.

Aggression and desire suddenly heighten, which can lead to a drop in grades, so I rely heavily on the student counselors when making this decision. They interact with the new adults on a personal level, acting as coaches and sounding boards for those in need during the final two years of extended education while they get used to their new bodies. It keeps me from basing my decision strictly on what the test scores say about a student.

With the stack of folders cradled against my chest, I lock my office before walking down the carpeted hall. Light glows from under Principal Ikeda's door, and Ko still sits behind the secretary desk at the front, his head-set fitted around his horns.

He glances up as I near and moves his thin microphone to the side. "I have coffee, tea, and water in the conference room, and the sign set up to direct parents to the right place."

I give him a grateful nod. "Thank you, Ko."

His shoulders pull back. "I'm a press of the button away if you need assistance tonight."

Heat stains my cheeks, and I know without looking that even my ivory horns blush. Compared to Ko's broad shoulders and hard biceps, I'm weak as far as horns go. He's had to step in more than once over the years when a parent's anger outweighed their good sense.

I force down my embarrassment. "I appreciate that, Ko, but with Ryuu there, I'm sure I'll be fine."

"He's still new. Keep the phone close." Ko moves his microphone back into place.

With another nod, I hurry out of the office and into the empty hall. Not every horned easily stacks on muscles or becomes aggressive, and I've had years to come to terms with not fitting into the standard mold. I was rarely emotional as a kid, and transitioning into my adult form didn't change that. I've only lost control of my senses once in my life, and I ended up eighteen with a pregnant wife who didn't love me.

Soft voices drift from the open conference room, and my steps slow as I struggle to pull myself into a professional mindset. I need my focus on the students and their parents right now.

The voices grow clearer, words trickling out, and I recognize Taro. "Stop it, we're still at school."

"No one's here yet," Ryuu's voice follows, low and coaxing. "This is my first parent-teacher meeting. I'm nervous."

Suspicion fills Taro's tone. "You don't look nervous."

Silence follows.

I frown, worried that the new horned counselor needs some reassurance.

Rounding the doorway, I freeze in surprise to find Ryuu, the large, horned counselor, embracing his slender counterpart in a passionate kiss. Taro's black tail wafts back and forth for a moment before curling around the other man's leg.

Embarrassment shoots through me for misreading the situation. The two men only recently announced their mate bond, and my reserved friend wouldn't appreciate such a private moment being witnessed.

As I hastily step back, my shoe scuffs on the linoleum, and Ryuu's head lifts, his eyes widening when he spies me at the doorway.

Taro begins to turn, but Ryuu pulls him into a

hug. "Thank you, Taro. My nerves are feeling much better."

The other man's voice comes out muffled against his chest. "I'm glad. Now, let me go before Juro gets here."

"Just one more second." Ryuu squeezes his now struggling mate tighter and mouths, *Sorry*.

Steps silent, I finish backing out of the room and lean against the wall to give them a minute to separate. Such moments should bring envy and perhaps yearning, but all I feel is disappointment that my one romance never attained the level of passion these two men displayed in a simple kiss.

Not for the first time, I wonder what's lacking in myself that I can't readily feel desire the same way other people do.

Ryuu and Taro begin talking at a normal level, and I take another deep breath before I walk back into the room, pretending like nothing happened.

"I hope you know I *will* be speaking to Principal Ikeda about your extreme incompetence," the angry woman hisses as she grabs her kid's arm and yanks her from the seat. "If this is the level of attention this school gives their students, then maybe it's not the right fit for my daughter."

"I understand your anger." I keep my voice calm as I look up at her. "But I assure you this decision did not come easily. This is a volatile time, and we believe that dropping your daughter to Class B will lessen some of the stress. When things have settled, she can retake the Class A Exam."

"And be behind all of her friends? I don't think so!" She pulls her daughter toward the door. "I'll have your job for this!"

I fight back a wince as she slams out of the conference room.

"Well, that didn't go well," Ryuu murmurs.

"I'm shocked this is the first one of the night," Taro responds. "We've usually had four by this point."

"Seriously?" Shock fills Ryuu's voice. "You didn't tell me that!"

Taro's tone softens. "You were already nervous."

The first time I did this was terrifying, and years of practice haven't made it easier. But we continue to make adjustments, such as rearranging the room to have limited options for things to throw and replacing the conference table with a desk set back from the three chairs left for parents and student to use. It puts distance between us and them, making it easier to see an attack coming and get out of the way. And they're less likely to fling a chair in use.

It's the small things in life, I suppose.

I scrub my hands over my thighs before I reach for the next file, relieved that it has a green flag on it. "Taro, can you ask Mrs. Iso to come in?"

The tailed counselor strides to the door and pokes his head out. A second later, he glances back over his shoulder. "Mrs. Iso couldn't make it tonight, but Mrs. Ito is here as a representative for Sota."

It's unusual, but not completely unheard of, especially with single parents. Usually, we end up rescheduling for later in the following week, but Sota and Masa are a special case, having discovered their mate bond almost as soon as they transitioned into their adult forms. They'd been best friends before, and their families have each other listed as emergency contacts, with the approval to make decisions for each other's child already on file.

Truly, a fated union.

I flip through the last two files on my desk and pull out Masa Ito's file, too. "We can bring both boys in at the same time."

With a nod, Taro gestures for them to enter.

Sota skips ahead of the other two, his little fawn

tail high with excitement as he claims the farthest chair. Mrs. Ito follows at a normal pace with her son, the two horned staring at the delicate tailed boy with equal looks of resignation and affection.

Mrs. Ito settles onto the chair in the center and folds her trim, black nailed hands in her lap. Masa sits beside his mother, his large body dwarfing the other two.

Side-by-side, it's easy to see the family relation. They both have straight black hair and deep brown eyes, and while Masa is masculine, he definitely gained his cheekbones from his mother. They're both calm and contained, which makes Sota's restless energy all the more obvious. He sits on the edge of his chair, his brown hair sticking up in the back and his blue eyes fixed expectantly on the folder in my hand.

"Right." I open both folders, though I already know their content. "As I'm sure you're aware, Mrs. Ito, we're recommending both Masa and Sota be moved up to Class A, with the condition that Sota continues to attend study sessions."

"Yes!" Sota thrusts his arms into the air.

Behind me, Taro lets out a resigned sigh. As Sota's counselor, I'm sure he's used to the boy's personality.

Mrs. Ito, however, glances at her son with a frown before she faces me once more. "While we're excited at this new jump in grades, we're also concerned the boys are pushing themselves too hard."

"*Mom*," Masa protests.

She turns to flick her nails at him. "If you could do this well before, why didn't you?"

Cringing, he hunches lower in his seat, the plastic creaking beneath his muscular frame.

Sota leans forward to smirk at him. "Because he's stupid with *love*."

Mrs. Ito whips around to pin him with another frown. "And why weren't *you* striving to do *better*?"

Blanching, Sota hunches his shoulders and mumbles unintelligibly.

"Too many video games, the both of you." Mrs. Ito faces me once more, and I can't help but feel the boys' pain when confronted with her firm stare. "Masa will *also* continue his study sessions, *separate* from Sota."

"*Mom*," Masa says again.

"No. It's obvious you're too easily distracted." At Sota's snicker, she gives him another frown. "You *both* are. You should stay in Class B until you have your hormones figured out."

"Mrs. Ito." Taro steps forward. "Sota has worked hard to get his grades up. He wants to go to a good university, and he needs a scholarship for that. Being in Class A will help tremendously. He's settled in well with his study group, and they push each other to aim for good grades."

She wavers in her decision. "Well…"

"Masa's also doing much better now that he's in the horned class," Ryuu adds. "He doesn't really need the extra study sessions, so it shows dedication that he's going that far."

She eyes her son. "I'm not sure his motivations are so pure."

Ryuu coughs to mask his laugh. "Well, all the same, his grades land him firmly in Class A."

Her dark brows arch. "And where do Sota's grades land him?"

I flip through his folder to his Class A test. "He did well, though he needs more work in math."

"I can help you with math," Masa offers.

"Nope!" Sota shakes his head. "That's what my study group is for!"

"There's a probationary option, is there not?" Mrs. Ito cuts in.

"There is," I say slowly. Most parents don't argue

against moving their kids up a class level. "Their files can be reviewed again in February."

Mrs. Ito nods. "We'll see how things go and re-evaluate then." She stands. "Come, Mr. Ito is making spaghetti for dinner. Sota, you will join us, of course."

Sota springs from his seat. "Yes, ma'am!"

"Why are you being so hard on us?" Masa grumbles as they stride for the door.

Her head tips back to look up at her son, her silver horns glinting. "Because I'm realizing I should have been harder earlier, you silly boy."

Sota skips ahead of them to hold the door open and waves back at us.

"He's so... bouncy," I murmur as they leave.

"Yes," Taro agrees.

"Were you ever like that?" Ryuu asks with interest.

"Never," comes the instant reply.

"Yeah, I figured." He leans over the desk. "Should I go get Mr. Akutsu?"

Setting Masa's and Sota's folders into their respective baskets, I drag the last folder over and stare at the yellow sticker.

This one is harder, on multiple levels.

Senichi's grades should really drop him from

Class A straight to Class B, but Ryuu's made the argument to keep him where he is. He believes Senichi's recent poor grades have more to do with outside influence than with his actual intelligence. It happens, sometimes, though usually not after the first year of transition. Senichi has had almost a full year as a horned, but he's also a transfer student, which is why we bring in the parents for an interview.

I can't decide without getting at least a glimpse of his home life. If he's not getting the support he needs, then the school will step in to provide it, if possible.

At my nod, Ryuu walks to the door and motions for the last of our interviews to come in.

A tall, elegant, tailed man strides into the room, his dark hair brushed back to display what most people would call classically handsome features. A long, straight nose, high cheekbones that aren't too sharp, a firm jawline without crossing the line into hard masculinity. His slender frame, silhouetted by a nicer than average suit, gives the impression of someone who takes care of themself.

My gaze lifts to meet his, and the other man's eyes widen in a brief flare of moss-green before his lashes sweep down, breaking the contact.

He stops at the desk, his hand out, and when I take it, his grasp is firm. "Hello, I'm Shig, Sen's uncle. Thank you for making time for us so late in the day."

"Of course, my name is Juro." I withdraw my hand and motion to the men behind me. "This is Taro, the tailed counselor, and Ryuu, the horned counselor." I glance behind him. "Is your nephew joining us?"

He glances over his shoulder, sighs, and turns, displaying a fluffy black tail that bristles with annoyance. He strides back to the door. "Come on, Sen. We don't want to waste more time than we already have."

The reprimand comes with a layer of tiredness, as if this isn't the first battle he's faced since taking Senichi in.

I remember reading the kid's file and how he moved here with his younger sibling after their parents passed away. Mr. Akutsu is younger than I expected to have a nineteen-year-old nephew. His sister must have been significantly older than him.

After a heated conversation, Mr. Akutsu returns with a sullen teenager in tow.

Senichi is everything his file showed him to be. Tattooed, pierced, and angry. His wavy black hair matches his uncle's, with inky black, feathered horns sweeping out on either side like an owl. He shuffles along, his shoes scraping against the laminate flooring, his hands shoved deep into his pockets, with headphones dangling from around his neck.

When they take their seats in front of my desk, Senichi slumps low, his eyes fixed on the tattered holes in the knees of his jeans instead of on me. Every line of his posture screams sullen teenager, forced to be here, and he has no problem making everyone aware of his displeasure.

Mr. Akutsu, on the other hand, sits straight in his seat, his tail still where it falls through the gap at the back. He faces me head-on, as if his attention will make up for his nephew's lack of manners.

I don't get the impression he's a man used to being disregarded, but neither does he give off any emotions heavier than frustration and resignation. He's young and was probably just establishing his career when he suddenly found himself the guardian of two children, one of them already an adult. He had to learn to be a father figure and support them while dealing with the death of his sister.

Sympathy tightens my chest. I'm well aware of the harsh realities of being a young, single father, and my heart goes out to him.

"Right." I tap the folder in front of me. "As I'm sure you can guess, we asked you to come in today to discuss Senichi's place in his class level."

"Just drop me to Class B and let us get on with our night," Senichi grumbles without lifting his eyes.

"Sen!" Mr. Akutsu hisses and casts me an apologetic glance. "I swear, he's not usually this rude."

And there, *right there*, is why Ryuu argues so vehemently against demoting Senichi.

The kid *wants* to fail.

Frowning, I close Senichi's file and fold my hands on top of it. "Are you being bullied, Senichi?"

That earns me an irritated flash of dark eyes. "I'm the one who bullies, or haven't you heard?"

"I've heard you skip class frequently, and when you're there, you ignore the lessons," I counter. "But you only get into fights with horned kids from other schools. You have the ones here handled quite nicely."

He juts his sharp chin out but doesn't argue.

I sigh. "Last year, you transferred in at higher than average for Class A. Intelligence and drive like that doesn't just vanish. Are you unhappy at home?"

Alarm flashes across his face, and he straightens.

"Shig takes good care of us. There's no problem at home."

"And you're *sure* there's no one in class picking on you?" I press.

His lip curls at the suggestion.

I let out a sigh. "Then, why are you trying to fail out of Class A when everyone knows you're more than capable of making good grades?"

His eyes drop back to his knees, and he crosses his arms over his chest in the universal gesture of *leave-me-alone* that every teenager masters.

"Okay, here's what we're going to do." I motion toward Ryuu. "Since you won't open up to us, you now have mandatory meetings with your counselor through the end of the semester. Mr. Morioka will update your teacher regarding the time of your appointments. Attendance is mandatory."

Head jerking up, Senichi's lips part to protest, but I lift a hand to stop him.

"This isn't a negotiation. If you skip, you'll be docked attendance credits." I catch his eyes. "And, before you scoff at that idea, know that I am making the decision to keep you in Class A. Right now, you are barely scraping by. If we dropped you to Class B, your grades *would* see you through to graduation. But in Class A, you *will* fail."

"Now, wait a minute." Mr. Akutsu leans forward in his seat. "Surely that's too harsh?"

"Senichi has the potential for a bright future, and he's currently throwing it away. Without a good reason to transfer him, I can't put him in another class where he will continue to waste the teacher's time." I keep my tone firm. "As of now, whether he graduates or not is completely in Senichi's hands. At any point, he can either choose to step up and be the student we all know he's capable of being, or he can drop out of school and give up the chance of going to university."

Anger flashes through Senichi's eyes, and he turns to his uncle. "I can just transfer, right?"

"No," Ryuu cuts in. "Not without moving, which would take your younger sibling out of their school as well."

Senichi springs to his feet. "You asked about bullying? *This* is bullying!"

"I'm sorry you feel that way." I glance at his uncle, who looks troubled. "We don't make this decision lightly. But neither can we sit by and watch our students sabotage their futures. If Senichi goes to his meetings with his counselor and stops skipping classes, we'll re-evaluate our stance."

Mr. Akutsu nods in acknowledgment. "We understand."

"This isn't fair!" Senichi fumes. "My grades put me in Class B! That's how this is supposed to work."

The uncle turns a tired look on him. "Did you ever stop to think maybe you're not as clever as you think you are? I don't know what game you've been playing these past three months, but you need to reconsider your actions."

"You don't know what you're talking about!" Senichi yells, his cheeks flushing red before he turns and stomps out of the room.

Mr. Akutsu runs a hand through his hair as he turns back to us. "I honestly don't know what's going on. He won't talk to me about it." His eyes shift to Ryuu. "Maybe he'll open up to another horned, because I'm not getting through. It's like a switch flipped at the beginning of the school year, and suddenly my sweet nephew is a constant ball of frustrated anger."

"There were no changes at home?" Ryuu asks.

"No." Mr. Akutsu shakes his head. "He and Deka had settled in well. They were dealing with their grief, Deka better than Sen, but he was doing okay. I've moved some of my workload so I can be home and available more, but he just locks himself in his room with his headphones on."

"I'll try to get him to open up," Ryuu says, and gratitude flickers through Mr. Akutsu's eyes. "I can even sit in on a couple of classes to see if I can suss out if he's lying about the bullying."

"I appreciate that. He's scrappy—far scrappier than I was at his age—so I know he can hold his own, but..." Helpless, Mr. Akutsu pushes to his feet, his hand coming out once more. "Thank you for your time."

We shake, and I stand to walk him to the door. "We'll meet again in February. There's only a little over two weeks left before Winter Break, but Ryuu's good at getting the horned kids to open up."

"I'll keep my fingers crossed." He reaches into the breast pocket of his jacket and pulls out a business card. "My direct number, if I'm needed, both at the office or at home."

I take it and stop at the door. Senichi leans against the wall across the hall, his headphones on, and his gaze angrily fixed on the floor.

"Good luck," I offer.

With a last nod, Mr. Akutsu goes to collect his nephew, and they head toward the front entrance.

I walk back to the desk to gather the folders and hand them to their respective counselors.

Ryuu takes his small stack and blows out a breath. "That was a lot rougher than I thought it would be."

"Are you kidding?" Taro's tail snaps against his mate's leg. "Tonight was tame. No one tried to punch Juro this time."

Ryuu's lips part in shock, his wide eyes turning on me. "That's happened before?"

I nod. "A horned dad tried to strangle me once. That was exciting."

Ryuu shakes his head. "Maybe we should petition to hold these meetings through bulletproof glass."

I smile, though I'm not completely against the idea. Horned can get dangerous when they start throwing their muscles around. It's scary, but also fascinating, when I'm not on the receiving end. I've never felt that level of passion, that drive to violence.

Before I transitioned at eighteen, I actually received counseling to prepare to join my tailed peers. I shocked everyone, myself the most, when I woke up with small, ivory horns sprouting from my brown hair.

Together, we walk out of the room, Ryuu and

Taro ahead of me as Taro regales his mate with all the tantrums he's witnessed parents throwing.

As they walk, Taro's tail curls around his mate's leg, their steps in sync. It must be unconscious, because Taro's never been one for public displays of affection. Finding his mate has been good for him opening up.

A pang in my chest brings with it a wash of disappointment. If only finding one's mate was always that beautiful.

UNICORNS OF LOVE

"Daddy!" Rin squeals as I walk through the front door.

Rin still wears the gender natural yellow smock from daycare, though it's now covered in flour. Until their body chooses a gender at age seven, they'll remain small and round, with chubby cheeks, a pointed chin, and large brown eyes.

Rin runs at me from the kitchen, bare legs pounding.

I catch Rin mid-flight, cuddling their soft body against me. "Where are your pants?"

Rin giggles. Pants are a constant, losing battle for me, and I fear the day they hit seven and pants become less of an option and more a necessity.

I tickle Rin's sides. "Did you have a good day?"

"Hana and I made cookies!" Rin lifts frosting and sprinkle-covered hands to shove in my face. "I made you a unicorn!"

"I can't wait to see it." As soon as I set them down, they race off, leaving flour footprints that lead back to the kitchen at the back of the house.

Glancing down, I sigh in resignation at the frosting and flour that smears the front of my padded blazer. I guess this one is destined for the cleaners after only one wear.

"We're just cleaning up, Mr. Ono," Hana calls from the kitchen. "There are leftovers if you're hungry."

My stomach rumbles, though the thought of cold fish sticks doesn't sound appealing. I would have stopped for something on the way home, but the meetings ran later than expected. I didn't want to keep Hana here longer than necessary. As a university student, she has homework and projects that I'm sure need her attention. I don't want to add any strain to her life.

If she quits, I don't know what I'll do.

I tug my tie loose and shrug out of my jacket as I head toward the kitchen. The old, worn wooden floors creak under my weight, and a cool draft pulls a shiver from me. The old house my grandparents gifted me needs a lot of work, but I haven't had time to make any of those repairs, yet. My administrative job doesn't pay much, and the only reason I can afford the three-bedroom house is because the mortgage was paid off before I moved in with Rin.

If not for their kindness, we would be in an apartment, and Rin would have no room to run and play.

I veer down the hall next to the kitchen to switch on the small space heaters in both of our bedrooms, hoping to warm them up before we go to sleep tonight. I don't like to use them when possible, but the news said we'll have ice tonight. By the way my breath fogged and with the metallic scent in the air on the way home, it feels more like snow.

In Rin's room, I double-check that the floor around the space heater is clear before switching it on, and the smell of burning dust fills the air as the element heats up. I turn on Rin's heated blanket, too, and check the lock on the window before lowering the blinds.

I cross the hall to my bedroom, add my blazer to the basket destined for the dry cleaners, then join Rin and Hana in the kitchen.

Hana smiles as she wipes down the counters, and I grab a broom to help sweep the flour from the floor. "You can head out, now, if you want. I can clean up the rest of this."

She straightens, the sponge still in her hand. "Are you sure? We kind of got carried away with the decorating."

Sprinkles, along with frosting and colored sugar, stick to the counter, and a cooling tray filled with misshapen cookies rests off to the side. It will take some elbow grease to clean, but I'm not the one with homework.

I give Hana a tired smile. "Yes, I'm sure. Go home before it gets any colder."

"Thanks, Mr. Ono, I really appreciate it." She takes the sponge to the sink and pulls off her apron. "You won't need me again until next week, right?"

"Yes," I crouch to brush the flour into the dustpan. "Rin's mom will be picking them up from daycare tomorrow and will have them over the weekend."

Hana turns to Rin with a big smile. "Are you excited to see your mommy?"

Rin looks at me, eyes round, before shrugging. "Mom's okay, I guess. Sometimes she gives me presents."

Hana winces as she glances back at me, but I wave to let her know it's fine.

She collects her school bag from the dining table and heads for the door. "Have a good weekend! I'll see you on Monday, Rin!"

"Wait!" Rin yells and leaps off the stool, running to the rack of cookies. "You forgot your hippopotamus!"

I eye the blob of gray cookie she grabs and consider calling the kindergarten to check what they're teaching my kid.

Hana crouches and solemnly accepts the cookie. "Thank you. I would have hated to get home and not had this yummy treat to eat."

"You can't eat it!" Exasperation fills Rin's voice, and I stifle a laugh. "That's your good luck hippo, so you'll pass your exams!"

"Oh, right." Helpless, Hana looks back at me.

Amused, I open one of the island drawers and pull out a plastic bag for her to take the cookie home.

She slips it inside and holds it out like a talisman. "Come on, hippo, you need to give me all the good grades."

Rin giggles as we follow Hana to the door.

"Drive safe!" I call as she walks down the stone path toward her car parked at the curb.

She lifts a hand in acknowledgment, and I shut the door, making sure to lock the deadbolt.

Rin races back toward the kitchen, slipping on the flour still on the floor. "Come one, Daddy! I want to give you your unicorn!"

I follow, sweeping up the flour as I go. Despite my best effort, though, my shoes still slip on the hardwood floor. I'll have to mop, too, or risk a fall.

When I walk into the kitchen, Rin stands in front of the island, hands behind their back with a wide, gap-toothed smile.

Understanding this is a special moment, I set the broom aside and kneel. "What do you have for me?"

"This is your *love* unicorn," Rin announces and presents a blob with three legs on one side and what looks like the fourth leg stuck to what must be the head. "This is so you can get married again."

Worry forms a hard knot in my stomach. I've tried hard to raise Rin in a happy environment since my wife asked for a divorce. Have I somehow failed? Do I need to find a new job that allows me to spend more time at home?

As I glance around the kitchen, regret pings through me. I should be the one making cookies, not the nanny. How many moments like this will I miss in Rin's life because of work?

Trying not to frown, I accept the cookie. "Why do I need a new spouse?"

"Aubrey at school just got a new daddy, and they get to go to Yipiland," Rin informs me.

"So, if I remarry, *we'll* get to go to Yipiland?" I surmise, relief easing the tension in my muscles.

Rin nods vigorously and leans forward, lifting a hand to whisper, "And Aubrey said the way to get a new mommy is to fall in *love*."

I smile, though it feels forced. "Yes, that's usually what comes before marrying someone. But, I can't marry someone new."

Rin's hands move to their hips. "Why not?"

With no way to explain how I just don't feel romance the way others do, I settle for, "Because I'm not ready."

"But mommy found Scott." Rin's face scrunches with dislike. "They live together now, so you can get married again, too."

If only it were that easy.

I force another smile and lift the unicorn cookie. "I will treasure this. Now, go brush your teeth. You've had way too much sugar for one night."

Rin throws their head back in a dramatic sigh before they march for the bathroom.

Smiling, I set the unicorn cookie back on the

cooling rack. I appreciate the sentiment and that Rin wants to see me happy again, but how do I explain that I can't just go out and find them a new mom? And that I don't have a desire to? Especially right now. They'll be turning seven soon, and that's already stressful enough.

My shoulders slump as I stare around the messy kitchen. This never would have been allowed if we still lived with Karen. She has a strict idea of how a house should be kept and how a child should act. We've gotten into more than one fight over her restricting Rin's creativity. Maybe that's what drove her to all those kissing parties, where she eventually found Scott, her destined mate.

After Rin was born, Karen refused to let a new baby hold her back from experiencing life. I had a feeling she was sneaking out on dates, that all those late nights with the girls were code for something else. But I buried my head in the sand, determined to do what I could to keep our family together.

It was almost a relief when she told me she was leaving. I just wish it hadn't meant she was abandoning Rin, too. At first, she made a show of coming over every other weekend, but then those visits drifted farther and farther apart as she settled into her new life. Her mate is a security guy at a club, and she spends most of her time there, sucking up to his bosses. It fits her personality. She was like that in high school, too. Always seeking out the next big party.

We hooked up at one, the only one I ever let my friends talk me into attending, and nine months later, we had Rin.

I wouldn't exchange having Rin for a normal end of high school or the four years at university I planned. I love Rin more than any what-if scenario. But being a single father is tough.

With one ear turned toward the bathroom, I listen to the rattle and splash of Rin getting ready for bed as I walk to the sink, grab the sponge to finish wiping down the counters, then mop the floor.

Rin stopped wanting my help getting ready for bed last year, which was a bittersweet moment. Soon, they'll switch over to grade school, hanging out with friends and hopefully following a different path than I did.

Rin runs into the kitchen in only a nightshirt, waving our latest storybook in the air. "Daddy! Time for Yip Yip and the Magic Tangerine!"

"I'll be right there." I dump the dustpan into the garbage. "Put on your pants."

"Never!" Rin shrieks and runs for their room.

Laughing, I hang the mop back in the utility closet, wash my hands, and walk to Rin's bedroom.

Rin already lays under the covers, all the pillows on the bed propped up against the headboard, and the book open to our current chapter.

I adjust the space heater before I settle next to them, and Rin instantly cuddles against my side.

I hug their soft body close. "Do you want to help me read tonight?"

"No." Rin traces the image at the beginning of the chapter. "Daddy?"

I look down at Rin. "Yes?"

Rin runs a finger over the princess's blue ballgown. "When I turn seven, will I be a girl?"

"I don't know." I set the book down on my lap. "Do you want to be a girl?"

Rin twists to gaze up at me, and my chest tightens at the uncertainty in their eyes. "Will mommy like me more if I'm a girl?"

"Oh, love." Tears sting my eyes at the question, and I lift my arm to draw Rin into a hug. "Your mommy loves you, and she'll love you whatever gender you end up being. She's going to come see you tomorrow and take you to the ice cream shop and to Bounce Palace."

Rin nods but doesn't look thrilled at the idea.

"Mom doesn't let me get a cone. I like cones. And she only lets me have vanilla."

I clench my teeth against my immediate response. We've had more than one fight about that, too.

Karen doesn't think children should be allowed to have cones or colored ice cream until they prove they can eat without making a mess. It takes all the fun out of going to a place like Twenty Scoops, where Rin can have ice cream cones turned into clowns with colored frosting and candy. Bringing a child there then limiting them to a scoop of vanilla in a cup feels like taking them just to rub in what they can't have.

"You're mommy..." I struggle to find words Rin will understand without bad-mouthing Karen. "She likes things a certain way, like how you line up your troll dolls by hair height."

Rin turns to look across the room, where trolls in various sizes and colors line the top of a green dresser. Rin spent an entire day carefully brushing out their hair and lining them up so it creates a rainbow slide of color.

"You like vanilla, right?" I squeeze Rin's shoulders.

"Yeah." They snuggle back against me. "But I like bubble gum, too."

The ache in my chest widens. "Then, when I take you next week, you'll get bubble gum. How does that sound?"

Rin nods, staring at the book until I pick it up, and my stomach sinks. I can't help but feel like I should fight for Rin's right to have whatever flavor ice cream they want tomorrow, but I know how that conversation will go, and it's been so long since Karen asked to see Rin that I don't want to ruin it over something as silly as dessert.

So, I swallow down what I feel to focus on making tonight a happy one and pray that tomorrow won't be a complete disaster.

BEING GENEROUS

The next evening, my cell phone rings at five-thirty, and I set aside the file I was reviewing to check the caller ID.

My stomach sinks when I see the name of the daycare on the screen. There's only one reason they'd be calling right now.

Motions hurried, I close up my desk and grab my jacket and car keys as I answer. "Hello, this is Juro speaking."

"Hello, Mr. Ono," a male voice says from the other end. "I'm calling because no one has come to pick Rin up yet, and we're getting ready to leave for the night."

I close my eyes in frustration. "I'm so sorry. My

ex-wife was supposed to pick them up tonight. I'll be there as soon as possible."

"Thank you. We'll keep someone here until you arrive." The line clicks off, and I wrestle into my jacket as I run for the school exit.

Outside, the cold December air slaps me in the face as I hit speed dial for Karen's cell phone.

She answers on the fourth ring, her voice slurred from sleep. "'ello?"

"Karen," I snap as I jog toward the parking lot. "The daycare just called. You were supposed to pick Rin up over an hour ago."

"Juro?" Awareness fills her voice, and a rustle comes from the background. "Was that today?"

"You know it was." Few cars still fill the parking lot, and I sprint for my SUV at the back. "You specifically asked for this visit. It's been on your calendar for three weeks now."

"God, you're such a nag." More rustling sounds. "I'm on my way now."

"Are you at home?" I reach my car and unlock the door.

"Where else would I be?" Irritation fills her voice. "You woke me from a dead sleep."

"You won't make it before they close." I slide

behind the steering wheel and set my phone in the cupholder as I start the engine.

The call switches over to my car speakers, bringing Karen back online mid-sentence. "—meet you at your house, then."

My shoulders tense. "Why don't I just bring Rin to you?"

"No, you know Scott doesn't like to be reminded of you," she says.

"I can bring the custody papers with me." Angry, I check my rear-view mirror as I back out of the parking spot. "He should be happy to see you sign them."

"You know I'm still looking for a lawyer to go over that," she deflects. "All that legal mumbo jumbo just confuses me."

My hands tighten on the steering wheel. "You've been looking for months now."

"I want to be able to trust the person in charge of my child's future," she snaps. "Show a little patience, Juro. I'll see you at your house in an hour."

The line goes silent, and I grip my steering wheel tighter. She's the last person who should talk about trust. I trusted her to stay and help me raise Rin. I trusted that when she said she was going to see her friends, that's where she really was. I trusted in our vows of marriage.

And she continues to make me pay for that trust.

The streetlights come on as I drive across town to the daycare near my house. Only one car remains parked out front, and I recognize it as Mr. Jacob's, who teaches the younger children.

Parking next to his sedan, I climb out and rush inside.

"Mr. Jacob," I call as soon as I'm through the door. "I'm so sorry to make you wait."

The preschool and kindergarten rooms are already locked up for the night, and the lights in the back of the daycare are dimmed.

"That's okay, Mr. Ono!" he calls from the locker area. "Rin's just getting their coat on."

I walk through the front room, where colored foam puzzle pieces pad the floor and drawings of snowflakes and starbursts decorate the lower walls. Glitter-covered pinecones hang from strings, and in a few places, clay Yule logs wait to be painted.

It warms my heart to see all the activities the kids do throughout the day. Usually, Hana picks Rin up, and I miss out on seeing all the projects in progress. I pause to study the different wreaths, wondering which one Rin worked on.

"Daddy!" Rin runs out of the back, their coat only halfway on.

Mr. Jacob follows a pace behind, holding Rin's teal backpack. "You shouldn't run indoors, Rin."

With a smile for the teacher, I crouch and catch Rin's small body as they leap at me. Standing, I reach out a hand for the backpack. "Did you have a good day?"

Rin nods. "I was super good today. I deserve ice cream." Then, their big, brown eyes move past me, and some of the happiness fades. "Mommy isn't coming, is she?"

"She's meeting us at the house." I look at the teacher. "I'm sorry about the mix-up. Thank you for staying late today."

"I'm always happy to hang out with Rin." Mr. Jacob reaches out to ruffle Rin's dark-brown hair. "We had a good time, didn't we?"

"I drew Yip Yip!" Rin snatches the backpack from my hand and digs inside, coming out with a drawing of the lime green hippo. "See? Yip Yip!"

"So I see." My eyes cross, trying to focus. "Very well done."

Mr. Jacob looks around at the other projects in the room. "Would you like to see what else Rin has been working on? It's been a while since you last came by."

I wince at the gentle admonishment. I know I shouldn't leave so much of Rin's care to Hana, but I frequently can't leave work until after classes are out. Most nights, I'm happy if I make it home by dinner time. "We shouldn't keep you any longer than necessary. I'll take a tour next time, during regular business hours."

Mr. Jacob smiles. "We'd be happy to have you in, anytime."

"Thank you." I bend to set Rin down and take their small hand. "Come on, Rin. Let's head home."

As we turn to leave, Rin looks up at me. "Is mommy really meeting us there?"

"I said she is, didn't I?"

"You said she'd pick me up today," Rin points out.

"She promised to meet us at the house." I push open the door and hold it for Rin.

"Will I still get ice cream?" Rin demands.

"After dinner." We walk out into the cold, and I unlock the car, helping Rin inside.

At six, they still need the booster seat in the back. When they turn seven and go through their first transition, that might change. A lot of kids grow a few inches, their soft, round bodies stretching out overnight.

It's not a comfortable process, and Rin will likely miss a few days of class before returning to school. I have their birthday already marked on the school calendar for time off. I can't trust that Karen will be there for the big event, and I don't want to miss it.

I've heard from other parents that time moves faster after age seven, and soon enough, Rin will be a teenager, then an adult and off to university. I want to be there for all the milestones.

On the drive home, Rin talks nonstop about all the things they plan to do over the weekend, and with each item added to the list, my heart sinks.

Karen won't do most of them, if any. She only takes Rin to remind me she can. From what Rin says, their visits with Karen involve sitting in front of the TV in the office where Karen sets up an inflatable bed for Rin.

If she would just sign the papers to give me full custody...

I've talked to a lawyer, and with how many visits she's missed, it can be argued she's abandoned Rin. But the process will be long, especially if Karen fights, which she will. She wants alimony, something I'm not obligated to provide now that she has a mate. They haven't married, but the mate bond pretty much equals the same thing, as far as most people are concerned.

When we arrive home, the driveway is empty. Karen would have had to leave right away to beat us here, even with the stop at the daycare.

I unbuckle Rin, and we walk inside, Rin running to their bedroom to store their backpack. In the kitchen, I pull fish sticks from the freezer and set the oven to preheat. I don't want Rin to starve while we wait for Karen, and if she shows up before they're done, I'll eat them myself.

Rin runs into the kitchen a few minutes later and scrambles up on the stool to watch me make dinner.

"Do you want to color?" I ask as I slide the tray of frozen fish into the oven.

Rin shakes their head. "I want to decorate a Yule log."

I smile. "We don't have a Yule log."

"We can make one!" Rin announces. "The older kids are doing that at school. All we need is clay."

"We don't have clay." When Rin's face falls, I add, "I can buy some this weekend. We can make it when you get back. How does that sound?"

Rin's face scrunches up, and I brace for the argument I see brewing.

Thankfully, the doorbell rings, stopping the tantrum before it starts.

Rin looks toward the door with none of the happiness a child should show at the arrival of their mother.

I pull a pad of paper and some pens from the junk drawer and set them in front of Rin. "Here, draw what you want your Yule log to look like, and I'll pick up supplies, okay?"

Nodding, Rin grabs the pen in one small fist and hunches over the piece of paper. Rin loves to draw, so this will offer a distraction while I answer the door.

I walk to the front of the house as the doorbell sounds again, followed by an impatient knock.

When I open the door, Karen pushes her way inside, her long, orange tail snapping with annoyance. "What took you so long? And why is the light off on the porch?"

"We just got home, and the bulb burned out again." I shut the door behind her, my muscles trembling with the effort it takes not to kick her back out.

"I don't know why you keep this dump. It's always having problems." She looks around, her thin lips pinched into a frown. "Where's Rin? It's a long drive back home."

"Then, you should have picked them up on time," I admonish.

She whirls on me, her finger stabbing the air near my chest. "And who's fault do you think that is?"

"Your alarm clocks?" I hazard a guess. "What were you doing sleeping so late in the day?"

Her chin juts out. "I had to take on a second job."

Unaware she had a first job, my brows shoot up. "Why?"

"It's not easy providing for Rin. And since you're so stingy, I have to work harder to make sure there's a nice place for them to come to." Her tail whips back and forth. "If you'd just agree to give me what I'm owed—"

"I don't *owe* you anything," I seethe through gritted teeth. "If you would just sign the custody paperwork—"

Her hands move to her hips. "There you go, trying to steal *my* child again."

"I wouldn't ask for full custody if you acted like you actually wanted Rin," I whisper fiercely.

"Mommy?" Rin calls, and I turn to find them standing at the entrance to the kitchen.

A fake smile spreads over Karen's face, and she crouches, her arms spread wide. "Rin, baby!"

Rin doesn't run into her embrace.

After a moment, Karen's arms drop to her sides, and she stands to glare at me as if Rin's behavior is my fault.

I glare right back. I won't force Rin to be affectionate toward Karen if they don't want to be.

"Well," Karen huffs. "Where's your bag? We need to go."

"Bag?" I question. "What happened to the clothes I sent last time?"

"Rin ruined them, and we had to throw them out," Karen snaps.

"I did not!" Rin yells, their face turning red at the accusation.

"Yes, you did," she insists. "Now, go pack some clothes. We don't want you wearing the same thing all weekend."

"Go." I nod toward the hall and watch as Rin stomps away.

"You need to teach Rin manners." Karen crosses her arms under her breasts, pushing them higher, and I notice she put on a low-cut shirt that displays her cleavage.

I notice, too, the makeup she applied, the glossy,

pink lipstick that gives her lips an artificial fullness, and the thick mascara and eyeshadow that make her look like a raccoon.

She hadn't gone to sleep looking like this, which means she's trying to draw my attention. But she should know better. Her attempts to be sexy never worked on me, not even at the beginning of our marriage.

I stay silent, and we stand like that until Rin returns, pulling a small suitcase on wheels.

Rin stops in front of Karen. "Are we getting ice cream like you promised?"

Karen crouches once more, her hands settling on Rin's shoulders. "I'm so sorry, baby, but mommy doesn't have enough money for treats. Maybe your daddy will buy us some?"

Rin turns wide eyes on me, and I clench my teeth to hold back the anger. I should have expected this. Karen knows I'll never say no when she already promised Rin ice cream.

With a forced smile, I pull my wallet from my back pocket and hand Karen a five-dollar bill.

She narrows her eyes on me. "What if Rin wants sprinkles?"

"Sprinkles, Daddy!" Rin yells, some of their happiness from earlier returning.

"I only have a twenty," I say, knowing full well Karen won't let Rin have sprinkles.

She sticks out her hand, fingers wiggling expectantly, and I reluctantly hand over the rest of my cash.

She tucks the twenty, along with the five I already gave her, into the tight front pocket of her jeans. "Come on, Rin, Daddy Scott is waiting."

"Scott isn't my daddy!" Rin yells instantly and points to me. "This is my daddy!"

"Don't you take that tone with me! That attitude just cost you your ice cream!" Karen grabs Rin's arm. "If you're good, *maybe* we'll get some on the way back on Sunday."

"Ow!" Rin protests, dragging their feet as tears fill their eyes.

"Karen," I say sharply. "You're hurting Rin."

She loosens her grip but turns angry eyes on me as she continues to pull our child toward the door. "If you'd support me more, Rin wouldn't be like this."

I follow after them, bringing Rin's abandoned suitcase. "I do ninety percent of the parenting."

"Well, maybe that should change." She yanks open the door. "We're thinking of moving to Oak

Harbor. Scott has a job offer there. We could take Rin with us."

Panic shoots through me, and I freeze. "You can't do that."

"Can't I?" Her lip curl into a sneer. "You were a worthless husband and a worthless father. I'm not sure I like how you're raising our child."

My gut tightens, and she yanks the suitcase from my numb fingers.

She leans closer, her voice dropping. "But maybe, if you were more generous with me, I'd sign those papers. Scott wants to start our own family, but children are so expensive, and we already have one." She pats me on the chest. "Think about it."

I stand frozen in the entryway, my heart pounding with terror, as she slams the door behind her.

I spend the weekend in a panic, searching the internet and calling my lawyer to try to figure out a way to force the custody issue. My lawyer isn't much help, probably because I can't afford one who specializes in family issues. He charges by the hour and hangs up once my retainer runs out.

On Sunday, a loud honk from the driveway announces Rin's return, and I pull on my jacket before I run outside.

Karen glares at me from the passenger seat of an expensive red sports car, and Scott, behind the wheel, ignores me completely.

I stride to the back and open the rear door.

Rin already has their seatbelt off and practically bolts out as soon as the door opens. I stare at the empty seat, then slam the door and walk to Karen's window.

She rolls it down, her brows arched.

"Where's Rin's booster seat?" I demand.

She shrugs. "We don't want it ruining the leather. And Rin's old enough now not to need one."

"Rin's not *tall* enough not to need one. Age has nothing to do with it," I snap, anger heating my face. "If you were in an accident—"

"Calm down, man," Scott drawls. "I'm a safe driver."

"That doesn't account for the *other* drivers on the road!" I look at Rin, who stands near the open door to the house. "And where are Rin's suitcase and jacket?"

Karen shrugs again, unconcerned. "Oh, Rin must have left them at our place."

My hands clench at my sides. "That's the third suitcase Rin has *left*."

She widens her eyes at me. "Are you accusing me of something?"

I'm pretty sure she sells everything I send with Rin, but I can't prove it. The stuff just never seems to make it back home.

"Did you at least buy Rin ice cream?" I demand.

"Sugar is so bad for kids." Karen shakes her head. "You spoil Rin too much."

"Give me back my money." I thrust my hand out. "I'll take Rin myself."

"I don't know what you're talking about." She looks at Scott. "Come on, baby, we need to get back before ice forms in the pass."

"Karen," I seethe.

"So much passion." She presses the button for the window, and it begins to roll up. "If you'd shown half this much emotion while we were married, I wouldn't have gone looking elsewhere. And now, I have Scott."

The blow stings, and I pull my hand back before she rolls the window up on it.

I tried my best to give Karen everything she demanded of me, even taking pills when she wanted to be intimate. I'm well aware I lack the passion most spouses bring to a relationship, but at least I tried. Karen just kept taking and taking, reminding me of all the ways I failed, and the more that happened, the less I felt for her, and the harder it became to sleep next to her every night.

And now, she treats Rin with the same disdain, using our child as a weapon against me.

"Daddy, come inside," Rin calls. "I'm cold."

Knowing her words hurt, Karen smirks as they back out of the driveway.

I turn away before they fully leave, focusing on Rin.

It doesn't matter that I couldn't give Karen the type of love she demanded. Whatever's broken in me that stops me from feeling romantic love doesn't extend to the love I feel for my child. I'll do anything to keep them safe, even put up with whatever barbs Karen launches at me.

I'll win my case and claim full custody of Rin, then I'll never have to see Karen again.

RIN'S FRIEND

Monday afternoon, my cell phone rings, and when I check the screen, Hana's name shows.

With a sinking sensation in my stomach, I press the answer button. "Hey, Hana, everything okay?"

"No, it's not, Mr. Ono," she says, her voice scratchy and stuffed up. "I'm so sorry, but I seem to have come down with a cold. I can't pick Rin up from school today."

My shoulders slump as I stare at the stack of files on my desk. "That's okay. Stay home and rest. Let me know when you feel better, okay?"

"I'm so sorry, Mr. Ono." She coughs, the sound muffled for a moment before she returns. "I'll get better as soon as possible."

"Really, it's okay. Take care." We hang up, and I check the time.

The bell for the end of school sounded ten minutes ago. I planned to stay until five before heading home, but I can leave now and take my work with me. I can finish once Rin goes to bed.

Loading the files into my work bag, I grab my coat and lock up my office.

The drive to Rin's school takes longer than usual, traffic congesting the road from student drivers and parents on their way to pick up their kids. When I finally pull into the parking lot, I have to wait for another car to leave to have room for my own vehicle.

Chaos reigns inside, children running back and forth screaming to their friends while their parents try to corral them.

Mr. Jacob spies me hovering off to the side and runs up to me. "Mr. Ono, you're earlier than usual."

"Yes, sorry." I look around for Rin. "Hana's sick, so I'll be picking Rin up for a few days."

"They're in the play yard." Mr. Jacob points to the back. "I can go get them—"

"No, it's okay." I gesture to the other waiting parents. "I can find them on my own."

With a relieved smile, he runs off, and I weave

my way through small bodies toward the playground attached to the back of the school.

I find Rin on the monkey bars with another kid of the same age. They take turns spinning cartwheels around the gymnastic bar, howling with laughter as they make themselves dizzy.

Warmth fills me at the sight, and I sit on one of the metal, picnic benches, happy to wait while Rin has fun. The other child must be Deka, the friend Rin constantly talks about. I'm glad Rin was able to make such a good friend after starting here. I'd been worried Rin would have a hard time opening up after moving to a new place.

"They're cute, aren't they?" a familiar voice asks, and I glance over in surprise.

Mr. Akutsu, Senichi's uncle, leans against the wall to my left, his eyes on the kids. Today, he wears a snappy navy suit with pale-blue pinstripes over a steel blue shirt. The tie around his neck hangs loose, and he wears his jacket open, his hands thrust into his pockets. He looks like he just came from a high-paying job, and I flush at my simple brown khakis and cream polo shirt, suddenly feeling underdressed.

Embarrassed and annoyed by the reaction, I follow his gaze back to the kids. "That's *your* Deka?"

"Sure is." He glances over, his eyes sweeping over me in quick assessment, and a soft smile spreads over his lips. "Is Rin yours?"

I nod, relaxing, as an equally soft smile spreads over my lips. "Yeah."

"Small world." His fluffy back tail wafts behind him as he turns back to the kids. "I haven't seen you here before."

The comment makes me cringe. Rin's been coming here for months now. It's horrible that I haven't met the other parents yet. Hana usually handles pick up, or I arrive after most of the kids are already gone.

Mr. Akutsu glances back at me, his eyes wide as if realizing how the comment sounded. "Hana's a very nice girl. The kids love her."

"She is." I rub my hands together against the chill. "She's come down with a cold."

He gives me a sympathetic smile. "'Tis the season, right?"

"Unfortunately." I look back at our kids and watch as Rin boosts Deka back onto the bar. "We should probably break them up. They're not showing signs of quitting on their own."

"Endless energy," he agrees. "I don't remember ever being that energetic."

"Me, either," I agree, and we share another smile.

"Hey, since Hana's sick, you want to have dinner with us?" Mr. Akutsu straightens away from the wall. "We can hit up Happy Palace and let them terrorize the playground there for a bit."

I consider the pile of files waiting for my attention, then Rin's excitement at playing more with Deka, and Rin wins. The files can wait a little longer, and exhausting Rin at Happy Palace will mean a faster bedtime, tonight. Besides, Rin deserves some fun after the weekend they had with Karen.

"We'd love that." I clap my hands to draw the kids' attention. "Rin, time to go!"

Twisting, Rin spots me next to Mr. Akutsu and shouts, "Daddy!"

Rin abandons the monkey bars to run toward me, chubby legs pumping, and I crouch, barely catching them as they launch at me.

As I stand, Rin's small hands clasp my cheeks. "Daddy, you came! Where's Hana?"

"Hana's sick," I squeeze out through fish lips.

Rin's eyes widen in alarm. "Did she eat the hippo? It was gonna bring her good luck."

"I don't think the hippo had anything to do with it." I make a kissy face, and Rin giggles, the sound easing away the troubles of my day. I lean back to free my face. "How does going to Happy Palace with Deka and Mr. Akutsu sound?"

Eyes wide, Rin bounces in my arms and squeals loud enough to make my ears ring.

A quiet laugh comes from Mr. Akutsu as he collects Deka, and over the kids' chatter, we agree to meet at the Happy Palace away from the Town Center in the hope it will be less crowded at this time of day.

Rin wiggles as I buckle them into the car seat, chattering non-stop about chicken nuggets and slides. I only have to add an occasional, "Sounds fun," on the drive over to Happy Palace.

By the time I park and walk around to Rin's side of the car, they already have their seat belt off and are wiggling the childproof door handle to escape.

Mr. Akutsu pulls up next to me in a sleek, expensive-looking black car, and I stare at it in amazement.

What kind of job does he have, to be able to afford such a nice car at his age? He can't be much older than me, and unlike me, he probably went to university. He has that polished air about him that I frequently feel I lack with only my high school degree and online certificate.

I got my first job directly out of high school to

start supporting Karen and Rin, who'd been a little over one by that point. It was a struggle, but I became a teacher's assistant through my last year of high school while working a part-time job at a Quick Mart, and Principal Ikeda liked me well enough to hire me after graduation. I worked as a helper while taking online classes, getting my certificate and taking over the position when my predecessor left to spend more time with her family.

For once in my life, I'd been lucky.

Deka's squeal jars me out of my thoughts, and I smile as Mr. Akutsu joins me on the sidewalk in front of the building, holding Deka's hand tightly so they don't escape. Rin wiggles and pulls on my hand, and I let myself be led to the front doors, helping Rin open one side as they struggle against the weight.

I glance back at Mr. Akutsu. "Do you want to take them to the playground while I order food?"

Deka yanks his arm back and forth, straining toward freedom, and he gives a relieved nod. "A number four and a nugget kid's meal, please. I'll pay you back with cash, if that's okay?"

"Perfectly." I crouch to draw Rin's attention. "You're going to be on your best behavior for Mr. Akutsu, right?"

They nod vigorously, reach out, and grab Mr. Akutsu's free hand.

Smiling, I stand and watch the two kids drag him toward the back, where the indoor playground can clearly be seen through the wall of windows.

I order the food quickly, getting the same thing as Mr. Akutsu to make things easy, then stand off to the side until a bored-looking teenager calls my number.

Balancing the tray of food and drinks, I turn and scan the restaurant. I spot Mr. Akutsu's black, wavy hair at the back where he sits at a four-person booth right next to the large window that overlooks the playground. The kids are already gone, and I walk over to slide into the booth across from him.

He points at the neon-blue tube at the top. "They're up there."

Staring through the window, I spot Rin through the little, round openings in the plastic just as they jump into the tube slide. Their shriek of delight travels through the glass before they pop out the bottom into a pool of colorful plastic balls.

Grinning, I turn back to Mr. Akutsu. "How long do you think that will keep them entertained?"

"We'll have to drag them out." He reaches for the tray and divides the food.

"I got orange soda and lemon-lime." I point to the two cups. "I hope you like one of them."

"I'm a fan of both." He smiles at me, his eyes warm and friendly. "Which do you prefer?"

"Ahh." I stare at them, liking each one equally. "Orange, today."

"Then lemon-lime for me." He takes the remaining soda and moves the tray off to the side to make more room on the table.

We eat in companionable silence, watching the kids play. It feels nice, being with someone my own age. I don't have a lot of time to make friends, and the people I'm close to at work have their own lives. I'm one of the few in my age group with kids, too, which complicates things. Rin's hard to entertain in an adult situation, and most adults don't have the desire to spend time at parks or other activities appropriate for a child Rin's age.

"How long have you been a school administrator?" Mr. Akutsu asks, drawing my attention away from the playground.

I take a sip of soda, the sugary drink tickling my nose, before I answer him. "I've worked for the school for five years, but I've been an administrator for the past three."

His eyebrows shoot up, and he scans my face. "You can't be more than twenty-five."

"I just turned twenty-five last September," I admit, blood rushing to my cheeks, and I lift a self-conscious hand to cover my horns, knowing they'll be pink, too.

"You must be very driven," he murmurs, his tone impressed.

My flush deepens. I don't receive a lot of praise, especially not when it comes to the parents of the students I meet. I don't really feel like I deserve his praise, either. My push to get a better job had nothing to do with a drive to rise within my field and everything to do with a desperate desire to do right by my family.

I clear my throat and take another sip of my soda. The carbonation tickles my nose once more, and I quickly cover my mouth as I sneeze. My eyes water, and I grope for a napkin only to find Mr. Akutsu already holding one out.

He grins. "Soda gets me like that, too, when I haven't had it in a while."

"Thank you." Embarrassed, I wipe my mouth. "It's one of those treat items I don't indulge in often."

"I'm more of a coffee all the time kind of guy,

myself." He takes a sip of his soda. "But carbonation is fun sometimes."

Dismayed, I stare at the two cups. "I'm sorry, I should have asked what you wanted to drink before ordering."

"But this is fun." A shriek from the playground draws his attention, and we watch as our kids race to the entrance to the tubes to climb back up to the slide. His expression turns wistful. "I should do this more often."

I feel the same way as I watch Rin play with their friend. I spend so much time at work, giving these special moments to Hana. Maybe I should talk to Principal Ikeda about cutting back my hours. But, if it means a cut in pay, I really can't afford it.

When I turn back, I find Mr. Akutsu's gaze on me, that considering look back in his expression before his eyes drop to my left hand, still curled loosely around my soda. "Will your spouse be upset we ate out tonight without them?"

"Oh, no." I tuck my hands into my lap, though he clearly already saw I don't wear a pair ring. "I'm divorced."

He nods as if confirming it in his head. "I apologize. That was rude of me."

"No, it's fine." I clear my throat. "It was two years ago."

"I've only ever seen Hana at the daycare when I pick Deka up..." He trails off and offers me a wry smile. "Again, I apologize. Asking invasive questions comes too naturally to me."

"What do you do for a living?" I ask, curious and wanting to shift the conversation away from my ex-wife.

"I'm a lawyer." He doesn't sound like he's boasting when he says it, though he's young to be a lawyer. He must have graduated recently, but the car outside says he did well landing his job. As if he senses my thoughts, his smile grows. "It's a family tradition. My sister was also a lawyer, as are both of our parents. You could say it's in my blood."

My chest tightens. "I'm sorry for your loss. I have no idea what losing a sibling must feel like."

"Thank you." His eyes move back to the window. "This isn't the life I had mapped out for myself, but it's an amazing gift, you know?"

I do, and the shared understanding passes between us. We're both single fathers with young children, not something anyone plans, but I wouldn't trade Rin for the world.

A quiet chime breaks the mood, and Mr. Akutsu

reaches into his pocket to pull out a sleek black phone. He checks the screen, then glances up at me. "It's Sen."

I motion for him to answer, and as soon as he does, a panicked voice floods out, loud enough for me to hear despite his phone not being on speaker.

"Shig, Deka isn't at the daycare. I came to pick them up, but they're not here, and no one signed her out—"

He blanches. "Sen, it's okay, I have them. I was distracted—"

Senichi's angry retort cuts him off, and he winces as he pulls the phone away from his ear.

The reprimand goes on for a solid minute before Mr. Akutsu's allowed to apologize again and promises to be home soon.

He grimaces as he tucks his phone away. "Looks like I should go."

"He cares for his sibling," I respond as I gather our wrappers onto the empty tray.

"Yes." Mr. Akutsu sighs heavily. "I just wish he'd show the same care for himself."

"He's young." Guilt rushes through me as I remember the ultimatum I gave Senichi at our last meeting.

That can't have made Mr. Akutsu's life easier. I

want to apologize and offer a way out, but I bite back the desire. No matter how guilty I may feel now that I'm getting to know Mr. Akutsu a little better, I can't let my personal feelings sway a verdict that Senichi's counselor believes will help him in the long run.

This is probably why school administrators and student parents shouldn't get involved. But I can't bring myself to regret letting Rin spend more time with their friend.

I stand, tray in hand. "It was a pleasure sharing a meal with you, Mr. Akutsu." I shuffle awkwardly, not sure how parents usually do this. "Perhaps we can do it again, sometime? To let the kids play?"

"Please, call me Shig. And I'd like that very much." He stands and pulls the line of his jacket straight. "Now, for the hard part."

With a quiet laugh, I head for the trash area, more than happy to let him deal with calling the kids in from their fun.

I'll let him be the bad guy, then win Rin's goodwill by bribing them with their cold kid's meal like any respectable father would do.

MY FRIEND

The next two days pass quickly as I split my time between work and picking Rin up from school.

I keep an eye out for Shig, but our paths don't cross. I regret not asking if I could use the number on his business card for personal calls. I feel guilty using it when it was offered for emergencies regarding Senichi. If I don't run into him by the end of the week, though, I'll break social protocol, because Rin keeps asking when we'll have another play date at Happy Palace.

On Wednesday night, Hana calls to let me know she's gotten worse, not better, and that she's heading in to see the doctor. I worry she has an infection instead of a standard cold and tell her to take care of herself despite the burden her absence adds to my shoulders.

Rin doesn't make working from home easy, and I find myself not sitting down to my files until after I put them to bed, which makes for long nights and early wake-ups.

By the time Thursday rolls around, I feel like death warmed over and start to worry I'll come down with a cold of my own.

With how unreliable Karen is, and with Hana out of commission, I really can't afford to be sick. On my way from work and pick-up, I swing by the Quick Mart and buy some Immunity Booster tablets and a bottle of water before completing the drive to Rin's school.

I park and grab the small shopping bag, pulling out my purchase. The tablets pop and sizzle, turning the water orange, and it tickles my nose when I lift it to my lips to take a sip. The first swallow coats my tongue with an imitation-orange, mineral taste that makes my nose wrinkle, and I cap the bottle before getting out of my car to walk into Rin's school.

Chaos reigns, the sounds overwhelming for my fuzzy mind, and I search the sea of kids for mine.

Mr. Jacob waves for my attention and wordlessly points to the back. Of course, Rin's outside. They love the outdoors, and no amount of chill in the air will change their mind.

Pulling my jacket closer, I step outside, and a cold wind knifes through me. It smells metallic and promises more snow tonight, despite what the weatherman claimed.

I spot Rin on the monkey bars, playing alone, and call out, "Rin, time to go home!"

Their eyes flicker in my direction before they resolutely ignore me and pull themself back up for another spin.

I sigh, in no mood to fight them to leave the play yard, but also wanting to get out of the cold. "Rin, come on! Time to go!"

They don't even glance my way this time as they spin in a fast circle, up, down, then back up again, brown curls flying.

Today won't be fun. I know it in my bones. Know it from all the other times Rin tried to assert their authority to have things their way. Tears and tantrums are in my future, and I tuck my bottle of Immunity Booster into my pocket as I prepare for the battle to come.

Just as I step out onto the soft rubber yard, a small body darts past me, and I recognize Deka's blue cap and mittens as they runs up to Rin.

My spirits lift, and I glance back to find Shig standing just outside the door, rubbing his hands together against the cold.

He offers me a hesitant smile. "They wanted to say goodbye before heading home."

"You don't know the reprieve you just gave me." I abandon the play yard to join him beneath the overhang, where the building blocks some of the cold. "I was preparing for war."

"Well, keep preparing, because it never stops." He tucks his hands into his pockets and glances at me again. "I was hoping I'd hear from you. Has work been busy with preparations for the holiday?"

"Ah, no. Well, yes, but that's not why." I pull my jacket tighter at the throat. "I forgot to ask about your number."

His brows sweep together in confusion. "Didn't I give you my card?"

"Well, yes..." Embarrassed now for my waffling, I drop my gaze. "But this wasn't school-related..."

"Ah, I see." The tips of his shoes fill my view as he steps closer, and he thrusts out a hand, his palm up. "Give me your phone."

I lift my head in surprise before digging my phone from my pocket and passing it over.

He swipes at the screen, then shakes his head at me. "You should really password protect this."

I shrug. "It slows things down, and it's just Rin and me. There's no one who would want into my phone."

"Rin's almost seven, you know." He taps at the screen, programming in his number. "More than old enough to learn how fun phones can be."

Chagrined, I make a mental note to set a password. "You sound like you speak from experience."

He snorts softly. "Not mine, thank goodness. But my sister learned that lesson well with Sen." He presses more numbers, pulls his phone out, and holds it up to show a new message on the screen. "There, now we have each other's numbers. For *non*-school business."

I take back my phone, cradling it in my hand. "I'm dreadful at this, aren't I? Rin's already six, and you're the first parent friend I've made."

His eyes widen for a moment before that thoughtful expression returns. "It's not easy for some people to put themselves out there. I think it's more dreadful that society makes that the standard expectation."

Relief rushes through me that he understands. "You must be pretty outgoing to do your job."

A soft laugh escapes him. "If you're saying I know how to schmooze, I can't deny it. And I had my fair share of friends in university, though most have drifted away since I got the kids. It's difficult to be out all-night drinking when there's a troubled teenager and a child at home."

"I get that." I tuck my phone away. "Most of my friends ditched me once Rin was born. Nineteen-year-olds don't know what to do with a baby around."

"You did well, though." He nods to our kids, laughing as they run around. "Rin's a happy child."

Another cold breeze cuts through the walkway, and I shiver as I shove my hands into my pockets only to have my water bottle get in the way. With a grimace, I pull it out and give it a small shake before uncapping it to chug the rest.

Shig laughs at my expression when I finish and toss the bottle into the nearby trash can. "What was that, and how do I avoid it?"

"I'm feeling a little run down, so I thought I should probably boost my immune system since it's cold season." I lick my lips, tasting the orange tang still there. "I'd almost prefer the cold."

"Hana's still sick, I take it?" At my nod, he gives me a concerned once over. "How many decent meals have you eaten this week?"

I give him a wry look. "Does Happy Palace count? Rin takes all my attention, so it's been frozen meals every night, then I'm up late catching up on work once they're in bed."

"Oh, no, this just won't do." He turns to the play yard and claps his hands. "Kids, time to go!"

An instant whine fills the air.

"You can play together back at the house where it's warm!" he calls before glancing at me. "You're coming over for dinner. I make a mean casserole."

My stomach rumbles at the offer, but I shake my head. "Oh, no, we can't possibly impose."

"I insist." He catches Deka as they crash against his side. "The kids can keep each other entertained, and you can get through some of your work while I make dinner. It's a win-win for everyone."

The offer of a good meal and going to bed on time is too tempting to pass up. "Okay, but only if you let me reciprocate next time."

"Deal." He crouches and lifts Deka before he turns toward the door. "We live in the Greenwich area. I hope it's not too far from your place?"

Greenwich is a nice area of town full of new

developments, but it's not that far from our house. Our city isn't huge to begin with, so even if we lived on completely opposite sides of town, it wouldn't be more than a twenty-minute inconvenience.

"Only about ten minutes. We'll follow you." I catch Rin's hand, and their small, icy fingers freeze mine. I glance down. "Where are your mittens?"

Rin rolls their eyes. "I can't hold onto the bar with my mittens on."

I release them. "Well, put them on now. Your hands are like ice."

They pat their pockets, then twist to scan the play yard, and I let out a sigh. "You lost them again?"

"No," they deny, but the mittens don't magically reappear.

"They'll show up in the lost and found tomorrow," Shig says from the doorway. "I can loan you a pair of Deka's if you don't have spares."

"No, we have spares." I sigh and lift Rin into my arms, hoping to share some of my body heat with my frozen child. "But we're going to run out of spares if this keeps happening."

"I don't need mittens," Rin announces. "They just get in the way."

"They keep your fingers from falling off," I counter.

Rin lifts their hands and stares at their fingers as if waiting for them to fall off this very second. When nothing happens, they give me a look that says they think I'm telling stories.

I bounce them in my arms. "Okay, but when you don't have pinkies anymore, don't come crying to me."

They giggle and reach up to squish my cheeks with their cold hands. "You're silly."

"No, you're silly," I squeeze out, and Shig's soft laugh draws my attention to him. I bounce Rin again. "Come on. Let's sign out so we can get out of here."

At the reminder of what happened last time, Shig studiously looks away, his chin up and his spine straight as he walks back into the chaos of the daycare.

Excitement quickens my pulse as I follow. Making a new friend is a big step for me, and I can't lie to myself and say it's just for Rin's sake. I like talking to Shig, like that we share common ground, and it's been far too long since I had a friend I could rely on. I've spent the last two years living for Rin, and the years before that putting everything within me into maintaining a family that was never stable to begin with.

But this feels different. New and hopeful.

I just need to not mess it up, for my sake as much as for Rin's.

"If you give me your coats, I'll hang them up," Shig says as he leads the way into his house.

As I help Rin out of their jacket, then mine, I glance around. While nice, it's smaller than I expected based on his car and the neighborhood we drove through to get here. His is one of the smaller houses on the block. A modest rambler in the middle of mini-mansions.

The entryway leads straight into a small family room, which flows into a dining room with a table designed to seat six. Past that, an island separates the living space from the kitchen. A large opening next to the dining area leads to a hall, where I assume the bedrooms hide. The furniture looks nice but well used, the leather couch worn and soft with a padded coffee table that invites guests to sit back and put their feet up. Soft lap blankets rest over the arms of the furniture, ready to be snuggled up in for a movie night.

As I pass Shig our coats, Deka grabs Rin's hand, and they scamper to the hall.

"Don't worry," Shig says as he hangs everyone's jackets in a small closet behind the door. "There's no way into the backyard from the bedrooms, unless they climb out the window."

"I wouldn't put it past Rin to climb out a window," I warn.

He grins. "Well, the fence in the backyard is pretty high, too, and they're not tall enough to reach the latch to open the gate."

I return his smile and glance around once more. "You have a nice home."

"Thank you. I bought it after the kids moved in." He turns and leads the way farther into the house, his black tail wafting back and forth. "My one bedroom wasn't going to cut it anymore, and the property is a good investment."

Gods, he has his life so much more put together than I do, and he's only a year or two older than me. Is that the difference between going to university instead of working straight out of high school?

"You can set up at the dining table, if you like." He motions to the dark wood table. "It will take a bit to get dinner prepped. Do you want something to drink? Coffee? Water?"

Coffee sounds wonderful right now, as I feel like I'm about to pass out. But I don't want him to go to more trouble than he already is. "Water's fine."

As he walks into the kitchen, I set my work bag on the table and settle onto one of the padded chairs.

It feels odd to come over here with the intention to work, and I hesitate to pull out my laptop. "Are you sure you don't need help?"

"I've got this covered." Shig sets a glass of water by my elbow. "Hurry up and get to work so you can relax over the weekend."

"I appreciate this," I murmur as I open my laptop. "If we were at home…"

"Rin would be demanding all of your attention." He pats my shoulder, his hand warm through my button-up. "Believe me, this is giving me peace of mind, too. When Sen isn't home, Deka is quite the handful."

"I bet." When he squeezes my shoulder, I look at his hand then up to his face, wondering if I missed something.

But he's looking at the front door, a troubled frown on his lips. After a moment, his hand falls away, and he heads back into the kitchen.

Is he wondering when Senichi will be home? Is

he worried about what his nephew is up to right now? It's a fair concern, based on my limited interaction with the kid.

The clatter of dishes being pulled out of cupboards fills the house, a familiar and comforting sound. "I hope you like chicken."

"Right now, I like anything that isn't a fish stick," I say as I open my first file and set it next to my laptop.

"Is that a must-have for Rin?" He opens the fridge and begins to select ingredients. "Deka is on a hot dog and macaroni with cheese kick right now."

"Rin will love that, too." I open my first spreadsheet, the numbers on the printouts demanding my attention.

As my fingers move over the keyboard, the sound of Shig bustling around in the kitchen fades to comforting background noise, and I lose myself in work.

CLIQUES

The smell of coffee pulls me from my work, and I lift my head, blinking the room back into focus. I don't know how much time passed since I started working, but Shig now sits at the table across from me, glasses perched on his nose as he works on his own laptop. A steaming mug sits on a coaster beside him, and he lifts it absentmindedly to take a sip.

Guilt rushes through me that I so completely ignored him and didn't even realize he finished prepping dinner. The way I lose myself in work was one of the many things Karen and I fought about. She thought that, when she was around, all of my attention should be devoted to her. I tried, I really did, but sometimes work spilled into personal time.

It was either stay longer at school and not see my family or bring the work home. If I waited until after Rin went to bed to pull out my work bag, it would only launch a new fight about how I ruined the romance of our marriage.

While Shig is far from being Karen, I still should have paid attention to him more than my work. He was making dinner for Rin and me, after all.

He lifts his cup again, tips it forward with a frown, finds it empty, and sets it back down.

Seeing a way to make up for my neglect, I push my chair back. Taking his mug, I walk into the kitchen, where I find the coffee pot on the counter next to the fridge. I refill his cup, then hesitate at the shaker of sugar that sits next to it. I have no idea how much he puts in his coffee, and if he uses creamer. Suddenly, my gesture of apology feels silly.

I stare in dismay at the dark liquid, hating to interrupt his work and hating the idea of bringing him back a cup he'll have to fix to his liking.

A warm hand touches my waist, and I jump in surprise as Shig leans past me to grab the sugar. "I like just enough to take the bitterness out."

As he adds a dash of sugar to his cup, embarrassment flushes my cheeks. "I should have asked. I'm sorry."

His head turns, his moss-green eyes soft as they meet mine. "I appreciate the thought. It's been a while since someone's done that for me."

"So, there's no significant other who pampers you?" I ask, then flush hotter for getting so personal. "I'm sorry."

His lips curve. "No, no significant other. There hasn't been a lot of time for that. And meeting new people is hard."

"Kids take up a lot of time," I agree.

I'm surprised Shig has problems even with his new family, though. He's attractive and obviously has a bright future ahead of him. People should be lining up for the chance to date him, kids or no kids.

"Are you and your ex still close?" he asks.

The question takes me by surprise, but turnabout is fair play, I suppose.

I shake my head. "I'm pretty sure she hates me."

He winces. "That bad?"

"Things didn't end amicably," I say, not sure how much I want to go into the dirty details of our divorce. "She's found her mate, though, so I like to think she's at least a little happier now."

He rubs my back in small, soothing circles, the gesture bringing with it an unexpected sense of comfort. He must have done the same for Deka so many times it's now ingrained in him to soothe away bad feelings, and the knowledge warms me. It's obvious he loves his sister's children, despite the havoc they brought to his life.

"What about you?" he asks.

Confused by the question, I stare at him blankly for a moment before I look away. "I don't hate her, but our marriage was never about love."

"Ah." Understanding, his eyes shift past me to the hall. "It was about responsibility?"

I nod, grateful I don't need to explain further. Shig's smart and can do the math. Rin's six, which means she was conceived as soon as I grew my horns. It's a volatile time, and doing stupid things is common. They just don't usually end with a baby.

Shig continues to stroke my back, and I suddenly become aware of how close we stand and the intimacy of our conversation. It's a lot for two people to talk about, especially when we're just getting to know each other, but I feel inexplicably safe with Shig. Maybe it's the way he treats his youngest charge and his worry over his nephew. I just *know* he's a good person and that he won't judge me for my failed marriage.

I look back down at the coffee bar. "Maybe I'll take you up on that coffee?"

"Of course." Shig reaches past me and opens the narrow cupboard next to the fridge to reveal an assortment of glasses and mugs. "Take your pick."

I study the options, giving it the serious consideration it deserves. There are standard, solid-colored blue mugs like the one Shig's using, but there are also a couple that look like Deka picked them out. I pull down one with Yip Yip grinning on the front, a favorite childrens' hippo celebrity.

Holding it up, I smile. "Rin likes hippos."

"They have good taste, then." Shig lifts the coffee pot from the warmer and fills my cup. "There's cream in the fridge if you'd like some."

"I take it black." We walk out of the kitchen together, and I gesture to his laptop. "Do you have a lot of work tonight?"

He winces. "It never ends. But I'll put it away when dinner's ready. Have to know when to draw the line, right?"

It's a line I struggle with, which is why I rely so much on Hana. Not having her here to help has been a big eye-opener on how much she does for Rin's care, and I'm not sure I like the picture it paints.

"What's the frown for?" Shig asks, and I look up to find him watching me.

I smooth the tension from my face. "I was just

thinking how it shouldn't have taken me this long to meet you." When Shig's brows shoot up in surprise, I rush to add, "Or any of the parents at the kindergarten. But you, specifically, I suppose. Since Rin and Deka are such good friends. I should have met you sooner."

"Ah. I actually thought the same thing." He brushes a self-conscious hand through his hair. "That I should have sent a greeting or something. Some of the parents at the kindergarten do that." He gives a short laugh. "They do lunches, too, though. And after-work drinks."

My lips part in surprise. "They do?"

He nods. "They're rather cliquish, actually. It's difficult being the new guy when they already have their little groups. I was happy when our kids became friends, but I figured you already had your clique…"

A surprised laugh escapes me. "Well, the joke's on me. I didn't even know I was being left out."

"That probably made the other parents quite upset." Shig lifts his mug to hide a smile. "They talk about you."

My stomach tightens at the comment. I didn't know they talked, but I'm not surprised. I'm sure they have a lot to say about the young, divorced father who can't even find the time to come to the kindergarten when it's not a scheduled meeting.

The front door bangs open, bringing with it a gust of wind, and I slap a hand over my papers before they fly off the table. Shig stands, his expression a cross between worry and irritation.

A moment later, Senichi stomps into view. He has new bruises on his face since the last time I saw him, and blood trickles from a split in his lip.

I leap up in alarm, and his eyes immediately jump to me, then narrow on Shig. "What is *he* doing here?"

"Did you get in another fight?" Shig crosses the room, his hand stretched out. "I told you—"

"I can take care of a couple of punks." Senichi dodges his uncle's touch and simultaneously grabs a pair of earbuds that hang from a wire around his neck. "I'm going to my room. I don't need dinner."

Without waiting for a response, he stuffs the earbuds into his ears and stomps to the hall that leads back to the bedrooms.

Feeling guilty I made things worse between Shig and Senichi, I turn to gather my paperwork. "I'll go. You have family matters to take care of."

Shig's shoulders slump. "No, please stay. If you

leave before dinner, I'll be eating this casserole for the rest of the week."

I pause and glance uncertainly down the hall. "If you're sure?"

"I'm sure." Shig hurries to the table, closes his laptop, then moves it out of the way. "Sit back down. I'll go check on dinner."

Resuming my seat, I watch Shig hurry back into the kitchen, and my eyes drop to his tail. Gone is the relaxed sway from earlier. Now, it tucks close to his body, with an almost questioning curl at the tip, and I remember how it felt to become a single dad. I had more time to come to terms with having a child, but Karen's leaving came as a shock, as did the sudden knowledge I'd be raising Rin practically alone. Shig didn't have any experience before he found himself saddled with a pre-gendered child and an angsty almost-adult.

As dishes clatter from the kitchen, I put away my work. I got far enough that the rest can wait until I'm back in the office tomorrow.

Standing, I walk to the opening to the kitchen. "Do you need help?"

I catch Shig about to open the oven, and he straightens in surprise. My attention shifts immediately to the pink, bunny potholders on his hands. They even have bunny ears on the backs.

Shig glances down at them, too, and laughs before curling his fingers toward his palms and bouncing them in a hopping motion. "Another gift from Deka. They make them smile."

They make me smile, too, and I lean against the counter. "They're cute."

Shig's tail tentatively perks up, and his shoulders relax. "I'd die of embarrassment if my co-workers saw this, so you have to promise to keep my secret."

I mime zipping my lips, then straighten. "Where are the plates? I'll set the table."

Shig points one bunny to the cupboard on the opposite side of the sink. "The adult plates are in the uppers, and the kid's plates are in the lower cabinet."

Nodding, I skirt past him to the opposite side of the kitchen. The galley layout doesn't lend itself to multiple people in the kitchen, and Shig's tail brushes against my legs as I pass. He doesn't seem to notice, though, as he bends once more and opens the oven to pull out two small casserole dishes. The scent of food grows stronger, and my stomach lets out a loud rumble. It's been a while since I had a good, home-cooked meal.

"Forks are in the drawer," Shig tells me as he

kicks the oven door shut and sets the hot dishes on the stovetop.

I try not to be obvious as I peek over at the dishes. One is clearly the promised mac and cheese with hot dogs for the kids, and the other looks like pasta, with a fragrant red sauce and melty cheese on top.

My stomach lets out another rumble of approval, and I catch the curve of Shig's lips as he smiles with amusement.

Before I can embarrass myself more, I gather the plates and silverware, then walk them out to the table before I head for the bedrooms.

"Deka. Rin," I call as I enter the hall.

Shig said Deka's room pointed toward the backyard, so I turn left and venture deeper into the house. The first door I pass is closed, and music pounds out from inside, identifying it as Senichi's room. He must have switched to a stereo system to drown out everything. I know that feeling. I've wanted to block out the world more than once.

I walk past his room with a pang of guilt, but even I know not to prod angry teenagers. He'll either come out for food later, or he'll go to bed hungry. He's old enough to make that decision on his own.

Light pours from the open door at the end of the hall, and quiet giggles drift out before silence falls.

I poke my head around the door. "Kids, it's time for dinner."

Soft greens and yellows fill Deka's room, with a poke-a-dot comforter on the bed and posters of kid's movies hang in frames on the walls. A small table sits against the wall surrounded by stuffed animals and an abandoned tea party at its center. Costumes spill from the chest at the foot of the bed, and I spy a feathered boa peeking out.

But Deka and Rin aren't in sight.

Smiling, I step farther into the room and rest my hands on my hips as I look around. "Oh, no, wherever could they have gone?"

Another muffled giggle sounds from behind me, followed by a *shh*.

I shake my head in dismay. "I guess I'll just have to eat all the hot dogs by myself."

As I turn to leave, the closet door flies open, and the kids shriek, "Boo!"

I lift a dramatic hand to my heart and fall to the ground.

They erupt in laughter as I sprawl out. "You got me!"

Cheering, they sprint circles around me before racing out of the room.

I climb back to my feet and follow at a slower pace. When I reach the dining room, I find them reenacting the scare for Shig, and my heart warms at how happy Rin looks right now. It's been a while since I've seen them play like this at home, and I'm glad now that I stayed, despite the awkwardness.

After the divorce, Rin became a little closed off. When Karen broke one too many promises to come pick them up for a visit, I began to worry my ex's constant wishy-washy behavior would seriously impact Rin's development. But seeing them with Deka eases some of that concern.

Behind me, a door creaks open, then Senichi shuffles past me to the dining table and takes a seat. His sullen expression contrasts sharply with his young sibling's until Deka climbs up the side of his chair and plops down on his lap. Then, the frown vanishes, and he squeezes Deka in a tight hug until they shriek and flail to escape. Grinning, Senichi ruffles their hair, and the tension breaks.

Shig glances over at me, his tail wafting back and forth. "Come on, before the kids eat all the food, and you're left to suffer with that growly monster in your belly."

Rin laughs and growls as they climb up onto the seat next to Deka. "Come on, daddy! The belly monster wants a hot dog!"

Smiling, I join everyone at the table and sit between Rin and Shig, feeling like part of a family for the first time in a while.

HALF MY MESS

Friday afternoon, Shig sends me a text message.

Shig: You should come do work at my house again.

The suddenness of the invite makes me smile. It feels like we've been friends for longer than a couple days. Like me bringing Rin to his house is not only normal, but wanted. Considering what to say, I text back.

Juro: You just want someone to distract Deka.

The reply comes instantly.

Shig: Am I really so transparent?

He follows it up with a puppy dog face.

A laugh escapes me as I respond.

Juro: How about I cook for you guys tonight?

Shig: Oh, I get to see your castle?

That makes me pause, and I take a moment to respond.

Juro: If you're expecting a castle, you'll be disappointed.

Juro: But you're welcome to come see for yourself.

Shig: Deal.

Bemused, I set my phone aside to focus back on work. I want to get through my files today before leaving so I can actually spend time talking to Shig.

I pull into my driveway and stay in the car with Rin until Shig pulls up alongside me, then climb out.

Shig takes in our house as he helps Deka out of the car seat. "Okay, I admit. It's not a castle."

I take a look at my house, too. When it was built back in my grandparent's day, it was probably considered a mansion, but by today's standards, it's just a regular house with a small turret. When Rin claimed that as their playroom, I was happy to give up a potential office space if it meant having a place to contain the majority of Rin's toys. It's also warmer up there than in the rest of the house, and there's no way for Rin to slip outside without passing through the living room. But still, it's far from being a *castle*.

I shake my head as Rin flings themself out of the back of my car as soon as I open the door. I need to baby lock the seat belt as well as the car door, if that's even a thing. "You really thought I lived in a castle?"

"It *is* a castle, daddy!" Rin yells, racing for the door only to come up short when they find it locked. They bounce up and down. "Come on, come on, come on!"

I jingle my keys. "Do you want to unlock the door?"

Rin instantly runs back to me, snatches the keys, then races back to the door, trying to fit every key on the ring into the lock.

"That's how locks break, you know," Shig whispers as Rin tries to shove the wrong key in.

I shrug. "There's access through the back, too. If the lock breaks, I can replace it."

Rin finds the right key and flings the door open, shouting, "I'm home!" Their voice echoes through the house, and Rin grabs Deka's hand. "Come on! I'll show you my tower!"

"Deka's been talking about seeing Rin's castle for

months," Shig informs me as we walk inside after them. "I had expectations."

Laughing, I gesture around the living room. "Sorry to disappoint, but it's just a normal house." I shiver as I slip out of my jacket. "And a cold one, too. Give me a second to turn the heaters on. The kitchen is back that way."

I point to the back of the house before I head around the house, turning on the space heaters, then spend an extra couple of minutes picking up Rin's room in case the kids switch locations. Overhead, their feet pound back and forth, and the noise fills me with a sense of happiness. It's been way too long since Rin laughed like that at home.

Walking back to the front of the house, I find Shig still in the living room, his coat in hand as he studies the narrow bookcase next to the TV.

At the sound of my footsteps, he glances over his shoulder. "You have some nice classics here. I didn't even know some of these came out on DVD."

"I'm going to be sad when my old disc-player dies. Most of them weren't converted for digital download." I walk over and hold out a hand. "I'll hang your coat up."

"Oh, thanks." Shig holds his coat out, and our fingers brush in passing.

Turning, I walk it to the coat closet. "Did you bring a lot of work with you today?"

His footsteps follow after me. "Left it all at the office for once. What about you?"

I hang his coat up next to mine. "There wasn't anything urgent I needed to bring home."

Shig gasps. "Does that mean we actually have a night to...*relax*?"

The way he says it makes it sound like a foreign word, and I close the closet with a laugh. "What's that mean? I don't think I've ever heard that word before."

When I turn around, I find him right behind me, his eyes twinkling and his tail wafting back and forth. "I *think* it's when people usually watch a movie."

I point to the bookcase. "One of *those* movies?"

He widens his eyes at me. "It's been forever since I saw *My Sweet Transition*."

Another laugh escapes. "That's the one you're going for?"

I never would have pegged Shig as a romantic comedy enthusiast.

He puffs out his cheeks at me. "You have a problem with *My Sweet Transition*?"

I shake my head. "No, I love it. I own it on VHS,

too. Not that I have anything that will play that copy, anymore."

"Excellent." Shig rubs his hands together, then shivers. "Please tell me you have a blanket we can snuggle under."

Guilty over how cold the house is, I motion for him to follow me into the kitchen. "Hang out with me in here while I get dinner into the oven, and we give the heaters time to kick in."

He chaffs his arms as he follows me. "Are you trying to save on the energy bill?"

"I wish, but no." Opening the fridge, I pull out ingredients. "The old boiler needs to be replaced, so we're making do with space heaters for now."

"Oh, yeah, you don't want to leave those on unattended." Shig scoots up onto the barstool that Rin usually claims when they help me in the kitchen. "There are always a handful of cases that come through the office every year about fires caused by space heaters."

"Yeah, I made sure to buy the electric ones that shut off if they tip over. They're supposed to be the safest." I drop fish sticks onto a tray before running my frozen fingers under hot water. "I'm hoping to replace the boiler before it gets too much colder."

"Here, I'll help." Shig hops off his stool and

comes around to my side of the island to survey the ingredients. "What are we making?"

I pause in the process of pulling out the cutting board. Karen never offered to help make dinner, even though she didn't work and frequently complained I never spent enough time with her.

"Um…" I set the cutting board on the counter, along with the knife. "I was going to make stirfry, if you'd like to chop the veggies?"

Shig's tail baps against my leg as he pulls the bell pepper, onion, and green beans over to sit in front of him. "I can totally do that."

Bemused by his excitement, I pull out a second cutting mat and another knife for the meat. Shig chats casually about his day and some of his clients as we work side-by-side, then goes with me to check out the 'castle' where we deliver the plates of fish sticks to Rin's little table that they have up there. I don't usually let them eat where I can't keep an eye on them, but I find myself selfishly wanting to continue our adult conversation. It's been way too long since I've had an adult conversation that didn't involve work or arguing with Karen.

When we head back downstairs, we grab out bowls of stir fry and return to the living room, where I pull out the promised lap blanket. Shig snuggles into a corner of the couch as I load *My Sweet Transition*.

Shig laughs at all the same parts I do, and soon, we're taking turns misquoting scenes from the movie.

When the more serious parts of the movie unfurl, we fall quiet as the main character goes through their final transition into a horned girl.

Shig leans forward to set his empty bowl on the coffee table before he stretches out, his feet near my hip. His toes nudge against my thigh.

Surprised, I look over at him to find his attention fixed on the TV, his expression wistful. "It's hard to imagine that will be our kids in a few years."

My throat tightens, and I pat his foot. "One transition at a time. First, their gender."

He glances over at me. "Any idea which way Rin will go?"

I shake my head. "They aren't leaning either way, as far as I can tell."

Shig scoots lower on the couch, his toes wiggling beneath my leg, the same way Rin does when their toes are cold. Worried, I reach out and tuck the blanket tighter around his feet. Rin always likes it when I turn them into a caterpillar, but I resist the instinct to completely swaddle Shig.

He lets out a contented sigh. "Is it bad I want Deka to be a boy? The idea of raising a girl is *terrifying*."

I laugh and point at the TV. "That's why we have movies like this for reference."

Shig turns his head to watch the scene and smiles. "This just makes it even more terrifying. Can you imagine Rin going through all of that in high school?"

I shudder, and Shig laughs, his toes wiggling. "See? Pray for a boy."

Feet thunder from the stairway, and we turn to peer over the couch. A moment later, Deka and Rin run into view.

"Daddy!" Rin shouts at the same time Deka shouts, "ShiShi!"

Shig cuts a glance at me. "You didn't just hear that."

I widen my eyes at him. "Hear what, ShiShi?"

In response, he pulls his feet out from under me to kick against my thigh.

Rin launches over the back of the couch, their round body getting caught on the back and their chubby legs kick. Undeterred, Rin grabs the back of my sweater. "We want dessert, Daddy!"

Deka takes the longer route around the couch

and bounces on their toes next to Shig, their large, round eyes silently begging.

"Well...." I grab the back of Rin's yellow jumper and pull them over. "There *might* be popsicles in the freezer..."

Shig yanks the blanket up to his chin. "Brr."

Helping Rin to sit up, I hold up a finger. "One popsicle. And I better not find fish sticks in the carpet upstairs, or it's dining table only from now on."

Rin and Deka exchange wide-eyed looks and bolt back to the turret.

I lean back with a sigh. "I'll have to drag the vacuum up there later."

"I can help," Shig offers from beneath his blanket. "Half my children, half my mess."

The kids thunder back down the stairs and race for the kitchen.

I pat Shig's leg. "How about you make sure they don't make another mess down here?"

"And abandon my blanket?" The blanket wafts, and after a moment, I realize his tail's wagging. "Oh, no, I really can't..."

"You're not at all convincing." With another pat, I stand and walk to the coat closet where I keep the vacuum.

"I'll do the cleaning tomorrow," he calls after me.

I pause, one hand on the vacuum. "Tomorrow's Saturday."

"So?" The couch cushions squeak. "Do you already have plans? I was going to talk you into a park date."

My chest tightens. I haven't taken Rin to the park in a while. I hadn't felt like I had the time. Weekends were reserved for chores and getting ready for the next week.

But Shig's suggestion reminds me that I need to do better. Is this how adult friendships are supposed to be? Pushing each other to be better? Because it's definitely what I've needed all these years. Someone to help out and remind me when to stop and breathe. My throat thickens with an emotion I can't identify. It feels like shame and gratitude at the same time.

Clearing my throat, I grab the vacuum. "Sounds like a plan."

PARK DATE

"Here you are." Shig returns from the coffee cart and passes me one of the to-go cups.

"Thank you." Eagerly, I wrap my cold fingers around it as I watch the kids. "I should have brought gloves. I'm always on Rin for losing theirs, but I didn't even consider how cold the park would be with us just standing around."

"Hold this." Shig passes me his coffee, then tugs the scarf from around his neck and loops it around mine, tucking it under my chin. "There you go. That should help."

"But what about you?" I protest as he takes his coffee back. "Now, you'll be cold."

"Ah, but I *did* bring gloves." He holds his hand up

as proof, displaying the black gloves he wears, and gives me an impish smile. "We can trade in an hour, so you can have warm hands and I can have a warm neck."

The offer pulls a laugh from me. "Deal."

"I'm just glad you wanted to come today." He takes a sip of his hot coffee as he looks at the park over the brim. "Not a lot of people are brave enough to risk a park date so late in December."

"I can't say I'll be jumping at the invitation in January, when the heavy snow starts." Rin's laughter fills the air, and I smile. "Though, I'll probably still come."

"I'm happy to hear that," he murmurs.

From the corner of my eye, I study his profile. It can't have been easy for him to suddenly become the guardian to one almost-grown child and another not even old enough to have gone through the gender transition. He's so young, but he stepped up when he was needed, not something everyone would have done, and I admire him for that.

I turn toward him. "Do you mind if I ask about your sister?

Startled green eyes lift to meet mine, and I suddenly realize how invasive that question was.

"You don't have to tell me," I hurry to add. "I just want to know more about you."

A sad smile crosses his face. "I don't mind. It's not an especially exciting story, though."

I shake my head. "I'm not asking you to entertain me."

"Most people who ask expect some grand tale, but it's pretty simple." He takes another sip of coffee and returns his focus to the playground. "Ena was a lot older than me. I was the surprise child long after our parents stopped trying. I was still in preschool when she found her mate and they had Sen." He laughs softly. "I was six and not interested in babies."

I chuckle. "No, not at the grand old age of six."

"Hush, or you won't get the story," he admonishes, his tail smacking me playfully in the leg.

I mime zipping my lips and sip my coffee to help keep me warm.

"By the time I graduated middle school, I had become the official babysitter of the family. My sister and her husband were both lawyers and focused on their careers. They planned to take over the family business once our parents stepped down, but then she became pregnant with Deka and their focus changed. Like our parents, they weren't prepared for a second child, so her husband took a more profitable job in Merch Hail, and they moved away."

His voice roughens, and he clears his throat. "They were busy a lot, and I only knew Deka through photos they sent of the kids. There was always a plan for them to come back, eventually, and our parents were getting near retirement age. They were actually preparing to return when they were in a car accident. Luckily, the kids were at school when it happened. Their car hit some ice and slid off the side of the mountain."

I step closer and place a hand on his arm. "I'm so sorry."

He reaches up and covers my cold fingers with his warmer ones. "We all thought we'd have more time to come back together as a family. Losing both of them took everyone by surprise, but Sen took it the hardest. He was always a serious child, good at school and keeping mostly to himself. My parents wanted to take the kids in, but my sister named me as their guardian, and I didn't want to disappoint her memory."

"You're a good man," I murmur, meaning it.

He steps closer until our arms press together to share our body heat. A fine tremor runs through him, and I lift a hand to rub his back, much the way I do with Rin when they stay out in the cold too long.

"I waffled on it for a while," he whispers, pain clear in his voice. "If it had just been Sen, I might have given in to my parents taking over. They knew how to raise children. They'd already done it twice. But they're also getting old, and their stamina isn't what it used to be. Deka would have run circles around them."

"There's no shame in hesitating." My eyes drift to Rin on the slide. "When Karen told me she was pregnant, my first instinct wasn't to marry her."

He turns to look at me. "Your parents pushed for it?"

I nod, remembering that argument. "They're conservative, and they have ideas about broken families."

Shig scoffs, making me smile.

"I don't think I would have stuck it out so long with Karen if I wasn't so worried about disappointing them. They wanted us to be happy together, but..." I shake my head.

Shig presses his arm against mine in silent support. "Can I ask what ended it?"

My lips thin, and I check Rin's location, making sure they're too far away to hear. "She cheated on me. She'd been doing it for a while, but then she found her mate, and that was the end of our family."

Shig's lip curls in disgust. "She should have ended it herself if she was that unhappy."

"I think she wanted to secure her next income before leaving me." The shame of that still burns. I put so much work into keeping us afloat, sacrificed so much while she gave up nothing. I shake my head to dispel the dark thoughts. "My parents weren't thrilled when I told them we were getting a divorce, but it's hard to argue when Fate's involved. I think they wanted me to try harder, though. If I'd been a better husband, she wouldn't have strayed."

"That's horrible." Shig grasps my hand and squeezes it. "I know we haven't known each other for long, but I don't get the impression that you failed in any way."

"I appreciate that." I squeeze his hand in return.

We smile at each other before shrieks pull our attention back to the playground. But Deka and Rin are fine, having fun on the monkey bars. They keep sliding off, though, and I sigh when Rin finally yanks off their gloves and throws them on the ground so they have a better grip on the bars.

"That's how we keep losing mittens," I mutter,

noting where these ones fell so I can grab them before we leave.

Shig grins. "Rin's fun. Deka's really opened up since they became friends."

"Deka's good for Rin, too. They didn't have many friends at their old daycare."

"Why did you make the change?" he asks, then quickly adds, "Not that I'm ungrateful you did."

"Their old school was farther from work and didn't have a good pre-gender setup. They were just a daycare. I liked that this place has preschool and kindergarten for the kids, so they'll be in a better position once they transfer to grade school."

Karen wasn't happy when I informed her of the change. It meant spending more on the new place, but I keep that part to myself. I already unloaded more on Shig than I planned to. He's just so easy to talk to, and I'm comfortable around him in a way I haven't been with my colleagues at work. There's just something about him that is open and accepting.

Funny that I would become friends with the guardian of my child's friend, but it also makes things easy and natural.

"That's why I picked that school, too," Shig admits. "And they have excellent online ratings, and they're open later than other places."

"That was definitely in their favor." While I have a nanny, too, sometimes Hana's classes go late.

She had messaged me yesterday with another update, once again apologizing for the inconveniences, but I told her to just focus on getting healthy again.

What I didn't say is that her illness gives me an excuse not to stay at work, and I've been enjoying my time with Rin while strengthening my friendship with Shig. I'd feel too guilty, otherwise, to take time off that could be spent working.

A cold breeze whips past us.

I shiver and hunch my shoulders.

"Oh, no, your nose is turning red." Shig reaches up to adjust the scarf around my neck, closing any gaps where the wind can sneak through. "Maybe we should relocate to someplace warmer? The kids should be ready to eat after all that running around."

"I wouldn't object." If I'm freezing, Shig must be doubly so since he gave me his scarf.

He smiles, his eyes brightening. "It might be a little fancy for the kids, but we can always drop them off with Sen if you're open to—"

My phone vibrates in my pocket, and I hold up a hand. "Give me a second."

"No problem, I'll get the kids."

As he strides onto the playground, yelling for them that it's time to go, I check the caller ID and frown before I answer. "Hello, Mrs. Thomas. What can I do for you?"

Mrs. Thomas lives across the street from us and has my number for emergencies, but sometimes, she calls to ask for help around the house or just to invite me over for tea and cookies. She's getting on in years and lonely after her husband passed away, so I always try to be accommodating.

"Juro, dear," she says, her voice warbling. "I'm so glad you answered. I knew you weren't home, and I thought you should know your wife is at the house. She and *that man* have been parked in the driveway for five minutes now."

"Ex-wife," I correct instinctively as dread pools in my stomach. "Thank you for letting me know. I'll give her a call."

"Do that," she instructs. "And make sure you stop by for tea soon. I have a fresh box of cookies to share."

"I will," I promise. "Thank you, Mrs. Thomas."

Pressing the End button, I walk farther away from the playground as I call Karen. I've been having such a good day so far that I hate to have her ruin it, but I also don't know why she's at my house when she saw Rin last weekend. She didn't message or anything, either, which has me worried. It's not a short drive over the mountains, and if she has money to waste on gas, then she should stop taking from me.

Her phone rings and almost goes to voicemail before she picks up.

I don't wait to hear her greeting before I demand, "What are you doing at my house? It's not your weekend to have Rin."

"Well, aren't you just a ray of sunshine?" she snaps. "Scott needed to come over for business, and we stopped to see if Rin was available for lunch, but you're not home."

The way she says it sounds accusing, like I should be sitting at home, waiting on the off chance she decides to show up unannounced.

"I'm out and won't be back until later." I carefully avoid telling her where I am. The last thing I need is for her to show up and have Shig witness us fighting. "You should have called to let me know you were coming."

"It's fine. It was spur of the moment, but we need to head back soon." Her easy agreement takes me aback. Karen never easily agrees to anything, especially when she had other plans. "Scott was nice enough to fix your porch light, so make sure to thank him next time we're together."

I pull the phone away from my head and check the screen to make sure I called the right person. In the four years we were together, Karen never lifted a finger to help around the house. Why would she do so now?

"Give Rin a hug for me," she continues, her voice distant until I return the phone to my ear.

"I will." Unsure how to deal with a friendly Karen, I add, "Drive safely on your way back home."

"We will. Bye!"

The call ends without waiting for my response, which is much more like the woman I've grown to know over the years.

Bemused by the entire conversation, I tuck my phone away and head back to Shig and the kids.

"Everything okay?" he asks as I join them.

"Yeah, we're good." Bending, I scoop Rin up. "Where are your mittens?"

Giggling, they press ice-cold fingers against my cheeks, and I mock bite at them, making Rin laugh harder.

"Here, you go." Shig slips the missing mittens

into my pocket before grabbing Deka's hand. "Now, about that meal..."

"Actually, do you mind if we pick something up and take it back to your place?" Knowing Karen's in town fills me with anxiety. I don't want us to accidentally run into her in town.

"Sure, that sounds good." He gives me a warm smile. "We can watch a movie, too, if you're up for it?"

Liking the idea of being hidden away where Karen can't find me, I nod eagerly. "That sounds fantastic."

"Great." Eyes bright, he scoops Deka up so we walk faster. "Let's get out of here."

TEA TIME FOR FIVE

The rest of the day flies by in the blink of an eye, and I forget about the brief irritation of Karen stopping by unannounced. Rin and Deka barely make it through dinner before they fall asleep on the couch, leaving Shig and me to choose a movie we want over the kid's one we originally pulled out.

It's so nice to have adult time that when he suggests going shopping the next day, I jump on the offer.

Sunday arrives with a freezing downpour, and we meet Deka and Shig at Happy Palace for a fast brunch of pancakes and cinnamon rolls before we take the kids shopping at the Town Center. We both have parents to buy Yule presents for and take turns distracting the kids as we buy gifts for them, too.

After that, I drag an exhausted and grumpy Rin home, just the two of us, so I can run a couple of loads of laundry and clean the kitchen before the weekend ends.

On Monday, the knowledge I'll go back to Shig's after work fills me with a happy warmth that carries me through the morning, until Ko appears at my office door during lunch break.

He still wears his headset with the microphone tipped up and the cord dangling down his chest. "Oh, good, you're here."

I frown and stand from my desk, which holds my usual sandwich and apple. "What's up, Ko? You look a little frazzled."

"Mr. Ernst just went home sick, and I can't get a temp in before lunch ends." He presses his hands together in supplication. "Juro, you're my only hope."

"Okay, yeah, sure…" Feeling a little overwhelmed by the sudden change in my day, I stuff my sandwich back in my lunch box. "Okay, just give me a minute, and I'll head up. Did he leave his lesson plan?"

"It's in the top drawer of his desk." Ko slaps a

small key down next to my phone. "Thank you. I'll find a temp to come in for tomorrow."

"It's no problem." I stuff my files into the cabinet, lock the door, then spin back to Ko. "Can you reschedule my after-lunch parent-teacher meetings to later in the week?"

While I already dealt with the difficult cases, I still have meetings with the parents whose kids won't be changing classes and simply need general updates on where everyone is at. Most prefer to do it over the phone, but a few, like the ones scheduled for this afternoon, like to come see me in person.

"I'll get right on it." Ko flips down his microphone and grabs the dangling cable as if he can plug it into thin air to start making calls.

He vanishes back out the door before I can ask any more of him, and I grab the key he left, my lunch box, and lock up my office.

Mr. Ernst teaches Class A for the horned students who will be graduating this year. It's more of a preparation class for what to expect when they either go on to university or set out to find jobs. Which means I don't need to know history, advanced math, or anything special. I just need to be there to point students in the right direction and go over Mr. Ernst's plan for the rest of the day.

I arrive in the classroom before the bell rings to signal the end of lunch. With just enough time to scarf down my sandwich, I read over Mr. Ernst's notes. Today is supposed to be about job study, with a focus on careers in trade companies and what students who go to university can expect versus those who'd prefer to seek out an apprentice-type position and do more hands-on training. Seems easy enough.

Footsteps sound out in the hall just before the bell rings, and horned students rush into the room, bumping against each other and talking loudly. They quiet, though, when they spot me sitting at Mr. Ernst's desk, and stare with curiosity until most of the seats fill and the final bell rings.

I stand and clasp my hands behind my back to stop the nervous flutters brought on by so many eyes on me. At the beginning of my career, I hoped exposure to these kinds of situations would squash the anxiety that comes with public speaking, but it's never faded, no matter how often I'm called on. I've just gotten better at hiding the signs I'm nervous.

Spine straight, I look out over the room without fixing on any specific student. "Welcome back. Mr. Ernst had to leave suddenly. You'll have a substitute tomorrow, but in the meantime, my name is Mr.

Ono, and I will be overseeing the remainder of your day."

A few calls of welcome come from around the room before they fall silent again.

Glad I had a little time to prepare, I smile at the class. "For the rest of the day, we'll be focusing on welding. Is anyone in the room interested in pursuing a career path in welding?"

A couple of hands go up, and my tension eases. "Excellent. It's good to see some of you have an idea of what you'd like to study. Welding is a high demand—"

The classroom door opens, cutting me off, and Senichi slouches into class. His eyes flick to me and widen for a moment before he continues on past my desk to take one of the empty seats by the window. He stares outside and stuffs his earbuds into his ears, ignoring the rest of the class.

I turn back to everyone and force another smile. "Now, about welding…"

As soon as the bell rings, students stuff their books into their bags and flee the room.

Ko cuts through the flood to catch my attention.

"Juro, I was able to move one of your appointments to later in the week, but the other two insisted today was the only time that would work. I rescheduled them for three-thirty and four-thirty."

"Oh, no." Dismayed, I check the time now. "I need to pick Rin up from kindergarten. My nanny's sick."

Shig had texted this morning that he was going to be late and asked me to pick up Deka, too, so I can't call him and change plans last minute.

Ko blanches. "I'm so sorry. I didn't even think. I'm used to you being here late, so I just assumed..."

"I'll pick them up," a quiet voice interrupts, and we turn to stare at Senichi, who shrugs. "What? I'd need to pick Deka up, anyway, right? They can burn off some energy walking home. I'll even take them to the park."

I stare at Senichi in surprise. "If you're okay with that?"

"I wouldn't offer if I wasn't okay," he grumbles as he stomps past us. "See you at the house later."

"Thank you, Senichi," I call after him. "I'll let the school know you're signing Rin out today."

Without looking back, he lifts a hand in acknowledgment before disappearing out the door.

Ko watches him go before spinning back to

stare at me, his lips parted in shock before he grins. "Juro, I didn't know you were back on the market. But one of the parents? I *definitely* didn't see that coming."

"Oh, no." I wave my hands between us. "It's not like that. Rin goes to the same school as Senichi's younger sibling. They're best friends, and I've made arrangements with his uncle to trade off nights making dinner while the other works and our kids distract each other. Absolutely not back on the market."

Ko's lips purse. "Well, you *should* be. It's been two years already. Stop pining over that woman."

"I'm not pining." At his doubtful look, I add, "Really, I'm not pining."

"If you say so." He holds out his hand, and I drop Mr. Ernst's key into his open palm. "You should come out drinking with the other staff. Bond more with the teachers."

Giving him a weak smile, I shake my head. "I'm not very good with alcohol."

"Then drink juice. Just come for the experience." He steps to the side and flaps his hand toward the door. "Hurry up. You have just enough time for a bathroom break and to chug some coffee before your first appointment arrives."

With a nod of thanks, I hurry from the room, my thoughts whirling with Ko's words.

By the time I pull up to Shig's house, it's dark outside, and the warm glow of his porch light encourages me to hurry into the house. The walk from the car to the house leaves me shivering. The house will be freezing when we get home tonight.

I give the front door a brief knock before walking inside. "I'm here!"

The warm smell of spaghetti and coffee greets me, and my stomach rumbles with eagerness. Either eating with other people makes meals taste so much better, or Shig is a superior cook.

"Come join us for a tea party!" he calls, and I hang up my coat before heading down the hall to Deka's room.

I find Shig perched on one of the tiny chairs at the table in Deka's room, a small teacup pinched between his fingers. Senichi sits with them and glares when I enter before Deka distracts him by smacking the teapot against his arm for attention.

Rin waves for me to join them, and I pick my way over stuffed animals to kneel on the floor next to

Shig. There aren't enough chairs or teacups for five people, but Deka solves the problem by setting the bottom half of an empty jewelry box in front of me. Rin takes the teapot and pours fake tea into my 'teacup'.

I lift the padded square and make a show of sniffing the rim. "Is that earl grey I smell?"

Deka giggles, and Rin gives an imperious nod. "With extra sprinkles."

I stare into the empty box. "So I see. That makes this extra special."

The kids giggle again, and Shig's tail baps against my side. When I look at him, he lifts his teacup, one pinky in the air, and we clink our glasses together.

He then turns to Senichi, and the sullen teenager cracks a smile before looking at Rin. "I bet we have more sprinkles in the kitchen."

Eyes wide, Rin and Deka both bolt for the bedroom door.

"Oh, no." Shig surges to his feet, smacking Senichi in the face with his tail as he passes. "If they make a mess, you're cleaning it up."

He vanished out the door, but not before a crash sounds from the kitchen.

Senichi laughs and stacks the tea set back into the center of the table. His dark eyes flash up at me through his lashes. "There was no other way we were getting dinner tonight. We've been having tea since we got home from the park."

"Thank you for picking Rin up," I murmur as I hunt around the floor until I find the top of the jewelry box and set it on Deka's dresser. "You really saved me."

"Any chance you'll drop me to Class B as a thank you?" he asks.

"Nope." I pick up a couple stuffed animals and toss them into the open chest at the end of Deka's bed. "You didn't participate at all in class today. Why are you trying to fail out so hard?"

He rolls his eyes. "I'm not going into welding."

"What do you want to do?" I try to keep my tone casual since he seems to be more open to talking tonight. "Something with music?"

"Why do you think that?" he asks. "You've read my transcript. I've never taken a music class."

"No, but you're always listening to music. And you don't have to play an instrument to do something in the field. You could produce, or work with the stage equipment, or headhunt bands." I drop a large stuffed rabbit into the trunk. "If it's something you're passionate about, you can figure out how to turn it into a career."

"I don't want to make music my job," he says after a long pause. "I think that would ruin the magic."

I nod in understanding. "I can see that."

"Did you go to university planning to become a school admin?" he asks after another long pause.

"No, I didn't make it to university." I cross my arms over my chest to stop myself from cleaning the rest of the room. "I took online classes to get my certificate."

His dark eyes search my face. "Did they kick you out of school when Rin was born?"

Shocked by the sudden question, I rear back, then dart a glance at the open door before I look back at Senichi with concern and lower my voice. "Are you worried you got someone pregnant?"

Now, it's Senichi's turn to look shocked, and he barks out a laugh. "No, that's not possible. I'm not into girls."

"Oh." I look again at the door. "No, I didn't drop out when Karen got pregnant with Rin. But I did take on a part-time job right away to support my family, then moved to full-time work immediately after graduation."

"And you're doing okay with your life." He scrubs a hand through his hair, ruffling the feathers that make up his horns. "You have a castle, and you're raising a kid alone. University isn't everything."

"But I *did* graduate," I feel the need to point out, afraid he's taking me as a shining example of why he can quit school. "And I'd be making a lot more right now if I had a four-year degree."

Senichi looks away from me. "What if I promise to get top scores in Class B? I won't miss any more classes, even if I'm sick. I'll be an exemplary student. Just... I *can't* stay in Class A."

Worried now, I step closer to him, my hand out. "Hey, if there's something going on—"

"Sen, come clean up this mess so we can eat!" Shig yells from the kitchen.

I see the second the moment passes, and Senichi's sullen mask slides back into place before he hurries from the room. I'd been so close to breaking through with the kid. He was on the precipice of telling me what's going on, but the chance slipped away.

Senichi stays silent through dinner, and Shig's attempts to pull him into conversation go ignored.

When we finish, I help with the dishes while Senichi disappears into his room, and the sound of music soon drifts out.

Shig sighs and shakes his head. "Am I doing the

right thing? Maybe I should have let my parents take care of them. I'm not equipped to be a parent."

"You're doing great," I reassure him. "Something's going on with Senichi that has nothing to do with your skills. He'll open up eventually."

"Thank you." He leans against my side for a moment before straightening. "Deka's been talking about decorating a Yule log. But they want a *real* one. From the mountains. I was thinking of taking a trip up to the pass. Do you and Rin want to come, too?"

"I've...never done that," I admit and realize I never made it to the craft store to buy clay to make one at home. There's only one problem. "I'm not sure Rin's snowsuit still fits."

"Deka has two." His tail baps against my leg. "It will be the perfect way to spend the weekend before Yule."

"That would be amazing." I stare down at the soapy sponge I hold. "I still need to go gift shopping."

"Me, too. If we go together, we can take turns distracting the kids, again," he teases with another bap against my leg.

I smile. "Excellent planning."

"Then, it's a date." He grins at me. "They'll have

so much fun hunting Yule logs. Maybe we can even get Senichi to join in."

I return his smile. "That would be nice."

We finish drying and putting away the dishes, then go out to the living room to find Deka and Rin curled up asleep together on the couch.

Shig's hand lifts to his mouth. "They're so cute. I'm not ready for this stage to end."

"Me, either." Gently, I bend to scoop Rin up and cradle their soft body against my chest.

"I'll get your jacket," Shig whispers and hurries to the closet to fetch our coats, shrugging his on in the process.

He opens the front door and follows me out to my car, waiting as I carefully set Rin into the car seat and buckle them up. Rin stays fast asleep the entire time. I just hope that lasts until we reach home and I tuck them into bed.

Straightening, I close the door as softly as possible and turn to find Shig behind me with my coat ready.

He swings it over my shoulders with a soft smile. "Don't want you catching a cold before we go Yule log hunting."

I laugh, and my breath creates white puffs in the air between us. "We can't have that."

"Definitely not." He tugs the collar closer around my throat. "I'm looking forward to it."

"I thought it was for the kids, ShiShi," I tease.

"Oh, hush." Smiling, he steps forward, his eyes dropping to my mouth a moment before he kisses me.

AS YOU ARE

I freeze, my mouth unmoving beneath the gentle press of his lips. All I can think is 'soft' and 'surprisingly warm'.

Then, he steps back and searches my face. "I read this wrong, didn't I?"

"I…" Lifting a hand, I touch my still warm lips. "I'm sorry, I don't…"

"No, I'm the one who's sorry." Briskly, he pulls my jacket shut and steps back. "You should head home before it gets icy."

"Shig, wait." Instinctively, I reach out to catch his arm. "Don't apologize. I didn't realize that's what this was."

Releasing his arm, I rub the back of my neck, embarrassed now as I realize all the 'dates' we've been on weren't dates for our kids but dates for Shig and me.

When Shig stays silent, I add, "I'm sorry."

He hugs his elbows as he glances at me then away. "Did I ruin this? What we have? I knew you had a wife before, but I thought... We get along so well..." He rakes a hand through his hair. "I'm so stupid."

"You're *not* stupid, and no, you didn't ruin anything. I enjoy spending time with you. I don't want that to stop." My pulse quickens with nervousness. "And it's not that I'm only interested in women."

When he looks at me, hope fills his eyes, and it just compounds the guilt I feel for being so slow to notice what was happening.

I lick my lips, tasting him there, and regret what I don't feel. "I'm not interested in *anyone*. I don't... Romantic feelings just don't happen for me."

His expression clears. "Oh. You're asexual."

"I don't know. Maybe?" I shrug. "I've never been comfortable with picking a label."

Shig's focus shifts to the backseat of the car, and his brow furrows. "But... You have Rin."

Now, true embarrassment sets in. "It was a party. There was alcohol. I...don't even remember hooking up with Karen. I just woke up next to her, and a few weeks later, she told me she was pregnant." Unable to hold his gaze, I look at the dark street. "It's not that I *can't* have sex, I just don't feel the urge to. It doesn't make for a great relationship."

Shig shakes his head. "No, it just means you've never been in the *right* relationship. You can be close to someone special without it involving sex."

My laugh holds a bitter edge as I remember all of the times Karen railed against my lack of passion in our marriage. "Who would commit to something like that?"

Shig ducks into my line of view. "I would."

My mouth gapes before I snap it closed. "What?"

He steps back into my personal space. "I like you. I like how I've felt the last week, and I like just being with you. If that's all this ever is, I'm okay with that." One side of his lips kicks up. "But I *do* expect you to warm my feet during every movie we watch."

"You can't..." I shake my head in disbelief. "That's not fair to you."

"That's for me to decide." He reaches out to catch my hand. "How about we just try it and see how it goes?"

"But..." I glance from our joined hands back to him. "You could be with someone who can meet your... physical needs. You'll grow to resent me, then we won't even be friends. I don't want to ruin Rin's only friendship by trying to be someone I'm not."

"I'm not asking you to be someone you're not. I like you as you are." Shig squeezes my hand, suffusing me with the warmth of his determination. "You can set the pace, and we won't do anything you don't initiate."

Pain tightens my chest. "I'll just disappoint you."

"Do you object to snuggling?" He slowly steps forward until his chest presses against mine, and the warmth of his body sinks through my jacket. "Do you hate this?"

Giving his question serious thought, I shake my head. "No, I like this."

He tugs my captured hand until my arm wraps around his waist in a half hug. "And this?"

I oblige and wrap both arms around him, testing how he feels in my arms. "I like this, too."

His head drops to my shoulder, his body sagging against mine until his weight presses me against the car. His next question comes with a flutter of warm breath against my neck. "And this?"

A sense of comfort sweeps through me, and I wrap my arms more firmly around him. "This feels nice."

"Then, I have perfect faith this will work." He shifts until he rests most of his weight against me. "Snuggles mean way more than sex. And I think we fit pretty perfectly, don't you?"

The bulk of our winter clothes make it a little awkward, but I have to agree our height and body sizes do fit pretty perfectly.

My voice comes out gruff. "Yeah. And I like snuggles. It's nice to hold someone who's not Rin."

"So, dinner at—" He cuts off and leans back, looking down between us. "Either you're more into snuggles than I realized, or your phone is ringing."

My cell phone vibrates in my pocket again, and I pull it out with more reluctance than I would have five minutes ago. Shig wanting to snuggle reminded me how lonely my life has been over the past two years—longer than that if I'm being honest—and I find myself wanting to hold onto the moment for as long as it lasts.

When I check the caller ID, my neighbor's name glows on the screen, and worry pushes away my disappointment. With one arm still loose around Shig's waist, I hit the answer button and lift the phone to my ear. "Mrs. Thomas? This is Juro."

"Juro, dear. Thank goodness you answered." Her

frail voice wavers with panic, and I straighten in alarm. "Where are you right now?"

Confused, I look at Shig, who arches his brows. "I'm over at a friend's house in Greenwich. What's going on, Mrs. Thomas?"

She releases a long, shaky breath. "Oh, honey, I don't know how to tell you this."

My hand tightens on Shig's waist. "Please, just say what you called for, Mrs. Thomas."

Sirens blare in the background, almost drowning out her next words. "It's your house, dear. It's on fire."

Shig stops his car next to the barricade set up by the fire department and shuts off the engine. He leaps out and hurries around to my side, opening my door. I stare up at him for a long moment, my thoughts racing so fast I can't focus on anything.

After Mrs. Thomas's call, Shig took Rin back into the house and asked Senichi to watch the kids before he shuffled me into his car. I was in no state to drive and was glad for his company because, while I can't seem to process what's happening, he keeps a level head. Which makes sense. As a lawyer, he would need to think clearly under stress. Something I've never been able to do.

He leans down and grasps my arms. "Do you want to stay here while I go try to find someone who knows what's going on?"

I stare at him, hearing the words, but they don't process.

He peers over his shoulder, searching the gathered onlookers, before he turns back to me. "I'll be right back, okay?"

As he straightens, his words finally penetrate, and I lunge forward to catch his hand. "No, don't go."

He squeezes my fingers in reassurance. "We need to know how bad it is."

"Don't go alone," I amend and struggle to pull my legs out of the car and stand.

I waver for a moment, and Shig stays right by my side until I nod to let him know I'm okay. I can do this. The house can be fixed, or replaced if it comes to that.

I'm just glad Rin wasn't inside when it happened.

A week ago, we would have been home when the fire started. At this time of night, Rin would usually already be asleep, and with how tired I've been lately, I might have been, too. Which means I might have caught it in time, but there's always the possibility I wouldn't have.

"Are you sure you want to do this?" Shig asks, concern clear in his voice.

"Yeah, I need to see how bad it is." I look past the people gathered on the street to the orange glow that fills the sky and swallow hard. "That doesn't look small."

"No, it doesn't." Expression grim, he reaches past me to close the car door and lock it.

Together, we push through the crowd gathered at a large, orange, plastic barrier. I recognize some of my neighbors, but others I've never seen before.

Did they come here, drawn by the fire, just to watch my home burn down?

Anger chases back the fog created by the news, and I stick close to Shig as he elbows people out of his way to make space for us to pass.

We find Mrs. Thomas at the front of the crowd with a young, horned police officer caught in her grasp. But I can't focus on them as I see the blaze of fire that rises like a torch from the turret of Rin's castle. Nausea rolls in my stomach, and I reach for Shig as the blood drains from my head.

The sound of the fire roars, louder than I ever imagined fire could be, and heat floods the street.

Even from this distance, it warms me enough to make my winter coat uncomfortable. Firemen dance back and forth in front of my driveway, but their hoses aim more at the neighboring roofs, putting out any sparks that travel from the blaze of my home.

"Juro, dear!" Mrs. Thomas calls, and my eyes jerk away from the fire to find her dragging the young officer over. "Young Theason here has all the information."

On autopilot, I stick out my hand. "Juro Ono."

Mrs. Thomas finally releases the officer so he can shake my hand. "Officer Theason. You're the owner of the house?"

"Yes." I pat my pockets, then pull out my wallet to show him my license. "What happened?"

"We won't know until it's safe to go inside. It's going to be a while." He glances at Mrs. Thomas nervously. "You'll want to get a hotel for the night, probably longer. They won't let anyone back in until they make sure it's safe."

"Do they have any idea how the fire started?" Shig asks.

The officer shakes his head. "Not without being able to go inside. All we know right now is that it appears to have started at the front and spread from there."

The words ring in my ears, and I grab Shig for support. If we'd been home, we would have been trapped inside.

Shing slips an arm around me. "You're safe, and so is Rin. No one was hurt."

Alarmed, my focus jumps back to the officer. "Was anyone hurt?"

He shakes his head. "No, as soon as we confirmed no one was inside, we focused on containing the fire to stop it from spreading." He gives me an apologetic look. "We'll save what we can, but with old houses like this..."

"I understand." I lean against Shig as my attention returns to the flames.

Shig pulls me closer, his voice a low murmur in my ear. "We shouldn't stand around. Let's go back to my house for now. They'll call once the fire's out and they know more."

Forcing myself to straighten, I turn to face Mrs. Thomas. "Thank you for letting me know what was happening."

She gives me a wavering smile. "I'm just glad you and little Rin weren't inside, dear."

I shift to face the police officer. "How will I be notified?"

"Give me your contact information." He pulls a

small tablet from his jacket. "I'll pass it along to the right people. You'll need to inform your insurance company, too. They'll want to do their own investigation."

My stomach tightens. I hadn't even thought of that.

"We'll take care of it," Shig says before giving the officer his name, address, and phone number, as well as my number.

"I should get a hotel..." My voice falters. "I don't have enough in savings for an extended stay at a hotel."

"Insurance will take care of that," Shig assures me. "Just stay at my place until things are settled. Rin can sleep on the trundle bed in Deka's room. And we have more than enough clothes to share."

I nod numbly, murmur another thank you to Mrs. Thomas, then let Shig lead me away from the home I'd made for Rin and me the last time our lives fell apart.

BEING SELFISH

I wake up the next morning warm and confused. The clock on the nightstand doesn't look right, and the location of the door is way off. I also shouldn't be this *warm*. We don't leave the space heaters on at night, and the house is usually freezing by the time morning comes around.

The bed shifts behind me, and something warm and soft brushes against my calves. For a moment, I have a weird sense of déjà vu from all the mornings I woke up next to Karen. Then, a warm, lean body presses against my back, a muscular arm draping over my waist, and the night before comes flooding back.

Shig's confession, my house burning down, then returning to his home.

When I offered to sleep on the couch, Shig had pointed out his king-sized bed was more than sufficient for two people. I didn't have the energy to go over all the reasons why that could be a mistake.

But Shig was a complete gentleman, offering me a spare set of pajamas and ushering me into the master shower to clean off the smell of smoke that clung to my hair.

When I came out, smelling of his soap and dressed in his pajamas, he thrust a cup of herbal tea into my hands and vanished into the bathroom. He came back out five minutes later, showered and dressed in matching pajamas, to find me still standing next to the bed, the cup of tea cooling in my hands. He coaxed me to drink it, then stuffed me into his bed before he crawled in behind me.

Then, he held me while I cried, murmuring soft words of reassurance and demanding nothing in return.

I lift a hand to rub away the crust from my eyes. My face feels tight and swollen, and a dull headache pounds behind my eyes.

Blinking, I look at the clock again. It's only five in the morning, but I should get up and get ready for work. The warmth of the bed and the comfort of

Shig's loose embrace lull me to linger but also push me to leave.

It was kind of Shig to take care of me last night while my world fell apart, but I can't become reliant on him. It will make his eventual abandonment all the harder. Because, no matter what sacrifices he said he's willing to make to be in a relationship with me, experience tells me his affection will eventually turn to frustration when I can't be the person he truly desires.

Someone like Shig deserves better than I can offer.

Slowly, I inch to the edge of the bed, Shig's arm slipping away, and sit up. The floor feels cold beneath my feet, and my bare toes curl against the hardwood as the unfamiliar pajamas I wear twist around me. They remind me I don't own any clothes to change into for work, or any outfits for Rin to wear to school. All of their favorite toys are gone, along with years of photos of them growing up and class projects I planned to put into albums to embarrass them when they're older.

Grief washes through me, a painful knot forming in my stomach, and I hunch forward to drop my head between my knees. The shadows in the room waver, and I squeeze my eyes shut as tears threaten to overflow once more.

I thought I cried everything out last night, but every time I think of something we lost in the fire, the grief grows. It's so stupid to mourn objects. I know it is. What matters is that Rin is safe and no one was hurt. But then, I'll remember the decorated pine cones they brought home a couple days ago and how we planned to hang them in the living room, and the pain in my chest grows.

"Hey," a soft voice murmurs, and Shig rubs my back. "Come back to bed."

Gently, he pulls me down, and I somehow end up on my side facing him, my face pressed against his chest as he reclines against the pillows. I clutch him like a child as tears escape to soak his shirt. He doesn't say anything else, just continues to rub my back in soothing circles until I finally exhaust myself.

But sleep refuses to come, and eventually, I stir enough to choke out, "I should get ready for work."

His hand moves to the back of my head, stroking my hair. "You should take the day off. I can call into the office, too."

I shake my head. "I need the distraction. And there's still so much to do before break."

"Then, rest just a little longer." He smooths the hair from my damp cheeks. "It's still early."

I nod and feel one of my horns press against him. "I'm sorry, this must be incredibly uncomfortable."

"Just the opposite." His hand drifts higher and tentatively strokes one horn.

Warmth rolls through me, followed by a sense of overwhelming comfort.

Startled, I turn my head into his touch, giving silent permission for him to continue. No one's really touched my horns since I first grew them. Karen called them stunted and colorless, much like my emotions.

"Is this okay?" Shig rubs a fingertip over the tip of my horn, and I melt against him with a nod. He chuckles, the sound vibrating through my ear. "I like your horns."

"They're small." My grip on his shirt loosens, and my hand flattens on his chest, right over the steady thump of his heart.

"If they were bigger, they'd be stabbing me." He strokes down the short length, then back through my hair. "I appreciate not being injured while I hold you."

"Thank you." I smooth the shirt over his chest. "For—" My voice chokes off, and I take a moment to collect myself once more. "Thank you for being there. I don't know what I would have done if you weren't."

"I think Mrs. Thomas was ready to take you home and wrap you in a blanket." He cups the back of my neck. "I'm glad I had the honor of doing that instead."

My hand drifts down to his waist, and I hug him closer. "How do I tell Rin? Will they even understand?"

"They may not understand fully, but they're young enough to bounce back from this." His fingers return to my horn, sending waves of comfort through me. "Wait a couple of days until you know how much was actually lost, and you have time to talk to the insurance company."

I tip my head back to frown up at him. "Rin will want to know why we're moving to a hotel, though. They're not *that* young."

He scoots down until our heads rest on the same pillow and we no longer struggle to see each other. The glow from the alarm clock illuminates his serious expression. "Stay here. I hate the idea of you and Rin at some impersonal hotel when I have plenty of room."

My brows shoot up. "You have a nice home, but I'd hardly call it large."

"Okay, fine, it's not a castle," he teases. "But there's space."

Worry fills me, though. It feels like taking advantage of Shig's feelings, which he only confessed to last night. We haven't known each other long enough to just move in with him. But outright rejecting his offer feels like I'm not taking him seriously.

Unsure what to do, I settle for the logical response. "Rin might be excited to sleep in Deka's room for a couple nights, but eventually, they'll want their personal space back. Not to mention your personal space. Or what this change might do to Senichi, who's already having issues. And—"

Shig places gentle fingers over my lips to stop me. "The kids will be fine, Sen's going to have issues whether or not you're here, and I don't need personal space. I don't even need to make room for your clothes. I barely fill half my closet right now." Then, his hand falls away, and concern fills his voice. "Unless you're uncomfortable staying here." He sits up abruptly and scoots off his end of the bed. "Don't let me force you into something you don't want."

I push up on my elbows to watch his shadowed form walk around the bed. "Shig?"

"I'm going to make some coffee." He pauses next to my side of the bed and tugs the blanket up to my chin. "Think about it. No pressure. I'll support whatever you choose."

Before I can respond, he straightens and hurries from the room, gently closing the door behind him.

Confused, I lie back in the bed we shared last night. It didn't feel uncomfortable or strange to sleep next to Shig, but that could be the shock of suddenly being homeless.

Even so, would I have been okay sharing a bed with anyone else I know? I like to think I'm amiable with Ko and Taro, but I would have insisted on going to a hotel if either of them were with me last night.

I lift a hand to touch one horn. How would I feel if either of them touched me here?

Instant rejection fills me at the idea, yet Shig touching my horns felt fine. Good even.

Restless, I climb out of bed and pad out into the living room. The scent of coffee fills the air, and I find Shig hovering in front of the coffee pot, his tail curled close to his legs.

He glances up in surprise when I enter before

returning his attention to the coffee pot. "I was going to bring you your coffee."

Stopping next to him, I grab his hand and lift it to my head. He looks back at me, his eyes wide, but he immediately strokes my horn. That sense of comfort fills me once more, proving it wasn't a fluke brought on by the intimacy of darkness.

Shig's tail relaxes enough to waft softly, and he turns to face me fully as he traces over the dull tip of my horn. "Is this what you want?"

Nodding, I step in closer and rest my head on his shoulder.

He takes my weight and leans back against the counter. "I should have just stayed in bed, huh?"

"No." I loosely wrap my arms around his waist. "I appreciated the time to think."

"You didn't take very long." His voice turns husky. "Dare I ask what you decided?"

"Are you *sure* this is okay?" I squeeze him a little tighter to let him know I'm talking about more than just our temporary living arrangement. "Even if this is all it ever is?"

His hand drops to my shoulders, and he pushes me back far enough to meet my eyes. "I like you, Juro. I don't know what that will mean long term, but I want the chance to find out. And if this"—he squeezes my arms tighter around himself—"is all we ever do, I'll be more than satisfied."

He sounds so *sure* while uncertainty fills me.

He must see it, because his expression softens, and he cups my cheeks. "Be selfish for once. Just focus on what *you* want, and let me know what that is. I'll follow your lead."

I search his face, searching for any sign of hesitation, and find none.

He releases a pain-filled sigh and gently pulls my head back down to his shoulder. "She really did a number on you, didn't she?"

Is it that obvious? I had years of perfecting the mask I showed to the world. Be the perfect husband and father, never ask for more, and put everyone else's happiness ahead of mine. Do I dare to be selfish now? To trust that Shig knows what he wants and to follow what makes me feel good?

The quiet creak of a door opening pulls us apart, and we peek into the living room in time to catch Senichi sneaking toward the front door. Despite the December chill, he wears a thin t-shirt and tight black jeans.

"Where are you off to so early?" Shig calls, and Senichi jumps before whipping around to face us.

"Sasha asked me to help at the cafe this

morning." His shoulders hunch. "It's only a couple of hours. I'll be at school on time."

"Okay," Shig responds easily. "Will you be home for dinner?"

Senichi relaxes and glances at me before focusing on his uncle once more. "Yeah, I figured you'd need me to watch the kids while you deal with…" He trails off, looking uncomfortable.

"I appreciate it," I say, trying to infuse my voice with sincerity. "And thank you for watching them last night."

"Yeah, no problem." He ruffles his hand through the feathers of one horn and shuffles toward the door. "Sorry about your house. That sucks."

Anxiety forms a tight ball in my chest. "Thank you."

Shig steps out into the living room. "Actually, before you go…"

Senichi hunches up again. "I won't get into any fights. It's just the cafe. It's in a good part of town." He checks his watch. "Sasha's going to be here soon to pick me up, and he'll give me a ride to school, so I won't even be on the streets."

Shig's tail baps with agitation before he stills it. "No, that's not what I wanted to talk about. Would you be okay if Juro and Rin stayed with us?"

Senichi's dark eyes jump to me before bouncing away. "Isn't that..." He scrubs his hand through his feathers again. "I'm one of the students he oversees. I mean, I don't care, I won't say anything, it's just...you know?"

"It's a valid concern," I say gently, "And I'll talk to Principal Ikeda today. She can confer with Ryuu about your schooling if necessary. I'm not a teacher, so there's more leniency."

"Okay." Senichi checks his watch again and glances at the door. "We good? Can I go?"

"Have fun." Shig walks him toward the door. "Say hi to Sasha."

Nodding, Senichi grabs his coat from the closet before slipping out into the dark morning chill.

Shig rejoins me in the kitchen and gives me a hesitant smile. "That went well."

Better than I expected, honestly. With how prickly his nephew is, I thought Senichi would kick up more of a fuss.

Shig tugs on the front of the pajama shirt I borrowed. "Now, let's grab our coffees and enjoy some quiet time on the couch before the rest of the kids wake up and our peace goes out the window."

HELD HOSTAGE

At lunch, I knock on Principal Ikeda's door.

She looks up, her long, ivory horns shining beneath the overhead lights. Her dark brows lift in surprise. "Juro, how may I help you?"

My heart hammers with nervousness. While confident this morning that my relationship with Shig wouldn't be a problem, revealing it to my peers now fills me with anxiety. Everyone who works at the school knows what happened with my marriage. Though they don't know the full details, it was a subject everyone carefully avoided discussing in front of me, then gossiped about behind my back.

Will my new relationship be gossiped about, too? And what if it doesn't work out?

"Do you have a minute?" I point at the door, indicating my preference to close it for privacy.

Principal Ikeda's stern expression softens. "Of course, Juro. Close the door."

Tall and lithe in a gray dress suit, she stands and strides to the sideboard against the left wall, where a teapot sits on a warming tray. As I close the door, she pours two steaming cups and walks to a pair of padded chairs set to face each other. She settles one cup on the small coffee table between the chairs before she settles into one and crosses her long legs.

Her grace and confidence make me feel ungainly in my own body, not something that's uncommon for me. I've never felt completely comfortable, like the body I inhabit came with defects no one else has. I resist the urge to fidget as I join her and perch on the edge of the padded seat.

She takes a sip of her tea, her gaze studying me over the rim.

Reminded of the courtesy, I reach for my cup, but my hand shakes, so I fold my fingers together in my lap instead and clear my throat.

Principal Ikeda sighs and uncrosses her legs to lean forward and set her cup down. "I have a feeling I know why you're here."

I straighten in surprise and no small amount of alarm. "You do?"

She nods, a pained expression on her face. "I know the recent school budget cuts have put an additional burden on you. Ko has mentioned more than once that your office light is on long after most of the staff have gone home. He has also reminded me, non-too subtly, that you are a single father and should be spending your evenings with your child."

"Oh, no." Dismayed, I shake my head, but she lifts a hand to stop my protests.

"I've gone over the budgets multiple times. Ideally, I would be able to backfill the missing transition counselors' positions and hire a second administrator." She runs a black nailed hand down her skirt, smoothing out a wrinkle. "Unfortunately, the funds just don't exist at the moment. But Ko and I have put our heads together, and we believe we've come up with a solution. I planned to discuss it with you, Ryuu, and Taro at the end of year meeting, but since you've come to me now, I'd like your opinion."

"Of course," I murmur, falling back into my role as part of her support system. "Any assistance I can provide is yours."

The sudden topic change from what I planned to discuss calms my nerves, and I lift my teacup and settle back in the chair. I'm comfortable when it comes to discussions about the school. I've been doing my job long enough to be confident that I know what I'm doing. It's the issues with my personal life where my confidence suffers.

She smiles. "I know I can count on your honesty. You were a good student, and you've become an excellent administrator. It's actually what sparked this idea."

I nod and take a small sip of tea, the sweetened chamomile relaxing me further.

"While we can't afford to hire more staff, I think we can open some positions for intern assistants." As if expecting a protest, she lifts a hand. "Not from the students here, but from graduates. We can work with the university to provide work studies, but I'd also like to leave it open for those who aren't at university, who would still like to explore other avenues of work that they could gain through volunteer experience and qualifying through certificates, like you did."

A smile spreads over my face. "That's a wonderful idea."

Her shoulders relax. "It would, of course, take some training on your end, but the hope is that it would ease your burden. They would be able to handle much of the paperwork involved and manage your schedule, leaving you open to put your focus where it needs to be. It would also, hopefully, mean your day ends when classes do, and you'd be able to spend more time with Rin."

Warmth and gratitude fill me that Ko and she put so much thought into this. I didn't want to bring up my workload, knowing that any funds the school came up with should be spent better than on hiring me an assistant, but having help would ease a lot of my burden. This sounds like the perfect solution.

Principal Ikeda smiles. "Wonderful. This is still in process, but I'm hoping to have some student references available early in the new year. I'll discuss the matter with Ryuu and Taro, as well, and I'd like to sit down with all of you to go over what tasks would be expected of an assistant."

I nod in understanding. "I'll give it some thought and make a list."

She leans forward to reclaim her teacup. "I'm so glad we're in agreement."

As she makes a move to stand, my heart lurches. "Actually, I had something else to discuss."

Her eyes widen, but she settles back in her seat.

Now, the nerves flood back, and I force the words out past the tightness in my throat. "I've started seeing someone."

Her smile broadens, warmth filling her eyes. "Good for you, Juro."

Her happiness only makes my palms sweat. "It's someone I met at school." Her smile dims, and I blurt out, "One of our student's guardians."

"Oh, my." She takes a long sip of her tea as she thinks things over.

"I realize this put me in a position to be biased toward this student, but I thought perhaps Ryuu could handle the academic decisions for him, and if there's something that needs a second opinion, he can discuss it with Taro, since he knows all the students so well?" My voice turns a little squeaky at the end, and I clear my throat once more. "The student is in his final year here, so it will only be an issue for another six months."

She hums softly as she stares down into her tea. "Is it possible you can keep this relationship downplayed until after graduation?"

I cringe, my shoulders hunching. "We're currently living together."

Her head snaps up. "How long has this been going on? You should have come to me sooner, Juro."

My stomach turns sour at the quiet reproach. "Our youngest children became friends at their school, but we only just met last week. My nanny was handling pickup, but she's caught a bad cold. We became friendly and started meeting up so our kids could play together." I set my tea back on the coffee table before my sweaty hands cause an accident. "This weekend, though, things changed, and I'd like very much to see where this will go."

Confusion pinches her brows together. "And you thought moving in together was the best way to do that?" She shakes her head. "I know that your relationship with Karen moved quickly, but—"

"My house burned down last night," I interrupt before she can dredge up all the pain from my past. Principal Ikeda was there through it all. Out of everyone at school, she's privy to the worst of it, but even she doesn't know how bad it got, or how bad it continues to be.

Revealing this new pain offers a distraction, and her lips part on a short, sharp breath, before she leans forward to grasp my hand. "Are you and Rin okay? Why didn't you say something sooner? And why are you *here* today? You could have taken time off, Juro. Ryuu and Taro can handle the remainder of the parent meetings."

"Thank you." I pat the back of her hand. "I wanted the distraction while I wait to hear that it's safe to go see what's left. Insurance will be sending someone out to investigate, too, which will take time. Luckily, Rin and I weren't home when it happened. My neighbor called me to alert me to the fire, but it was far too late at that point."

"I'm so sorry." Sincerity fills her voice, and she squeezes my hand once more. "Are you sure you want to stay with your new partner, though? This kind of thing can put a strain on any relationship, and with the holiday coming up and this being so new..."

"If it starts to be an issue, we'll go to a hotel," I assure her, though I don't think it will be an issue, at least not for me.

She shakes her head and straightens with a firm expression on her face. "Nonsense. I have rental properties around town. Say the word, and I'll make one available for you to move into. A hotel. As if that's any place for a child."

Tears sting my eyes, my voice thickening with emotion. "Thank you."

She shakes her head again, as if the offer is nothing, but we both know it's just for show. "If you need anything in the meantime, my door is always open to you." She stands and brushes invisible lint from her suit. "Don't forget to inform Ko of your change in address. He'll pass it on to payroll."

"Thank you," I say again as I stand.

"And, if you need time off to sort things out, just let me know, okay?" Her voice turns gruff. "It's okay to ask for help, Juro. You don't need to always shoulder your burdens alone."

Throat too tight for words, I nod in acknowledgment and head for the door.

The brighter lights of the hallway help push back the emotions that swirl through me, and I take a moment to collect myself before striding toward Ko's desk, glad I remembered—or Shig remembered—to write down my new address before I left for work this morning.

Ko's eyebrows lift when I pass over the piece of paper. Curiosity lights his eyes, but he stays silent. I can only hope it remains that way, at least for a little longer. I'm not sure yet where this new relationship with Shig will lead, and I want more time before the curiosity seekers come knocking to ask questions I don't have the answers for.

As Shig makes dinner that night, my cell phone rings. When I check the caller ID, a hard ball forms in my stomach to see Karen's name on the screen.

Rin's and Deka's happy voices drift from the hall, safe in Deka's room, but I stand and walk toward the sliders that lead to the backyard, just to be safe. I hate for Rin to hear me fight with Karen. I want them to have a good relationship, unbiased by the tension between Karen and me.

As I step out onto the small deck and close the slider, cold wind whips through my button-up. "Hello, Karen, how are you?"

"Why haven't you been answering my calls?" Karen demands without greeting. "I've been calling all day."

The kind Karen from a few days ago was clearly a fluke, and tension fills my body.

I've known Karen long enough to know when she wants to fight, and her tone says she's rearing to go. "I only just got home. You know I can't answer personal calls when I'm at work."

While technically a lie, few of Karen's calls are ones I want to take where my coworkers can overhear.

"Well, you should take mine," she snaps. "I'm the mother of your child. Every call from me is important."

"What do you want, Karen?" I ask with resignation.

"Yule is coming up," she says sharply, as if I could have forgotten.

"Yes, I know," I acknowledge. "And it's my year to have Rin. We already agreed to this when you took them last year."

"You can't possibly think it's okay to keep a mother from her child over the holidays," she seethes, even though she kept me from Rin last year. "My parents expect to see Rin."

My hand fists at my side, my nails cutting into my palm, but the pain helps keep me calm. "Then, you should have made them aware it wasn't your year to have Rin for the holiday."

"What does it matter to you if I take Rin?" she sneers. "It's not like *your* parents will be there to celebrate with you."

No, my parents live too far away to make the trip during winter, but that's beside the point.

At my silence, she digs deeper. "You can have Rin after the holiday."

"No." I keep my voice firm. "We agreed Rin would stay with me for Yule this year, and that's what we're sticking to."

"Fine," she snaps, but a note of victory underscores her sharp acceptance. "Then, I need money to mail all of Rin's gifts to you so they can open them on the holiday."

And there's the real reason she called.

I grip the phone tighter. "You can give Rin the presents next time they come to visit. When will that be, by the way?"

"I'm not sure," she hedges. "You know I had to take on a second job. If you could send a little extra, maybe I can afford to take time off to drive over."

"You had no problem driving over last Saturday," I point out.

"That was for work," she snaps. "It's different."

"How about I drive Rin over on New Year's Eve, and you can sign the custody paperwork, too," I counter. "You can give Rin your presents then."

"No, I have to work on New Year's Eve. It's a big night for tips." Anger fills her voice. "With all the trouble you put me through during our marriage, you owe me. We're really struggling here, Juro. Do you want us to have to move to a bad part of town? Would you feel comfortable letting Rin come to a place surrounded by *gangs*?"

"There aren't any gangs in Clear Helm," I sigh. "You're being dramatic. What about Scott's job? Doesn't he make enough to cover the rent on your apartment?"

"You know he's saving to open his own security company. He has to reinvest his income." Warmth fills her voice. "He has big plans for our future. He's going to make sure we live the way we deserve."

Unlike you. The implication hangs in the silence between us.

"I'll need at least two hundred to ship Rin's gifts," Karen continues. "You can wire it directly into my account."

"Two hundred for shipping?" I exclaim. "That's ridiculous."

"They're big gifts, and you know how holiday shipping is," she wheedles. "If we want to make sure they arrive on time, they'll have to be overnighted at this point."

"I don't have that kind of money just lying around." And I wouldn't give it to her even if I did. I don't believe she has gifts waiting for Rin. "You'll just have to hang onto these presents until you can make time to see Rin in person."

"Fine," she snaps. "You explain to our child why they don't have presents to open on Yule, you stingy bastard!"

The line falls silent, and when I pull the phone away from my ear, a dark screen greets me.

I sigh, tuck it back into my pocket, then stare out

at Shig's small backyard. Grass peeks through the parts of the yard the sun reaches, but snow and ice lay in the shadows under the trees and near the fence. Icy December wind cuts through me, determined to freeze me to the bone. The air smells metallic, and gray clouds fill the sky. It feels like it will snow again.

Behind me, the slider opens, and Shig pokes his head out, releasing a draft of warm air that smells like stew and warming bread.

When he sees I'm off the phone, he steps out and shuts the door.

He stands quiet and shivering, his shoulder pressed to mine in silent comfort, here if I want to talk but undemanding.

The back of his hand brushes mine, and I realize it's still fisted. I force my stiff fingers to uncurl, then stare numbly at the bloody crescents left in my palm. "Oh."

"Let me see." Shig cradles my hand, then rubs his fingers over the sharp points of my black nails. "You need to trim these, or you might scratch Rin."

"I kept meaning to..." My eyes sting. "My file's back at the house."

He nods in understanding. "I can get Sen's for you."

When he turns toward the slider, though, I grab his hand to stop him from going back inside yet. "I spoke to Principal Ikeda today. She's fine with our relationship."

He turns back to me and squeezes my fingers in acknowledgment.

I drag in a deep, icy breath that hurts my lungs and release it on a shudder. "She wants money."

Shig squeezes my fingers again, and I know he understands I'm no longer talking about the principal.

Tears blur my vision. "I told her I wasn't giving her any more, but that just means she'll come take Rin away again, and I can't stop her because, legally, she has the right. I'm trying to gain full custody, but as long as Karen knows she can extort money from me by holding Rin hostage…"

Shig releases my hand to wrap his arms around me, and I turn to bury my face against his warm neck.

I clutch the back of his shirt, my next words muffled by his skin. "When she finds out about the fire, it's just going to be another weapon in her arsenal. What if she threatens to fight for full custody? What if she uses the fact we're homeless to take Rin from me?"

"You're not homeless." Shig's soft reassurance fills my ear. "And from what you've said, she doesn't actually want Rin."

"No, but she'll use my baby to get anything she can out of me." I clutch Shig tighter. "She knows I'll do anything for Rin."

"We can take her to court." Shig rubs soothing circles over my back. "In case you forgot, you're dating a lawyer now. I'll tie her up in so much paperwork she'll have to pay *you* child support for every time she's missed taking Rin over the last two years, which I'm guessing is a lot."

It is, and if it were that easy, I'd jump on his offer. I lift my head to meet his eyes. "It's more complicated than that."

He reaches up to wipe the tears from the corners of my eyes. "What makes it complicated?"

I glance at the slider to make sure it's closed before lowering my voice. "I'm not sure Rin is biologically mine. If we go to court, I could lose them for good."

NOT A HOARDER

Shig stares at me, his eyes wide with shock, before he steps back, taking his warmth with him. "Give me a second, okay?"

Before I can protest, he vanishes into the house, leaving me out in the cold with wet eyes and confusion.

A moment later, a giant, puffy blanket balloons through the slider, and I rush over to help pull it through.

Shig grins around the bulk. "I thought we might want something to keep us warm."

Together, we arrange the padded bench so we have an eye on the inside of the house through the slider, our backs to the yard.

When I take a seat on one side, and Shig tucks

the comforter between me and the arm of the bench. "I'll be right back."

He dashes back into the house and returns a moment later with two steaming cups of coffee. He passes them to me before he returns to the slider and closes the door. When he comes back, instead of taking his cup of coffee, he reaches into his back pocket and produces a beanie, which he carefully fits over my head, making sure to cover my ears.

His thumbs rub over the bumps my horns make in the hat, and he smiles again. "See? They're the perfect size for me to take care of you. Any bigger, and your ears would be left freezing."

I stare up at him, my chest tight with too many emotions to put a name to, before I clear my throat and ask gruffly, "What about you?"

Smile broadening, he produces a second beanie, this one green with little hippo ears on top. His cheeks turn pink as he pulls it over his wavy black hair. "Another gift from Deka."

"It suits you." I mean it, too. The silly hat makes his green eyes pop, drawing my attention to the warmth that fills them.

"I put a movie on in Deka's room," Shig explains as he lifts one side of the blanket to slide beneath. "It should distract the kids for a while."

I wait until he settles on the bench, then pass him one of the cups of coffee.

He takes it, wrapping his fingers around the mug for warmth. "Okay, tell me why you're not sure Rin is actually yours."

The segue back to my earlier admission takes my breath away, and I sip my coffee while I collect myself.

At last, I balance the cup in my lap, focusing on the warm interior of his dining room. "Karen got pregnant at a party."

Shig nods. "I remember you saying that. You had just transitioned."

I fiddle with my mug. "Right, so emotions should have been high with excitement."

"But not for you," Shig says quietly, without even a hint of judgment in his tone.

"It was the first time I realized I didn't, and wouldn't, feel things the same way my peers did." I stare down into the depths of my coffee to avoid looking at him.

I've never talked to anyone about this, and in a handful of days, I'll have laid myself completely bare to Shig.

I swallow hard before I continue. "I thought my lack of interest before then was because I hadn't transitioned. I had never had crushes the same way my classmates did, but the counselor assured me not everyone did. That those feelings would come when I shifted into my final form." One side of my mouth ticks up. "I was predicted to grow a tail."

"Because you didn't express any of the physical or dominating attributes most horned have prior to transition?" Shig guesses.

I nod in agreement. "I've never been interested in sports or working out, and I'm not especially tall. I'm not slender, either, though. I'm very average, all around."

Shig leans over to press his shoulder against mine. "Average isn't bad from where I stand."

Smiling, I glance over at him. We stand about the same height, and our frames are about the same. It makes holding and being held comfortable. There's no awkward bending or stretching; our bodies just line up right.

"No," I say softly. "There's nothing wrong with being average."

He reaches out to cup my cheek, his palm hot from holding his mug. I lean into it, thankful for the warmth against the icy outdoors.

After a moment of comfort, I pull away. I don't think I can continue the story if I keep looking at him, so I focus on the dining room once more. "When I transitioned into a horned, the expected urges didn't develop. I didn't look at my tailed counterparts and feel the need to dominate them. I didn't fight with my horned peers. I didn't have any issues controlling aggression. My counselor was impressed by my quick ability to overcome instinct, while I hid the fact that instinct just didn't exist for me."

Shig reaches out and takes my hand, lacing our fingers together in a silent show of support.

"Some of my classmates were throwing a party." I lick my cold lips. "A kissing party. I hadn't tried that yet, and I thought…"

When I trail off, Shig squeezes my fingers. "You thought it would kick start your libido."

I nod jerkily. "There was a nice tailed girl. We tried it out, but while she got excited, I didn't." I feel the question brewing and shake my head. "It wasn't Karen. Karen was part of the popular crowd, someone all the horned in my year talked about. We had only interacted during class projects before, and she mostly used her attractiveness to get the other teammates to do her parts of the homework."

"I knew a few like that in school," Shig murmurs

with an edge of bitterness. "Real life came as a shock for them."

Real-life had come as a shock for Karen, too. It *still* shocks her, which is why she's always trying to get money out of me.

I shake my head. "So, while my intended partner left to go find a more aggressive horned, I found the keg."

"Oh, no." Amusement fills Shig's voice.

"Yeah, it was a night for firsts." I laugh at how stupid I was. "I got very, very drunk and blacked out. I have no recollection of what happened after that, but when I came to, I was in a stranger's bed with Karen. Our clothes were missing, so I assumed something had happened, and she confirmed it when she woke up. It was beyond awkward, and she insisted I not tell anyone."

"She sounds like a real—" Shig cuts off and squeezes my hand. "Sorry, she's the mother of your child."

"She's a raging bitch," I say concisely. "Manipulative, greedy, and self-centered. But, yes, also the mother of my child."

We lapse into silence for a bit, before I take a deep breath. "Six weeks after the party, Karen showed up at my house during dinner with my family and announced she was pregnant. My parents were *thrilled*. I think they had given up hope I would find a mate. Our parents arranged our union within the month."

"No one questioned if you were really the father?" Shig demands, his voice incredulous.

I shrug. "Something happened at the party, and the timeline was right. I was talked into doing the right thing."

"Marriage wasn't the right thing," Shig protests. "You were eighteen."

"Now, as an adult, I realize that. But as a scared teenager being pressured by our parents…"

Shig growls low in his throat but doesn't comment further on the topic. "So, what made you suspect you're not Rin's biological father?"

My lips tighten. "Karen was never happy that I settled for a school administration job. She wanted me to make more money, to get a job that more than covered our expenses so that she could live the lifestyle she preferred. Over the years, we got into a *lot* of fights, and sometimes she made comments about how she should have set her sights on someone else, or other things that made me doubt I actually sired Rin." I look quickly at Shig. "But Rin is *mine*. I raised them while Karen was out partying, and after Karen left, it's been mostly me alone. Rin is *my* child, whether or not we share blood."

"Of course, they are," Shig soothes. "Anyone who knows you knows you adore that child."

My eyes sting, and I blink away the tears. "But what if they're *not* mine by blood? What if Karen really takes Rin away?"

Shig's expression softens. "Have you ever considered a paternity test?"

I shake my head. "I never wanted to know for certain. I don't think it would change anything for me if Rin's not, but there's a chance, you know?"

Shig nods in understanding. "Even so, if Karen follows through and takes you to court, you'll have to do a test. It would be the first step in the battle. After that, it's a matter of proving that your actions are what matters most."

Anxiety fills me, and I drop my head to stare at my lap. "I've never told anyone this. I was too afraid it would come back to haunt me, or that Rin would find out and ask questions. I didn't think Karen would ever follow through, but she's been getting more and more aggressive with her demands for money, and even though she agreed to sign the paperwork to make me Rin's sole guardian, she's been dragging her feet for over a year now. Her mate doesn't want Rin around, though, so I have that in my favor."

"Do you mind if I talk to my parents about this?" Shig asks softly. "My mother specializes in family court. She might have some better insight than I do."

My instant reaction is to refuse. I've spent so long staying quiet about this that even one more person knowing about what's going on fills me with fear. But I trust Shig, and if he thinks it will help, then I should take it.

I nod. "Yes, thank you. I've started a file with a lawyer already, and I have letters of reference about my character. I can give you his contact. I don't have much for legal fees—"

"Hush." Shig's finger covers my lips. "We're just talking right now. There's no need for money."

Reaching up, I pull his hand down. "This is your job, though. I don't want to abuse that just because we're..."

Shig's eyes light up, and he leans forward. "We're...?"

"Boyfriends?" I say, my voice squeaky.

His lips twitch. "That sounds rather high schoolish, don't you think?"

Lover doesn't fit, though, since we're not. I bite my lip for a moment before venturing, "Partners?"

"I like the sound of that." His eyes drop to my lips, and for a heart-racing second, I think he'll kiss me, but he pulls back instead and stands, taking my coffee mug from me in the process. "Come on. We should head back inside before the kids realize we're not watching them. And I want to clean your wounds."

Something flutters in my chest. Disappointment? Relief that he didn't push for something physical. I don't know, but it leaves me restless.

I busy myself gathering the comforter and notice that dirt now covers the side that was on the ground. "I don't think we can put this back on the bed."

"Don't worry, I have a spare." Shig glances at the soiled hem and shrugs as he pulls the slider open. "That one needed to go in the wash, anyway."

I struggle to contain the large, fluffy mass as I follow him. "You don't take it to the laundromat?"

He casts me a horrified look. "Goodness, no. There's a full-size washer in the basement."

"You have a basement?" I've been here multiple times now and never noticed a spare door.

He nods. "The access is in the garage. It's not very convenient, but I haven't had time to renovate."

"I can take it straight down," I offer, heading for

the door to the garage. Shig doesn't use it to park his car, so I've never been inside.

"Oh, no, I can do it." He rushes after me and tries to take the comforter from my arms. "You should go wash your hand, then wait patiently on the couch."

His eagerness to do the task sets off my alarm bells, and I narrow my eyes on him. "What are you hiding that you don't want me to see?"

He flushes with more than the cold from sitting outside. "Nothing. I'm absolutely not a hoarder."

My brows shoot up. "Well, if you're absolutely sure about that..."

I tug the comforter out of his arms and pull open the garage door. As I step through, a light automatically comes on.

"Oh, God," Shig groans as he follows me into the cold space. "Just don't trip, okay?"

It's difficult to see over the comforter's bulk, but stacks and stacks of boxes fill up every available space. I stare in amazement. Nothing about the inside of Shig's house could have prepared me for this wall-to-wall jungle of cardboard.

"There's a path." Shig edges past me and tugs the comforter from my limp grasp.

With the bulky material gone, I see a path along the back wall that leads to another door.

He fumbles it open, tosses the blanket down, then peeks back at me. "Less risky that way. So, I can see the stairs."

I nod, my attention returning to the boxes.

Shig's shoulder's hunch with self-consciousness. "A lot came from when I moved out of my parent's house, and there's stuff I collected while at university. Then, the kids brought more. I just haven't had time to sort through everything and figure out what to keep and what to donate. Sometimes, I consider just hiring a company to clear it all out, but then I worry I'll be getting rid of something that has sentimental value for the kids. So, it just all sits here."

"I can help you go through it," I offer, my hands itching to organize. "I have two weeks off for the holiday. At the very least, I can sort things into categories to make it easier to go through them."

"I was considering taking that time off, too," Shig says as he starts down the stairs to the basement. "Deka and Sen will be out of school. And we have those plans to take the train up to the mountains to go Yule log hunting."

In all the chaos, I completely forgot Shig brought up doing that, but I should have known he'd remember, even with everything else going on.

"So, we clean out your garage and go hunting for Yule logs over the break." Warmth fills me, pushing back the anxiety that always comes from talking to Karen. "Sounds like the perfect way to spend the holiday."

Shig glances back as he takes the last step into the basement. "Then, it's a date."

And, this time, I know it's more than just so our kids can play. It's a date for Shig and me, too.

I smile as warmth fills me. "It's a date."

GROOMING

I look around the basement in amazement as I follow Shig to a spot behind the stairs that holds a large washer, dryer, and utility sink. He must know the way by heart because, once he picked the comforter up off the floor, it completely blocked his view.

The basement runs the entire length of the house, with ceilings that have to be eight feet over our heads. The ducting for the house fits in snuggly between the beams, and the builders ran outlet boxes down the walls. While it's all cement and wood framing now, it could easily be finished for extra living space. Is that the renovation Shig was talking about doing? No wonder he hasn't started it. It will be a full-scale project once it begins.

"Here we go." Shig struggles to contain the comforter in one arm as he struggles with the front load washer with the other.

Laughing as he pats around blindly, I step forward. "Let me help."

When I reach for the blanket, though, he turns away, his tail waving in the air between us to keep me away. "No, you're wounded."

"It's not a wound," I protest. It feels strange to stand by and watch someone else do chores. I'm so used to being the only one to take care of the house that doing nothing leaves me with an odd sense of helplessness. "I just cut myself because I wasn't paying enough attention to my grooming."

"And we're going to fix that in just a moment." He gets the washer open and shoves the blanket inside before he grabs soap from an overhead shelf to fill the dispenser on the front of the machine. With a press of the button, he turns and grins. "See? Not hard at all. Now, back upstairs where the heat is on."

He shoos me ahead of him as we walk back to the stairs.

I peer over my shoulder as I head up. "How come you didn't just put the boxes down here?"

Shig grabs the railing on either side of the steps.

"Watch where you're going before you hurt yourself more."

His concern makes me happy, and I face forward once more.

Once I'm paying attention to where I'm going, he answers my question. "It's a lot of steps to go up and down, and I kept thinking I'd get to it."

"Well, once we go through what's in there, your poor sports car will appreciate being back in the garage." I reach the top of the stairs, look around at all the boxes once more, and shake my head. "Has it ever been in here?"

"No." He shuts off the basement light.

I look over at him in surprise. "Why would you buy such a nice car to leave it out in the cold like that?"

"Oh, I didn't." He smiles. "My parents bought it for me so I could impress clients."

"And here I thought it was because you're super-rich," I tease, while secretly happy that maybe he's not quite as out of my league as I originally assumed.

"Oh, no, I *am* super-rich. I come from a family of lawyers, and my job pays extremely well." He catches my uninjured hand and pulls me back into the house. "I just didn't throw money away on a flashy sports car. Cars, in general, are poor investments unless you get a classic, and those come with whole other issues."

I try to picture my parents buying me a car and come up blank. They hadn't even helped with a down payment on the SUV I bought used after Rin was born.

"Oh," I say weakly. "That was nice of your parents."

He laughs at my expression. "I know I'm coming from a place of privilege, but it also means I can provide for my family."

Is he concerned I'm worried about money issues because of Karen? If anything, I'm worried *I'm* the one taking advantage of *him*. Up until now, he's seemed so confident that I didn't realize he worried, too.

My tension eases. "You don't have to sell yourself to me as a good partner. Who you are as a person means more than money ever could, and I like that person very much."

He grins. "Yeah?"

"Yeah." I use our joined hands to pull him closer. "I'm living here, aren't I?"

"Well, yes..." Uncertainty flickers through his eyes. "But if you had other options besides a hotel..."

"I do, actually." My pulse flutters. "Principal Ikeda offered me one of her rental properties today."

His breath catches. "And you turned her down?"

"I want to explore what we can have together." I squeeze his hand. "I've never felt this comfortable with someone before, and it's scary, but you being you make me feel *less* scared. And none of that has to do with your house, your car, or your bank account. It has to do with how you take care of Senichi and Deka, and how you treat me. I feel like an equal when I'm with you, someone you genuinely want to spend time with instead of someone to be tolerated."

"Oh." His eyes shimmer, and he swallows hard. "That... I *do* like being with you. Very much. I'm not trying to treat you differently. This is just who I am."

"I know, and that's something else I like about you." I tug the beanie from his head. "You're an open and caring person, and it shows in everything you do."

His gaze flickers to my lips, then back up, and he clears his throat. "Go wash your hands while I get Sen's nail filer."

And that makes me like him even more. He really did mean it when he said he'd follow my lead in our relationship. I'm not so unaware that I don't know this situation would usually lead to kissing, and other things, but he doesn't push me for something I'm not ready for. But how long will that patience last?

I'm starting to think kissing might be nice with Shig, too. Our first kiss took me by surprise, and I hadn't been thinking of Shig that way. But I *do* like all the touches and cuddles, and kissing is kind of like hugging with our lips. But what if that's as far as I ever want to go?

The more I like Shig, the more I worry about losing what we have, but I refuse to pull back now that I'm committed. I feel, in my heart, that I *need* this, and it has nothing to do with what's best for Rin and everything to do with what's best for me.

Does that make me a bad father? I don't think so. Shig's already helped remind me I need to take time away from work, and Rin laughs so much more these days. Me being happier means Rin's happier, too.

After dropping our beanies in the basket in the closet, I go to the kitchen to wash my hands. When I come back out, I find Shig waiting in the living room. He has one of the blankets in one hand and a towel draped over his shoulder.

"Sit." He points at the floor, and I notice he

pushed the couch back to make room in front of the coffee table.

Eyebrows raised, I sit on the floor, then laugh in surprise when Shig sits in front of me.

He wiggles and leans back. "Make some room."

I unfold my legs and shift them to either side of Shig's hips. "Like this?"

Nodding, he scoots backward until he reclines against me, then drapes the blanket over us both.

Once we're full ensconced, he lays the towel over his stomach. "Hands."

Dutifully, I wrap my arms around him and rest my hands on the towel. "Are you really going to groom me?"

He lifts a metal file, one end sharp and pointed. "I'm going to try."

I curl my fingers against my palms protectively. "Not sure how I feel about that."

He raps my knuckles with the file. "I do this for Deka. I'm sure I can manage for you."

"Deka doesn't have claws," I remind him.

"Well, no." He uncurls one of my fingers to reveal a sharp, black nail. "But this can't be *that* different."

"Uh, huh." I splay my fingers out once more. "We'll see about that. But later, I'm brushing your tail."

His tail stirs against me. "Oh, yeah?"

"I'm getting out *all* the tangles," I promise.

He twists to frown at me. "I don't have *tangles*."

"You won't when I'm done with you." I wiggle my fingers at him. "I'll base how gentle I am by how well you do here."

"I feel…" He pauses to consider. "Threatened?"

"Warned," I correct. "Are you going to back down?"

"Not at all." He sets the metal file against the point of my nail. "Don't you know lawyers thrive on challenges?"

BUILDING A HOME

Late the next day, the fire department calls to confirm that the fire started at the front of the house due to faulty wiring, which doesn't surprise me. The house was old, and the wiring was just as old.

It was one of the big-ticket items on a never-ending list of things to take care of. My grandparents both blessed and cursed me when they gave me the house. It provided a home for Rin and me, but they had never done more than minimal maintenance on it. After seventy years, almost everything needed to be fixed.

The firemen were able to dig out the safe, though, which holds all of my and Rin's important documents, as well as a computer backup with digital copies of all the receipts for the more expensive items I owned.

I leave work after my last meeting, drive over to pick up my safe, then swing by my house to take a look at what remains. As warned, most of the house is blocked off, and the areas I *can* access are completely drenched in fire retardant, burned away, or both. The most critical area, the turret with all of Rin's favorite toys, is completely gone.

When I get home to Shig's house, I forward the necessary files to the insurance company to include in my claim. Every little bit helps, because the house isn't salvageable.

On Thursday, the insurance company contacts me with follow-up questions while I'm still at work.

"It appears that the fire started at the front door," the representative tells me.

I frown down at the file I have open on my desk. "Are you thinking it was arson?"

"No, but we did have a question about your security system." Papers rustle in the background. "In the paperwork you filed, you said you didn't have one."

"That's correct," I say.

"There was wiring found that look to be security-related," the agent says, sounding suspicious.

"The light kept burning through lightbulbs." I rub the bridge my temple because that's yet another item that was on my to-do list. "Maybe it was something to do with that? My grandparents gave me the house a couple of years ago, so I'm not sure what all was done to the house before that, but they never mentioned a security system, and there were no panels inside the house that indicated there was one."

"We'll send another investigator out to double-check." The clack of computer keys sounds. "The determination will be that the house is a loss, though, so you'll receive a lump-sum payment. If you use it to repair the house, it will have to go through another review before it can be insured again."

"I understand," I say tiredly.

"I don't show a record of the hotel you're staying at. You'll need to submit receipts of anything you've paid for so far, and—"

"We'll be staying with a friend," I interrupt, not wanting to extend the call further.

"If you change your mind, you have coverage for up to thirty days," they drone on. "I've emailed you a copy of your policy for reference about how much we cover per night. Anything above that will be out of pocket."

"Thank you. Have a good rest of your day." I hang up, a headache pressing at my temples.

As I already knew from my brief trek through the wreckage, there isn't enough house left to repair. When I receive the insurance payment, I can use it to go toward building a new house, but it won't be enough for a full reconstruction, and I have nothing in savings to bulk up what's missing. I'll be better off selling the lot to a developer and looking for a new home.

The knowledge both hurts and eases a weight I've carried for a long time.

I'm sad to see the house where my grandparents lived, and where Rin and I built memories, destroyed. But without the laundry list of repairs it needed, I suddenly find myself freed of that financial burden. With what the insurance company will pay, Rin and I can find a smaller, newer house that's easier to take care of.

The idea of moving, though, brings with it its own issues.

That night, when I update Shig of the news, he gives me a smile that doesn't reach his eyes. "I'll help you hunt for a house. Maybe we can find something nearby?"

The lack of enthusiasm in his voice makes it obvious he's not thrilled, and neither am I, if I'm being honest with myself.

While I haven't known Shig for long, I enjoy our evenings together and don't want those cut short by the need to pack Rin up to go home. But I also don't want to continue to impose on his hospitality, especially when there really isn't enough space for us here.

While Rin and Deka are enjoying playing sleepover, for now, that won't last forever. Eventually, they'll want their own rooms. And what about Senichi? He's rarely home, and when he is, he locks himself in his bedroom. If our presence here makes him uncomfortable, we need to fix that as soon as possible. I don't want to be responsible for him dropping out of school.

"Juro?" Shig nudges my foot with his under the table.

My head jerks up, my eyes meeting his as I realize I stayed silent too long.

His brows pinch together in a troubled frown. "If

I'm being too pushy, please let me know. Of course, you don't have to find a house near here if you don't want to. I know this isn't exactly the neighborhood you're used to. And you don't need to take me into consideration when choosing a home, either. I don't want to push in where I'm not welcome."

"No, that's not what I'm thinking at all." Chest tight at the pained look in his eyes, I stand to walk around the table to his side and lean against the tabletop. "The truth is, I'm worried us being here is affecting Senichi's behavior. He rarely comes out of his room—"

Shig's hand on my thigh stops me. "Sen is acting exactly like he did before you and Rin moved in, so don't take that personally. He's having troubles of his own that he refuses to talk about."

Some of the tension eases from my shoulders. "I also worry about being a burden on you. I know you said I don't have to pay rent while we're here, but I don't want to take advantage of your hospitality, either."

Shig's expression softens. "It's really not necessary, but if it makes you feel better, we can share the cost of groceries." He stands, putting us on the same level, and cups my cheeks. "And if paying rent will make you be in less of a hurry to leave, then pay all the rent you want." He leans forward to press his forehead against mine. "I feel selfish, but I'm not eager to let you leave now that you're here. I don't *want* you to leave. I don't want to go back to being alone at night. I sleep better when you're by my side."

"I sleep better, too," I admit quietly. "I want to be selfish and stay here, but what about the kids? They can't keep bunking together."

"Why not?" He straightens and lifts a hand to caress one of my horns. "We can buy them bunk beds. They'll be fine."

"What about after transition?" I melt into his touch. "What if they develop into different genders? Rin will turn seven in August."

"Deka's birthday is in March." He bites his lip for a moment. "You know, if you're serious about helping me clear out the hoard in my garage, we can convert that into a room for Sen, give him a little more space to do whatever he's going to do, and Rin can move into Sen's room. It's the same size as Deka's."

Surprised, I reach up to pull his hand away from my horn. I need a clear head to have this discussion with him. "You'd renovate your house just to make room for us?"

He smiles. "Well, not *just* for you. If you remember, I did say it was a plan I just hadn't gotten around to doing."

I frown at him. "Don't you want to park your car in your garage? You wouldn't have to scrape ice off your windshield, then."

He shrugs. "I was going to convert it for Sen, anyway." He glances at the dining table, where our laptops and paperwork fill the space. "I need a home office, too."

Which he'll lose if he gives Senichi's room to Rin.

"Why the garage and not your basement?" I ask, because that's what I thought he planned to renovate to begin with, and it's already wired for a living space. "It just needs some drywall and flooring. That way, you don't lose the garage, Senichi can have his own space, and there would be more than enough spare room for a secondary living room and an office."

"Something to consider," Shig agrees. "It would be a good investment, too, and increase the property value." Then, he shivers. "But I'm not sure I want to go out into the garage to get to a new office."

I lift my brows at him. "The garage is big enough to create an interior walkway and still park your car. You could even have a mudroom."

"True." He reaches up to pinch my cheek. "I knew I liked you for more than your good looks."

Blood warms my cheeks, and I drop my eyes to hide my embarrassment. "Only consider that option, though, if it's really something you already planned to do. Don't spend unnecessary money just to make room for Rin and me."

"Oh, no, there's no backing out now. You're committed." Playfulness fills his voice as he steps back to put space between us. "Now, I do believe it's *your* turn to make dinner tonight?"

"Hot dogs and macaroni?" I ask as I head toward the kitchen.

His tail bats playfully at the back of my legs. "I demand veggies. And *real* meat."

Shig's preference for meat surprised me at first, since most tailed lean more toward vegetarian meals, but it certainly makes it easier when planning out dinners.

"You'll get what I can make," I warn as I open the fridge to look at the contents. "We seriously need to go to the store."

"Yes, *we* do," Shig says, pleasure in his voice.

I glance back over my shoulder to find him leaning against the doorway watching me. "Shouldn't you be working?"

His tail wafts back and forth. "This is more fun."

"I'll put you on onion cutting duty," I warn, and he throws his hands up in defeat before vanishing back into the dining room.

I smile as I return my attention to the fridge and pull out ingredients for mushroom stew. Shig's out of luck as far as *real* meat goes until we can go shopping. Based on the limited spices, and the emptiness of the fridge, I get the impression a lot of the meals in this house came pre-made or from delivery up until recently. Which isn't surprising with how much work Shig brings home at night. I'm glad my being here can help change that, at least.

And Rin seems happier lately, too. I always regretted they didn't have a sibling to play with, but Deka fills that role. I'm just not looking forward to their first fight. That's going to be tricky while living under the same roof.

The front door opens and closes as I sauté mushrooms and onions with garlic on the stovetop, and Senichi's low voice fills the dining room.

I peek around the door and wave my wooden spoon. "Dinner should be ready in twenty minutes if you want to wash up."

Senichi sniffs the air. "What are you making?"

"Mushroom stew." I glance at Shig. "No meat unless you want hot dogs."

Senichi shudders. "Vegetarian is fine with me."

Shig gives me puppy dog eyes. "No meat?"

I shake my head. "Not unless you have a second refrigerator hidden in that labyrinth of a garage."

Senichi's snicker draws his uncle's attention, and Shig says, "We have a project for you over the school break."

"Oh, do *we*?" Senichi's eyes jump from Shig to me with suspicion. "What do *we* have planned?"

"We're going to clear out the garage and go through those boxes," Shig informs him.

Senichi's eyes widen in alarm. "*All* the boxes?"

"Yep." Shig nods decisively. "And then, we're going to look into doing something with the basement."

Reluctant interest creeps across Senichi's face. "What are you doing with the basement?"

"I think we can have some walls put up, actually make use of the basement space besides just for laundry." Shig glances at me. "It was Juro's idea. I was just going to stuff you in the garage."

Now, Senichi looks excited. "I'm getting my own space?"

"Only if you help clear out the garage," Shig

warns. "And we'll have to hire people to frame it in, put up walls, and lay flooring."

"I can help with that." Senichi bounces on his toes. "Can we put a gym down there? And a rec room? And maybe—"

"Whoa." Laughing, Shig holds his hands up. "Get ready for dinner, then we can go over your wish list and see what's possible."

For the first time that I've seen, Senichi smiles, and it completely transforms his face from sullen teenager to happy youth.

As he races toward the back hall, Shig runs a hand through his hair. "Well, if I'd known it would make him that happy to have more personal space, I would have done this last summer."

"A little gym isn't a bad idea. Might help him work off some steam," I say before I duck back into the kitchen to stir my mushrooms.

Shig joins me, coming up behind me and wrapping his arms around my waist as he stares at the pan of veggies. "Thank you."

"I didn't do anything," I protest as I push mushrooms around. I need to add the flour and broth soon, but it can wait a couple more minutes while I enjoy being held.

"Left to myself, I'd probably still be thinking

about renovations when Deka is getting ready to graduate from high school." His lips press to the side of my neck, and my pulse leaps. "So, thank you."

"You're welcome." I nudge him. "Now, go clear off the table. Dinner will be ready soon."

"Yes, sir." With another quick peck against my neck, Shig vanishes back into the dining room, leaving me with a confusing swirl of emotions.

My pulse continues to race, and warmth pools in my hips. I didn't want Shig to go, and not just because I was enjoying his hug.

Blindly, I add the next ingredients to the stockpot as I struggle with this new sensation rushing through me that feels dangerously close to desire.

CONFUSION

That night, I'm still not sure what to do as I get ready for bed alone in Shig's room.

I hadn't been able to focus on the conversation at dinner and was grateful Senichi's excitement over the basement renovation kept Shig occupied. Otherwise, he would have noticed that something was up with me. He's way too intuitive.

The pajamas I put on still smell like the plastic they arrived in, and I pull the tag from the waistband. I should have washed them first, but I was too excited to have clothes of my own again. I placed the order online for emergency items for Rin and me, since we couldn't keep wearing Shig's and Deka's clothes forever. I also ordered my preferred shampoo and body wash, and a couple things for

Deka as well, since I couldn't give presents to Rin without taking Deka into consideration, too.

They were too young to understand that Rin's new clothes and bedding are replacements for what Rin lost, not actual presents. I bought both kids matching hippos, since they both love Yip Yip so much, and a matching pillowcase for Deka's pillow.

My new slippers now rest on the side of the bed closest to the door, and my new phone charger sticks out from the wall. Slowly, I'm invading Shig's space, adding myself to the mix, and it makes that warmth in my body grow. I *like* seeing my things in this room, like that I have a side of the bed, like that Shig and I have a pattern to how we get ready at night.

In under a week, I've become completely domesticated, and it helps to push away the sadness that came from losing my home.

If not for our forced cohabitation, would we have progressed this far? I don't think we would have, and I'm secretly grateful that I was pushed into taking this risk.

Otherwise, I may have waffled forever, questioning Shig's continued happiness in a relationship with me. Karen had spent so many years letting me know I couldn't make anyone happy that I gave up on finding a partner after she left.

But Shig takes me as I am, even *wants* me, if his sudden desire to follow through with his plans to remodel the house is any indication. Karen would have scoffed at the expense and the time it would take, demanding we simply move to a bigger, nicer house. Shig wants to make an already welcoming house a home for all of us.

How did I get so lucky as to catch Shig's eye?

From the hall, I hear the bathroom door open. While the master bathroom is big enough for both of us to share, Shig gives me privacy at night and uses the bathroom in the hall that the kids share. Before he comes into the room, I quickly crawl under the covers. They used to smell like Shig, but they now smell like both of us, and it makes my pulse race once more.

Quickly, I pull the comforter over my waist, not wanting to acknowledge the semi-hard-on I've sported most of the night. It doesn't seem to want to become more nor go away, and it leaves me in a state of utter confusion.

In the past, with Karen, I needed pills to get hard, no matter how much she tried to stimulate me. Shig wasn't even being sexual when he kissed my neck earlier in the kitchen, so where is this excitement coming from? I don't even feel like acting on this half-reaction. It just confuses and somewhat alarms me.

What changed? And will it continue to change? Or will I go back to my normal disinterest in the morning?

Shig pads into the room, still rubbing the water from his hair. He brings with him a cloud of clean soap and a hint of the raspberry shampoo we have for Deka and Rin. He wears soft flannel pants that hang low on his hips to leave room for his tail to move without obstruction and a soft white t-shirt that fits tight over his shoulders but hangs baggy at his trim waist.

Did I always look at him like that? I can't remember, and I tug the comforter a little tighter over my lap.

He smiles as he tosses the small towel into the laundry basket next to the dresser. "Kids are settled down for the night. They've traded hippos."

As Shig climbs in on his side, I scoot down in bed. "They'll trade again, I'm sure."

"Most likely." He settles on his side, his head propped on his arm. "Thank you for getting one for Deka, too. Not that they need more stuffed animals."

I turn onto my side, too, curling my knees up. "Kids can never have too many stuffed animals."

"You say that now, but you haven't been with Deka in the toy section. You'll learn." The comforter rustles, and my heart leaps as he finds my hand under the blanket. He squeezes my fingers. "Sen was a lot more engaged at dinner tonight than he has been in a while. I think he's serious about helping with the basement remodel. Maybe his issues stem from feeling a lack of direction?"

"Maybe," I agree, though I have my doubts.

Being aimless doesn't make someone get into fights and skip school, does it?

Ryuu would know better as the horned counselor. It makes me want to abuse my privileges at school to ask about how Senichi's sessions are going. He's on probation right now, so it wouldn't be amiss to check-in, but my relationship with Shig makes that feel like I'd be crossing a line I shouldn't cross.

I wake with a jolt, not sure what disturbed me. Shig still lies facing me, his eyes closed in sleep, so it wasn't our alarm.

Rolling over in bed, I check the clock. It's only three in the morning. Shig and I stayed up late talking, and I've only been asleep for a few hours. But now that I'm awake, my bladder won't let me fall back asleep.

Quietly, I slip out from under the covers and walk out into the shadowed hall. Not wanting to wake anyone else up, I pad barefoot to the powder room in the main area.

The tiles turn my feet to ice, and I make quick use of the bathroom before hurrying back toward our bedroom. Shig has the heater in the house set on a timer that drops it down to sixty at night. It warms back up an hour before anyone has to be out of bed, so it's not usually an issue, but right now, my toes are regretting me skipping past my slippers.

I rub the goose bumps on my arms, already dreaming of the warm comforter that awaits, when a flicker of star lights in the hall catches my attention.

Frowning, I veer left down the hall to Deka's room, where the door stands open. When I check inside, the lamp on the short dresser slowly spins, painting the walls and ceiling in stars that illuminate the rumpled, empty beds.

Panic shoots through me, and I step farther into the room, my eyes sweeping the small space in case I just missed the kids. I even check the closet because they like to hide there, but I can't find them.

My heart races as I run out of the bedroom and make a sweep of the hall bath, then go out into the living room to check the couch in case they snuck out to watch a movie. Still not finding them, I race into the bedroom I share with Shig and throw on the light.

Shig bolts upright, his dark hair sticking up on one side. His eyes aren't even open before he's halfway out of the bed in a panic.

When his sleepy eyes meet mine, they widen in fear. "What's going on? What's happened?"

"I can't find the kids." My hands shake, and I back out of the room, half-turning toward the star-speckled side of the hall.

Maybe I just missed them? I should go check again.

Shig's warm hand on my arm stops me. "Juro, it's okay. They're probably in Sen's room. Let's go check."

I stare at him in bewilderment. "Why would they be in Senichi's room?"

"Deka used to go there all the time when they first moved in with me," he whispers.

Quietly, he leads the way down the hall, past the hall bathroom, and opens the door next to it. Quiet music drifts out, and Shig looks inside.

His shoulders relax, and he steps to the side to let me look in. "See? They're safe."

Pulse still racing, I creep forward and look into Senichi's room.

A screen saver plays on the computer on his desk, casting blue light over the room. I haven't been in here before, and it takes a moment for me to find his full-sized bed shoved up against the same wall the door is on.

From this vantage point, I see his slender form on the edge of the bed, while Deka and Rin take up the other two-thirds of the bed against the wall. Deka sleeps upside down, one chubby leg on top of Senichi's head, which rests under the pillow instead of on it. From the position, I imagine Deka probably kicked him until he loved. Rin lies near the bottom of the bed, face close to Deka's.

I back out, keeping my voice low. "Should we bring them back to their beds?"

Shig shrugs. "Sen's used to it." Quietly, he shuts the door and tiptoes back toward our bedroom. "I think that's partly why he's so excited about the basement bedroom. Though, I'm sure Deka will just sneak down there, too."

The adrenaline rush dissipates, leaving me shaky, and I lean against the wall for support. "I thought…" I scrub a hand over my face. "I almost had a heart attack."

"Hey, it's okay." Shig comes back and leads me to the bedroom.

As soon as we cross the threshold and close the door, I pull him closer, wanting his support and needing his comfort. After the fire, my mind went to the worst place possible when I saw Rin's bed empty. I thought I was dealing with everything okay, but the thought I lost Rin brings all those emotions flooding back.

Shig murmurs soft reassurances into my ear as he steers us to the bed, then somehow gets us back under the covers. I don't know how he does it, since I can't bring myself to let him go. He feels like the only stable part of my life at the moment, and it terrifies me.

What happens if this ends? What will I do then? I feel like I'm risking everything to be in this relationship. It's not just about me; it's about Rin, too. How will Rin react if we have to leave here after making it our home?

I gasp, but air won't enter my lungs.

Shig's hold on me turns firm, and he pushes me back.

My arms protest, wanting to stay tight, wanting

to maintain this contact for as long as possible.

"Juro," Shig says my name firmly as he cups my face. "Juro, look at me. Rin is safe. Okay?"

It's not just Rin I'm worried about, though, and that thought fills me with a mix of shame and fear. Rin's been the center of my universe for the last six years. And now, here's Shig, throwing everything off balance in the best and worst way possible. And there's Deka and Senichi, whose lives will change because of me.

Shig strokes my cheeks, then his fingers move up into my hair. He caresses my horns. Shivers roll through me, and I bow my head, silently insisting he continue. But the position leaves my arms empty, which I hate. I need to hold him, need to feel his solid body against mine, need to know he's not leaving.

With frantic movements, I knock his hands aside, then lunge forward to wrap my arms around his waist, shoving him down on the bed. My body lands on top of his, my head on his chest and my hips between his parted legs. He lets out an *oomph* of surprise, and I release my hold on him long enough to catch one of his hands and bring it back to my head.

"Okay, this is okay," he soothes as he resumes

stroking my horns. "I'm sorry I pushed you away. That wasn't my intent."

I'm glad he's so intuitive and understands what I need because I can't express my desires. I don't even understand what I need, except that it involves Shig being right where he is now.

He shifts beneath me, one leg lifting to curve against my hip, and he settles a little more evenly on the mattress, all without pausing his comforting strokes.

It feels so good to have someone to soothe me. Before Shig, I can't remember the last time someone reached out to comfort me. I've been the one always reaching, trying to be what Karen wanted, being the father Rin needed, but I was so lonely and didn't even realize how starved I became for touch. For the most basic contact between me and another adult.

I shift, snuggling against Shig, and feel something hard nudge against my stomach.

Shig's touch on my horns pauses. "I'm sorry, just ignore that. It will go away."

Blood rushes to my cheeks, and I feel that stirring from earlier flow through me. How am I supposed to ignore what's pushing against me? I shift again and feel Shig harden further.

Yes, I definitely can't ignore that.

Bracing my arms on the bed, I sit up and realize for the first time the position I put us in.

Shig lies sprawled on the mattress in front of me, his legs spread on either side of my hips. The thin t-shirt he wears is pushed up to reveal a broad expanse of bare skin over his stomach, and the tip of his hard cock pokes up past his waistband.

In the bright lights of the bedroom, I can see everything, and he makes no effort to cover himself as he lets me look.

Sweat breaks out on my palms, and I wipe them on my thighs as uncertainty fills me.

"Juro," he says, his voice soft and undemanding. "It really is fine, and it *will* go away. But if it makes you uncomfortable or feel pressured, I can go to the bathroom and take care of it."

My pulse leaps, and I lick suddenly dry lips as I look down the length of his body once more. "What if you *don't* go to the bathroom, but take care of it here, instead?"

EXPERIMENTATION

Shig's breath hitches, and his hand lifts toward his waistband, fingers skimming along the elastic. "You want to watch me?"

My eyes jerk back up to his. "Is that okay?"

His lashes drop to half-mast, and he licks his lips. "Whatever you want, honey."

My heart lurches at the endearment, then picks up speed as Shig's hand slips beneath his waistband. Through the fabric, I watch him fist his cock, and his hips arch as he lets out a soft groan.

His hand moves in slow, easy pulls, his hips flexing, and another quiet moan escapes him. My eyes lift to his face to find his gaze still on me, his cheeks flushed pink with desire, and my pulse quickens. He's enjoying having me watch him pleasure himself, enjoying putting himself on display.

But he hasn't really *shown* me anything. My focus drops back to his hips, to the fleece pants that stretch and flex, hiding what he's doing.

Hesitantly, I reach out and grasp the material on either side of his hips, pulling it down. Shig's stomach muscles contract on a sharp breath, and he lifts his knees, encouraging me to pull his pants completely off. He releases his hard cock to yank his t-shirt over his head, then lies back on the bed, fully exposed in front of me.

Lean muscles cover his body, giving strength to his slender frame. A light dusting of dark hair covers his chest, swirling around his small, tan nipples and forming a path down to his belly button, then lower, joining the thicker strands of hair that circle his hard cock. Like the rest of the man, it's slender, but long, tapering at the tip, where his skin turns dusky and cum leaks from his slit.

Strong, smooth thighs flex with strength as he parts his legs wider, giving me an unobstructed view of his tight, delicate balls and the seam of his ass. His dark tail, which lays next to my hip, curls and baps against me.

He really is beautiful, though that's not limited to

his physique. He's beautiful on the inside, too, someone I admire and hold dear.

Unable to hold the words back, I look up to meet his eyes once more. "You're beautiful."

"So are you." His hand trails down the line of hair on his abdomen. "Do you want me to keep going?"

"Please," I say, my voice thick with a burning sensation.

"If you want to touch, you can," Shig says as his hand drifts lower. "You can direct, too. Or you can just watch. Whatever you want."

I nod in acknowledgment, though I wouldn't even know where to start. Shig is so different from what I'm used to, but not in a bad way. No, far from bad. My eyes are drawn to the length of his body, though I don't feel the urge to participate. I want to see what Shig likes, what brings him pleasure.

Shig's hand curls around his cock once more, squeezing the slender shaft to illicit another moan before he slowly starts stroking himself again. Cum leaks more heavily from his slit, dribbling onto his stomach, and he scoops it up, using it as lube so his hand glides smoothly over his cock.

Soon, he glistens, his pace speeding up. His quiet gasps and groans fill the bedroom, and my skin flushes at the sound. I've never heard someone enjoy themselves like this. Shig gives himself over to the experience with complete abandon, not embarrassed or ashamed as he seeks his own pleasure.

The tip of his flushed cock pops in and out of view as his hand moves, cum dripping over his knuckles.

Shig lifts a leg and braces it against my thigh as he gasps, "Is this okay?"

"Yes." My hand curls instinctively around his slim ankle as my attention fixes between his legs to where his free hand dips lower.

He spends a couple minutes massaging his balls, cupping and squeezing them gently, before his foot presses against my thigh, his hips lifting, and his hand dips lower still to find the crease of his ass.

His fingers slip between his round cheeks, disappearing into that dark crevice to massage against his entrance.

I stare, mesmerized, as he lifts his hips higher, his fingers pushing deeper. The angle isn't perfect for me to see what's happening, though. It would be better if his knees were pushed higher, his spine curved and his ass fully out.

The direction trips down my tongue before I bite

it back. If this is how Shig likes to do this, then he knows best.

Soft fur brushes against my forearm, and I reach down to grasp Shig's tail, fisting the soft fluff.

He gasps, his spine arching, and I can't take it anymore.

My hold on his ankle tightens, and I push his leg up toward his chest, curling his body into a position that gives me a better view of what his skillful fingers are doing.

Shig moans, curving beneath me without protest, and putting his ass on display to reveal one finger shoved inside himself, his little pink pucker stretched around it. So small, but I know it can stretch wider. I may never have been with a man before, but I know how it's done.

"Lube," Shig groans out. "Nightstand."

My hold on him tightens, unwilling to release him.

He moans again with excitement. "Please, Juro, I need…"

His breathy plea gets me moving, and I lean to the side and stretch out to grasp the nightstand drawer, grateful we somehow ended up on his side of the bed so I don't have to release him completely.

I find the lube and straighten with it held in my

hand. What do I do now? Give it to him? But both his hands are busy.

Chest tight, I flip the cap open and drizzle a thin stream over the finger shoved into his ass. He pulls the digit out slowly, and my stomach tightens, the heat inside me building, as I imagine seeing that little hole stretched wider.

As if he knows what I want, he gathers up the lube, rubbing it over his hole. "More."

Without hesitation, I pour more lube onto him until his ass is slippery and shiny with the stuff.

He groans in encouragement, then presses two fingers against his entrance, slowly pushing them inside. His hole stretches, and he moans, his tail bapping against me once more for attention. I reach down and grab it again, holding it in place, too caught up in watching those fingers thrust in and out of Shig's body.

The front of my pants grow tight, heat flooding my stomach and between my legs.

Shig's other hand starts moving on his cock once more, jerking himself in time to the plunge and withdraw of his fingers into his body.

The leg I hold trembles, his muscles tensing, and his toes form beautiful points as he pushes against my hold. It doesn't feel like he's trying to escape, though, as gasps of pleasure fall from his lips.

His hand on his cock moves faster, the motions jerky with urgency before his whole body stiffens. His mouth opens on a long moan as he throws his head back against the pillows. He drives his fingers in deeper, past the second knuckle, and his cock pulses, thick ropes of cum splashing across his tense stomach.

The musky scent of him fills the room, making my mouth water with the need for something, though I don't know what. It's like a craving for a food I can't name but know will haunt me until I find it.

With a gasp, he sags beneath me, and I ease his leg down, only now realizing I may have left bruises on his ankle with how tightly I held him.

Shig's chest heaves as his body slowly relaxes, and his eyes slit open to stare at me. "Did you enjoy that?"

I trace my fingers over the red skin around his ankle. "Did I hurt you?"

"No, I liked it." He trails a lazy hand through the cum on his stomach. "How do *you* feel?"

I lick my lips as my gaze sweeps over his flushed and glistening body. "I'm...confused. And worried."

"It's okay to be confused." He reaches across the bed to grab his abandoned t-shirt and uses it to clean the mess off his stomach and hands. "What are you worried about?"

I pet his tail absently as I dig through the mire of thoughts that flood my find. "You're very sensual."

He props an arm behind his head and leans back against the pillows, unabashed in his nudity.

My eyes drop to his waist, to his thighs that still glisten with lube and his spent cock, nestled in his black curls like a treasure. "I'm worried if someone who so obviously enjoys sex will ever be satisfied with me."

He reaches down to caress his limp cock. "Do I look unsatisfied?"

My pulse flutters as I look back at his face. "No, you look very satisfied."

"That's because I am." His expression turns serious, and he sits up in an easy flex of muscle. "I would have been satisfied *not* doing anything, as well."

I duck my head to hide my disbelief. No one who enjoys sex that much could be happy skipping it.

"Juro, look at me." Light fingers on my chin lift my head so I meet Shig's earnest eyes once more. "Sex is a physical release for me. I can do it with or without a partner. What we did here tonight thrilled me, but it was because you were enjoying it, too. If you hadn't looked interested, I wouldn't have done anything. Because I don't *need* that in a relationship. What I *need* in a relationship isn't brief moments of sexual release. I need someone who's my friend, my confidant, the person I come home to on a rough day, and someone I share happy times with. I need someone willing to share my burdens as well as my successes, and I need someone who I can seek comfort from and who I can comfort in return. *That's* what I want from our relationship. Anything sexual that does or doesn't happen between us won't change that."

A lump fills my throat as everything he says he wants finds an echoing desire within me.

"As for your confusion..." His hand drops to my hip, to where my semi-hard cock still tents the front of my pants. "Is it because you liked what we just did?"

Staring down at his hand, so close to me, makes my dick jump. Warmth fills my skin once more, but that's it. I don't feel a need to do anything about what's going on with my lower half. There's no driving need to seek the same release Shig did.

At last, I nod, and my voice trembles as I speak.

"Why now, when I couldn't for my wife? It's why she left me. Because I couldn't perform how she wanted. I've watched porn, lots of porn. Mixed-gender and same-sex. None of it did anything for me. I thought I just didn't have those urges. So why is this happening now?"

Shig stays silent for a moment before he finally ventures, "Did you actually *like* Karen? Even at the beginning? Before the fights got bad?"

My head jerks up. "Everyone liked Karen. She was very popular at school, very pretty."

"I'm not talking about everyone." He presses a hand against my chest. "Did *you* like her? Even as a friend?"

"I... No." The admission comes with a bitter tinge of regret.

I always thought those feelings would come later, that we married for Rin but would learn to love each other, too. But it never happened.

I shake my head. "No, I never liked her. We had nothing in common. Not even our values where it came to raising Rin. And as time went on, our marriage turned into just getting through one day to the next. I was...*relieved* when she left." I cover my face with my hands. "God, that sounds horrible. I tried so hard to keep us together, but I was *glad* when she found someone else."

"It's not horrible. She sounds like someone who would be hard to like." Shig pulls my hands down. "I ask because… Have you ever heard of demisexuality?"

I shake my head, then my eyes drop to his bare chest, to the goose bumps rising on his skin, and I realize I've left him naked in the cold during this conversation while the heat of the moment wore off long ago. Reaching back, I grab the edge of the comforter and drag it forward, curling it around us both so we sit in a warm cocoon.

Shig smiles and shifts closer, straddling my lap and waiting until I slip my arms around him before he continues. "Demisexuality is when a person doesn't feel sexual attraction unless there's an emotional bond first. You were never able to be with Karen the way she wanted because you didn't have a bond with her. Whereas with me…"

"I like you." My arms tighten around him. "More than I should so soon after meeting."

"Thank you." He grins at me, displaying a dimple I hadn't noticed before. "I like you, too. Very much."

"So, if we bond more, I'll want to have sex?" My

cheeks flush hot with embarrassment, but I want to understand.

He lifts his shoulders in a show of uncertainty. "Maybe? The grayscale of sexuality is broad. You could be demisexual but lean more toward asexual. You may never want to act on sexual urges yourself. We'll work through it and explore together, at whatever pace you want. If tonight was a fluke, that's fine, and if you want to do this again, that's fine, too. Just be open with what you want, and I'll do the same."

Overwhelmed by all this new information, I nod and pull him closer to rest my head on his bare shoulder. "Thank you, for not saying I'm broken."

He strokes my hair. "No, you're definitely not broken. Not even a little."

Nuzzling against his neck, I breathe in his musky scent. "I think I like you even more, now."

"Good, keep liking me more and more." His arms loop around my shoulders. "Like me so much you don't know what to do without me."

My heart lurches, and I cling to him tighter, until there's no space left between us, because I'm too afraid to admit out loud that I might already like him that much.

BABY DADDY

Friday arrives with exhaustion from limited sleep, but also with a weight lifted off my shoulders.

It's a good thing it's the last day before the holiday break, though, and no one expects work to actually get done. After waking up—then staying awake—I find myself struggling to process any information.

I had completed the last of the parent conferences yesterday, so today is all about filing, making last-minute notes, and general prep work for the new year, when school opens back up.

At lunch, I realize I forgot to pack anything to eat and lock up my office to make a quick trip to the nearest fast-food place. It's not ideal, but beggars can't be choosers, and I refuse to go to the cafeteria to see what they have to offer.

With the end-of-year meeting scheduled for the end of the day, I order a small hamburger and skip the fries. I just need enough to tide me over. Principal Ikeda always provides something to eat as a token of appreciation.

I scarf down my burger on the way back, careful not to let any of the ketchup drip on my sweater. I'd forgone the usual button-up for something more casual, to celebrate the coming holiday. Shig had smiled at the ivy knit with leather patches at the elbows and commented that it made me look like a professor. The compliment pleased me far too much. I don't know when I'll get used to his flattery, but the blushes need to stop. I'm twenty-five, for goodness's sake.

When I pull back into the packed parking lot, I find my spot filled with a blue sedan. Only Principal Ikeda gets an assigned spot, leaving the rest of us to fend for ourselves.

I pull my car around to the side of the school, where the shadow of the building doesn't allow the snow to melt, and park nose first in an icy drift. No one likes to park over here, so I'm one of the few cars on this side of the school. So long as it doesn't snow again before I leave, it should be fine.

Climbing out of my car, I brush the crumbs from my sweater, before raised voices draw my attention.

Concern fills me, and I pull my cell phone from my pocket, prepping a call to Ko in the front office in case I need backup. I'd love to say I'm not afraid of students, but horned can get aggressive, and many of them are larger and stronger than I am. Add more than one to the mix, and I don't have a chance.

My steps slow as I near the edge of the building and peek around the corner.

As soon as I see what's happening, all thoughts of calling for backup fly out the window.

Senichi and a tailed kid stand back-to-back in the middle of a group of three horned guys I don't recognize from our school. Right now, they're only shouting, but by the clenched fists, it won't stay that way for long.

"Hey!" I shout as I stride into view. "What school are you from? I want names, now! You're not allowed on school property!"

The group spins toward me, scowls on all their faces. They don't seem especially ready to back down.

My eyes narrow on the biggest of them, the

ringleader, and I lift the phone in my hand. "Police will be here in under five minutes. I suggest you start running."

He spits on the ground and turns back to Senichi. "This isn't over, Akutsu."

With a jerk of his head, the three horned boys jog in the opposite direction.

Senichi and the tailed kid slowly relax, their hands unclenching as their arms drop back to their sides.

I gesture for them to get moving in case those guys change their minds. "Come on, I didn't actually call the police."

As they near, I notice they didn't come out of the fight completely unscathed. A new bruise already blooms on Senichi's cheek, and blood dribbles from the split in his lip that's busted open again.

"Thanks," Senichi grumbles, wiping the blood on the back of his sleeve. "I could have taken them, but this guy might have gotten hurt."

His friend's tail curls around his leg. "I love you, boo, but I would have kicked them in the balls, and you know it."

I glance between them. The tailed guy is more slender than Senichi, and a couple inches shorter. He wears his bangs long and hanging over his face in a rocker style, while silver rings line both his ears.

With the familiar way he touches Senichi, it's clear they're friends, or possibly more, though I'm a horrible judge of these things. "Senichi, this is your…"

"Sasha," he grunts, stuffing his hands into the pockets of his skinny, black jeans.

"Yes, I'm his Sasha," the other guy teases and nudges Senichi in the side. "Introduce me properly, you prickly pear."

"Mr. Ono." Senichi obediently gestures to his friend. "Please let me introduce Sasha, whose mom owns the cafe I work at sometimes. Sasha, meet Mr. Ono."

Sasha looks vaguely familiar, but not enough to be one of the students who has sat across from me for an interview. Which is surprising, since I've conducted parent interviews with most of Senichi's gang in school, at one point or another. I probably recognize him from passing in the halls.

I stick out my hand. "Nice to meet you."

"Oh, we've met before." He shakes my hand with an impish grin. "Picture me uptight with glasses." Releasing me, he pushes his blond bangs off his forehead, giving me a better look at his face. "You commended my studies last year and moved me up to class A."

"So, I did," I say faintly as I recognize him, though he looked completely different the last time we met.

Before, he resembled any other strait-laced, straight-A student on the path to university. But now, he looks like one of the bad boys who get called into the principal's office for fighting and skipping classes. Much like Senichi.

Is he part of the reason for Senichi's shift in character? Or did whatever cause it affect them both?

Now's not the time to ask those questions, though, so I focus on something more pertinent. "Those guys who were ganging up on you?"

"They're dropouts from Taft High." Senichi shoves his hands into his pockets once more. "They're trying to recruit for their gang."

The blood drains from my face. "And they want you to join?"

Senichi shrugs noncommittally.

"Senichi…"

"Are you going to tell on us?" he cuts in. "We didn't start the fight, and we're not joining their stupid gang."

I should report this to security, at the very least, but Senichi's on academic probation right now. I don't think it's fair to have him kicked out of school for a fight he didn't start.

Rubbing the chill from my arms, I shake my head. "No, since they ran away, I won't report this, though I will be asking security to make extra rounds outside during the lunch hours." I glance at Senichi's face. "Your uncle is another matter. I don't feel comfortable keeping secrets from him."

"*Ohhh.*" Sasha's eyes widen. "You're *that* guy. The baby daddy."

Startled, I almost slip on a patch of ice. "Excuse me?"

"The one shacking up with Sen's uncle," he elaborates.

"Sasha, shut up." Warning fills Senichi's voice, but his friend ignores him.

"The one with the adorable kid." Sasha pulls his phone from his pocket. "I have so many pics of them with Deka. Sen won't stop talking about how cute they are."

"Shut up, Sasha!" Senichi yells, his cheeks flushing red as he yanks the phone from his friend's hand.

"Well." I cough into my hand. "Rin *is* adorable. And Senichi is a big help with both Rin and Deka."

"I just want to pinch their cheeks." Sasha mimes the gesture before he turns a glare on Senichi. "But *someone* won't let me come over lately."

"Because you're like this," Senichi hisses, clearly embarrassed, then his dark eyes flash to me. "Also, I didn't know if I *could* invite people over."

"Oh." My lips part in surprise at his consideration. "I'm so sorry, Senichi. I didn't realize that was worrying you. Principal Ikeda knows. It's not a secret."

He gives a brief nod. "Okay, whatever."

Sasha dances in place. "Does that mean I can come over today?"

"No," Senichi snaps, and when his friend's face crumples, he adds, "You have work after school. You can come on Sunday."

Sasha slumps. "My mom's such a slave driver." He suddenly turns wide eyes on me. "Be my baby daddy, too. Then, I can come live with Sen and be pampered."

As I gape in shock, Senichi spins on his friend. "No one is anyone's baby daddy. Will you quit with that?"

"Sorry, boo, didn't mean to make you jelly."

Sasha makes a kissy face at him. "You know you're my only daddy."

"Forget Sunday. I don't want to see your face until the new year." Senichi lifts the headphones that dangle from around his neck and shoves them into his ears before jogging ahead of us.

Sasha watches him leave, the smile vanishing from his face as he turns to me, his expression now serious. "Those Taft High guys are serious about getting Sen to join up with them. Tell that rich uncle he needs a car, because I can't always be the one picking him up and dropping him off."

Before I can respond, the teasing smirk returns to Sasha's face, and he runs after Senichi. "Don't leave me like this, lover boy! You know I can't live without you!"

Despite the headphones, Senichi's angry stride slows, and the two men round the school building together, leaving me with too many thoughts and unsure what to do with them all.

Not for the first time, I check the clock that hangs on the wall as Gorou Hirota nods off again in the middle of his farewell speech. The old horned counselor hasn't been doing his job for a while now, but he held onto his position long past the time he should have retired. The birth of his first great-grandchild finally convinced him to shift his focus from work to family.

He stayed on through the end of the year to *train* his replacement, Ryuu. But everyone knows the real person who trained the new horned counselor is Taro, his tailed counterpart and fated mate. I don't know if it's Taro's skill as a teacher or Fate choosing a perfect complement for Taro in work ethic as well as personality, but they're a fantastic team. Our transitioned students are finally receiving the support they need.

This end-of-year party is a bit of a sendoff and celebration rolled into one. And it would have been over before the last bell for the day rang, if not for Gorou's bad habit of falling asleep anywhere, at any time.

Ko, near the front of the room, clears his throat loudly, and when that fails to rouse the old, horned counselor, he coughs and bangs his fit on the table.

With a snort, Gorou's head jerks up, and he blinks rheumy eyes around the room. "Right, where was I?"

Principal Ikeda's gaze flicks to Ko, who stands

and claps. "Lovely speech, Gorou, we'll miss you. Don't forget to send us pics of the new baby when you get to your granddaughter's house."

The rest of us follow suit, clapping, and Gorou's chest puffs out with pride. "Yes, I'll make sure to mail them as soon as I get the film developed."

The promise is met with coughs to hide laughter, and Principal Ikeda stands. "Now, we have cake and punch for everyone."

I check the clock again. I promised Shig I'd collect the kids on my way home today. I have both car seats in the back of my car, so even if I message him now, he can't pick them up instead.

"What do you think of the principal's big idea?" Taro asks quietly as he slides into the empty seat beside me. He holds two cups of punch and sets one in front of me.

"Thank you." I tear my eyes away from the clock and turn to face him. "It will ease some of my caseloads, once they're trained."

His lips tighten with unhappiness. "Yeah, it's the training that has me concerned."

"That's just because you're a worrywart." Ryuu strokes his mate's black hair as he claims the open seat on Taro's other side. "It will be fine. Look how well you trained me."

"You're permanent, so you were worth training," Taro grumbles as he swats the other man's hand away. "We'll get a student aid working efficiently just in time for them to leave, and we have to start over with a new one."

That occurred to me, too, but I have more hope. "We'll get students who want to go into these fields. They'll be eager to learn as much as possible." I release a wistful sigh. "Imagine not taking work home anymore."

"Whatever will we do with all that spare time?" Ryuu grips his mate's shoulders. "We can make more trips to Bell House Books."

Taro's black tail curls with interest. "We'll see."

"Don't let him curb your enthusiasm." Ryuu gives Taro a little shake. "He's excited. He just likes to be contrary."

Taro's tail snaps against his mate's leg. "*You* like to be contrary."

Watching their interaction brings a smile to my face. They really do complement each other, and it gives me hope that Shig and I will find the same happiness together.

Ryuu leans forward, draping his arm over Taro's shoulder as he focuses concerned eyes on me. "So, how are you doing? How is Rin taking the big change?"

I had to tell them about the fire when I informed Ryuu he'd be in charge of Senichi's academic probation going forward. "I haven't actually talked to them yet. Right now, they're so happy living with Deka that I just can't bring myself to burst the bubble. I'm still coming to terms with it, as well."

Taro's brows pinch together. "How did Karen take you moving in with your new partner?"

Dread pools in my stomach, and I fiddle with the plastic cup of punch in front of me. "I haven't told her. I was waiting until I had concrete information about what our next step was. And now..." I give Taro a wane smile. "Things aren't going well with Karen, and I'm worried this will somehow be another weapon in her arsenal."

Ryuu frowns. "You don't have a clause in your divorce contract about introducing new partners, do you?"

"No, thank goodness." I take a sip of punch, and the bubbles tickle my nose. "She tried, but because of the reason for our divorce, she didn't have a leg to stand on."

The question makes me uneasy, though. It's been a while since I read the document. Maybe I should pull it out and ask Shig to go over it with me over our two-week break. With his legal background, he'll better understand the language.

I check the clock again, worried I'm late picking the kids up, even though I still have hours before the daycare closes.

Taro follows my gaze. "Do you need to leave?"

"My nanny came down with a severe cold and has been struggling to catch up on schoolwork since she recovered. I promised to pick the kids up today." I check around the room, but no one else seems in a hurry to leave. "I hate to be the first out the door…"

"You have more than one good reason to leave first." Taro flaps his hand toward the door. "Go. We'll make excuses if anyone asks."

"Thank you." I peek over at Gorou, who slouches in a chair at the back, faint snores rising from him. "Think he'll remember I didn't wish him farewell?"

"I don't think he remembers much of anything, anymore," Ryuu murmurs. "Just go."

"Thank you," I say again, grateful for their willingness to cover for me.

Taro, and now Ryuu, are good people, good *friends*, and the realization startles me.

I've spent so long feeling alone that suddenly

being surrounded by people who care leaves a warmth in me that just keeps growing.

This feels like a second chance to do my life right, and I plan to grasp it with both hands and never let go.

YIP YIP DANCE

When I pull up to the school, I find the parking lot almost empty. Not unusual for a Friday, which just makes my guilt for running late more real.

Climbing out, I hurry inside, my eyes sweeping the room in search of the kids.

"They're out back with Sen," Mr. Jacob calls as he strides over. "He's been keeping them entertained for the last hour."

My brows shoot up in surprise. "Senichi has?"

"Yeah." Mr. Jacob walks with me to the back door to the playground, then lifts a hand to his lips. "Listen."

Confused, I tilt my head toward the door.

Senichi's voice coming from outside. "Happy happy, he he ho, spin around, away we *go*!"

The sound of Rin's excited squeal fills the air a moment later.

"Again!" Deka shouts.

"Come on," Senichi groans, sounding tired. "You said that was the last time."

"Again!" Deka insists.

"They've been doing that since he got here," Mr. Jacob whispers, affection clear in his voice. "Sen used to come by more often, you know, to volunteer here. He was a big hit with the kids, but I think he wanted to keep an eye on Deka."

"He did?" I ask, trying to imagine the sullen teenager I know having the tolerance to care for a whole herd of kids.

Of course, he's really patient with both Deka and Rin and even seeks them out to play without being asked.

"Yeah, when they first moved back to town." He bites his lip as he glances at the door to the playground. "We had to ask him to stop coming, though, when things got rough for him. We can't have him covered in bruises and taking care of the kids. It made the parents worry."

Sadness sweeps through me for how Senichi must have taken that blow. Whatever caused this change, I doubt he realized how much it would cost him. So, why does he keep it up, if he wasn't always like this?

"He told me, once, that he was considering going into childcare," Mr. Jacob whispers, almost too low for me to hear. "It's a hard field for horned to join. Parents worry, you know? But if he got his act together, stopped with the fighting, I'm sure the director would take him back as a volunteer. He really is good with the kids."

"I'll talk to him about it," I promise, though I'm not sure it will do any good.

Senichi hasn't exactly opened up to me, despite Shig's hope that we'd somehow bond over both being horned. He probably senses that I'm not the same as him, despite being in the same group.

Senichi's voice disrupts my thoughts. "Okay, last time."

Giggles and claps answer as Senichi begins the Yip Yip song again.

Stepping forward, I slowly open the door and peek outside.

Senichi stands on his tiptoes, his arms straight at his sides and hands pointed outward as he sings and spins in a circle with his eyes closed. The kids dance back and forth around him, trading places.

"—away we *go!*" Senichi shouts, his eyes popping open as he swoops down, grabbing Deka, who stands closest to where he stopped.

His sibling giggles as he lifts them into the air, swinging them above his head, while Rin cheers from the ground.

As soon as Senichi sets Deka down, they yell, "Again!"

He groans and rubs his lower back.

"Okay, I think Senichi's had enough," I announce as I push the door open all the way.

"Daddy!" Rin shouts and dashes over. "Play Yip Yip with us!"

I laugh and shake my head. "I'm not nearly strong enough to lift you above my head like that."

When I look up, red stains Senichi's cheeks, and he kneels to fuss with Deka's hat, pulling it down over their ears.

"Ready to go?" I ask the kids, then frown at Rin. "Where are your gloves?"

Rin holds chubby hands in front of their face and studies them before shrugging.

"They were on the balance bar when I got here." Senichi stands and jogs onto the playground. He disappears around the slide, then returns a moment later, holding a pair of purple gloves in one hand with a grimace. "They're soaked, so they won't be much help now."

I sigh as I stare down at my child. "It's going to be a sad day when your fingers all fall off."

"Daddy!" Rin rolls their eyes, then reaches out to grab Deka's hand. "Can we play in my castle today?"

Pain squeezes my heart. My mouth opens, but no words come out.

"I thought we were painting pine cones today," Senichi jumps to the rescue as he points to a small pile next to the door. "Isn't that why we gathered all those?"

"Oh, yeah!" Rin runs to the pile, dragging Deka along, and they struggle to gather all the cones into their chubby arms.

"Thank you," I murmur.

Senichi shrugs. "Just reminding them we had plans." His dark eyes flick up to meet mine. "There will be glitter involved."

"Understood." I stride over and grab the door to hold it open. "Come on, everyone, we have decorations to make."

As soon as we step into the warmth of the daycare, Mr. Jacob rushes over with a plastic bag to help carry the pine cones, and the kids take turns dumping their armfuls in.

Senichi takes the bag and carries it out to the car, then helps buckle Deka into one side while I fasten Rin into the other.

"Are you coming home for dinner?" I ask, keeping my tone casual. "The front seat is open, if you'd like a ride."

Senichi pauses before shoving the last buckle home and checking the straps for tightness. "Yeah. Any chance we're having pizza tonight?"

"Text your uncle and see if he's started anything, yet," I suggest. "If not, we can stop and pick a couple up on the way home."

Senichi grins and closes the back door before moving to the front seat.

By the time I double-check Rin's straps and give them another firm tug, he already has an answer. "Caught him before he started. Does Frank's Pizzeria sound good?"

"Sure." My stomach lets out a growl, reminding me I had a light lunch and no cake at the party. "Get me something with meat. And some cheese bread for the kids."

"Uncle Shig will like that." Senichi pulls up the app on his phone and punches in our order as I slip behind the wheel and start the car. "Can we get cookie dough?"

"Cookies!" Deka yells, and Rin joins in.

I laugh. "Well, now we have to."

Senichi grins and adds the dessert to our order before pressing send. "It will be ready in fifteen."

"Perfect." I glance into the rearview mirror before backing out of the parking lot.

Leaning forward, Senichi fiddles with the stereo, finding a kid's channel and putting it on the rear speakers. With the sound barrier in place, he turns to look at me. "So, how are things going with you and my uncle? Is this serious? Do you have good intentions toward him?"

The questions catch me off guard, and I smile as I keep my focus on the darkening road. "Things are going well, and I have the best intentions where your uncle is concerned."

"Are you guys planning to test for a mate bond?" Then, Senichi leans over the center console and drops his voice. "You haven't, yet, right? You'd have said something if...?"

I peek at him from the corner of my eye. "Isn't that something you should be asking Shig?"

"Oh, my God. Have you *met* my uncle? No way

am I asking him that." Senichi slumps back against his door. "So, have you?"

"No, we haven't." I glance at him quickly before returning my eyes to the road. "That kind of thing shouldn't be tested lightly. It's better to know what you both want, and what you're willing to sacrifice, before going into it."

Senichi stays silent for a block before asking, "If you're not, are you going to dump him?"

I tighten my hands on the steering wheel. "Your uncle is one of the kindest, most considerate people I have ever had the good fortune to meet. Whether or not we're Fated doesn't negate that."

Another silence follows, this one longer. "You won't feel like you're missing out if you commit to someone not destined for you?"

Worry fills his voice, and I risk another look. Senichi stares out the window, a pensive expression on his face.

I keep my tone gentle. "What are you really asking, Senichi?"

His dark gaze darts to mine, and he reaches out to turn the music up a little higher. "What if..." He licks his lips and swallows hard before shaking his head. "Sasha isn't my boyfriend."

"Okay." It's not the statement he originally

planned to make, and I stay silent, waiting for him to work up his nerve.

Senichi drums his fingers on his knees. "We let the school think we're dating, though, because it just makes things easier, you know?"

Unsure what he's getting at, I give him a nod to continue.

"But he's not my type. And I'm not his." Senichi turns to stare out the passenger window. "Do you get it?"

I think I do, and I think I understand, now, why he's struggling so much in his horned class.

Taking a deep breath, I let it out slowly as I pull into the parking lot in front of the pizza place and park. "You can't control how you feel, okay? Don't ever let anyone tell you otherwise. Love is beautiful, whatever form it takes, even if Fate isn't involved."

He looks at me, then away. "You really think that?"

"I do," I say, trying to infuse my voice with sincerity. "And if you want to talk more about it, I'm here."

"It's frustrating." He clenches his fist. "All the time. And it just builds and builds until I have to let it out. The clubs help, so does working at the cafe. They're distractions. The fights aren't something I go looking for, but I don't step back from them, either." He touches his lip. "Like today. We could have run. But then, they'd just catch me somewhere else. I know Sasha said something to you, so you don't have to pretend."

"You should really talk to Ryuu and your uncle about the gang thing," I encourage. "And about the other part of what's bothering you, when you're ready."

"I'm meeting with the counselor. I'm trying. But what I really need is to graduate and get out so they'll lose interest." His head turns toward me. "I'd be less frustrated in Class B."

My shoulders slump. "I can't drop you a class level unless there's a good reason, Senichi. If one of them is trying to force something with you, or if you feel in danger—"

"Never mind," he cuts in. "I'll go get our order." He pushes open his door and slides out, but pauses. "Um, can I get some cash?"

I pull my wallet out and pass him a couple of twenties.

He takes them, starts to close the door, but pauses again. "Thanks for listening. I'll think about what you said."

The door slams shut before I can respond, and I

watch as he jogs into the restaurant, unsure what to do with Senichi's revelation. On the one hand, I feel like I finally know what's going on with the kid, and on the other, it's not my place to talk to Shig or Ryuu about it. That's Senichi's secret to reveal when and how he wants to.

As for the gang that wants him to join them... I can help with that, as much as I'm able to. Security at school already agreed to make extra patrols around the exterior during times when classes aren't in session.

And I'll talk to Shig about getting Senichi a car. We can work out the finances for it, and maybe even give him chores, like grocery shopping and picking the kids up and dropping them off. We can make this work while giving Senichi another layer of safety.

Because, with the path he's walking, he's going to need it.

DATE NIGHT

As I open the front door for Senichi, the kids barrel past us, dropping pine cones along the way as they swing the plastic bag between them. They shed gloves, hats, scarves, and coats on their dash to the dining room.

"Watch your step," I warn Senichi as he walks inside, the pizza boxes balanced in his arms.

He ordered two extra larges, two cheesy breads, cookie dough, and soda, which makes for quite the armload. I offered to help carry them in, but he refused, so I hurry ahead of him and scoop up any pine cones that could become tripping hazards.

"Don't dump those out!" Shig yells, laughter in his voice.

We enter the dining room to find the table

littered with pine cones and dried dirt, Deka and Rin standing on chairs surveying their haul.

Shig stands over them, shaking his head. "Where are we supposed to eat now?"

"If you get out the decorating buckets, I'll sit with them at the table while you guys watch a movie," Senichi offers from behind his stack of boxes.

Shig's eyes light up. "Oh? You're offering to let us have a date night?"

Senichi drops the boxes far enough to glare at his uncle. "We'll literally be ten feet away, so keep it low-key." Senichi balances the boxes on one hand, finagles the top pizza box out of the stack, and shoves it at Shig. "Here. I made this special for you."

"So talented." Shig inspects the box. "Did you hand draw these designs, too? It looks so much like take out, it's amazing."

"That's me. Your super amazing nephew." Senichi walks past him and shoves pine cones out of the way to make room for their dinner before he looks at the kids. "Where are your art aprons?"

They jump off their chairs and run for the closet where the art supplies are stored.

"Well, it looks like he has them handled." Shig sidles up to me. "Can I interest you in a *homemade* pizza?"

Laughing, I nudge him toward the couch. "Pick out a movie while I hang up everyone's coats."

"Grab some drinks, too." He nuzzles his head against my shoulder before carrying our dinner to the living room, where he sets the enormous box on the coffee table.

I pause next to Senichi on my way to the kitchen. "You know he's going to see your face eventually, right?"

He flashes me a cocky look. "I'm really good at dodging."

Which might explain all the time he spends in his room or out of the house.

"I'm sure you are." Shaking my head, I continue on into the kitchen and open the fridge. On the top shelf sits a bottle of rose wine that hadn't been there this morning, and I hesitate before leaning back out the doorway. "Shig, do you want the Rose?"

"Will it go with dinner?" He peeks into the pizza box, and his tail starts wagging with excitement. "Oh, you got me *all* the meats."

I've never been much of a wine drinker, but it can't be horrible to have with pizza, right? I grab the bottle and two glasses, then dig around until I find a bottle opener in the miscellaneous utensil drawer. With a roll of paper towels tucked under my arm, I carry everything out and set them on the coffee table.

Shig pops a stolen pepperoni into his mouth. "A client gave me the bottle as an end-of-year gift. I make no promises it's good."

"I make no promises to know the difference," I reassure him.

His hand sneaks into the partially open pizza box and comes back out with another pepperoni. "I'm so glad you guys wanted pizza. I was *not* willing to stop at the store on a Friday night during rush hour."

"We'll go in the morning." I sit on the edge of the couch, pull the wine bottle closer, then stare at the corkscrew uncertainly. "Okay, here's where I admit I've never bought anything without a screw top."

"Here, I'll show you." Shig wipes the grease from his fingers, then settles on the couch next to me, his tail draping over my lap. He turns the corkscrew over and flips a small knife out from the handle. "First, you cut away the foil." He does so with ease before tucking the knife away once more and positioning the corkscrew over the cork. "Then, you just twist, twist, twist, and yank!"

The cork pops free but a large split in the center

breaks it in half, and the pieces fall to the coffee table.

Shig turns wide eyes on me. "I think we may have a cheap bottle of booze on our hands."

"If you hadn't said so, I wouldn't have known." I grab the two glasses from the table and hold them out. "Good thing there are two of us to split the burden."

Shig laughs and fills both glasses nearly to the top.

I stare at him in amazement. "Were you trying to fit the whole bottle in there?"

He shrugs. "We can't re-cork it, now, can we?"

"I suppose not." I take a sip, and sweetness fills my mouth. It tastes like red wines I've had, but lighter and crisper. "It's good."

"It is?" Shig sips his, then looks at me. "Oh, honey, we need to educate you."

I laugh and take another, deeper sip before setting my glass aside. "Naw, this just means I'm a cheap date."

Grabbing the pizza box, I pull it onto my lap and open the lid to find an entire half of the pizza devoid of pepperonis.

I turn narrowed eyes on Shig, who gasps and

stares down at the box. "Oh, no, they didn't put pepperonis on your half!"

"Really?" I ask drily. "That's what you're going with?"

He steals another pepperoni and pops it into his mouth. "I have a weakness."

I file that away and rotate the box so the side with the pepperonis faces him.

"I knew there was a reason I liked you so much." He picks off a couple more pepperonis, making them into a little stack that he pops into his mouth.

Leaning in, I whisper loudly, "Should I go steal the ones off Senichi's pizza, too?"

He pauses with another pepperoni pinched between his fingers. "Think he would notice?"

"Literally ten feet away," Senichi calls. "And you're not getting anywhere near my pepperoni."

"Shoot." Shig licks the grease from his fingers and grabs the TV remote. "I hope you're ready for sappy Yule movies, because that's what we're watching *all* night."

Senichi lets out a loud groan of protest, but we both ignore him as we snuggle together on the couch. "What's the first one about?"

"Runaway princess hides in a small town that devotes itself to Yule all year long and discovers the meaning of love." Shig plucks off the last of the pepperonis. "There will be snow and a kiss at the end."

"Sounds wonderful." I grab a slice as the opening credits begin to roll.

This is something else I've never done before with another adult. Cuddled on the couch to watch sappy movies. If movies were on in our house, it was always something Rin picked, and they'd either lose interest halfway through and wander away, or we'd watch the same thing on loop until I could recite it by heart.

Adult movies weren't a thing, and certainly not cozying up next to another adult.

I slip my arm over the back of the couch, and Shig leans in closer, tucking himself in like he was always meant to be there.

We make it halfway through the pizza before closing the box and trading it for our wine.

When I finish my glass, Shig refills it, and a warm, pleasant sensation uncurls in my stomach.

His tail moves on my lap, and I stroke my fingers through his soft fur, loving the way it feels through my fingers.

My attention shifts from the movie, focusing instead on watching the black fur as my hand moves over it. I've never touched such a fluffy tail before. I can actually hide my entire hand if I try. His tail moves beneath my hand, pushing up against my fingers, and my pulse jumps, the heat beneath my skin spreading.

"Are you enjoying yourself?" Shig breathes into my ear.

I turn my head to find his face inches from mine and lick my lips. From this close, his eyes look impossibly green. "I think it's been a while since I drank wine, and it's affecting me more than I thought it would."

"Do you want to go lie down?" he asks.

My eyes move back to the movie still playing. I have no idea what's going on besides that there's snow and an ice rink.

"Come on." Shig stands and grips my elbows, urging me up.

"But... the movie..." I protest.

"I'll grab my laptop, and we can watch it in bed until you fall asleep," he offers gently, then raises his voice. "Sen, you okay out here alone?"

"Got it," he responds. "But I'm not cleaning up the glitter bomb."

"I'll do it in the morning," I call back to him as Shig steers me toward the back hall.

On my feet, I feel tipsier, and I lean against Shig. He smells so nice. Have I ever noticed before how nice he smells? Something musky, with a hint of floral undertone.

Leaning over, I nuzzle behind his ear, where the scent is strongest. The black strands of his hair brush against my cheek, and I lift my head to rub my cheek against them. "Your hair is so soft."

Amusement fills his voice. "Thank you."

I drop back to that warm spot behind his ear. "I like your cologne. It smells nice."

"I'll be sure to wear it more often." He kicks the bedroom door closed and moves me to sit on the edge of the bed. "Come on, I'll help you into your pajamas. I don't think you're going to make it through the movie."

When he makes a move to step away, I reach out and grasp his hips to hold him in place.

My heart pounds as my thumbs slip beneath the hem of his sweater to find bare skin beneath.

"Juro?" Fingers under my chin tip my head up, and Shig stares down at me. "What do you want?"

"I want to..." My throat tightens, and I lick my lips. "I want to please you."

He brushes the hair back from my forehead, his

fingers light caresses on my horns. "You do please me."

"Not like that." Mustering up my courage, I drop a hand to the front of his pants and feel his cock jump beneath my touch. "I want to give you pleasure. But I don't know how."

His fingers trail down behind my ears and along the sides of my jaw. "Do you want to receive, too? Or just give?"

"Just give." I stroke his hardening cock. "Is that okay?"

"Yeah, that's okay." A shiver rolls through him, and he touches my lips. "Do you want to use your hands? Or your mouth?"

My pulse quickens, and my lips part on an excited gasp. I want to do this, to see that look of pleasure on his face and know I put it there. "Show me how to use my mouth."

His fingers nudge at my lips. "Open for me."

I do, then shiver as his fingers push past my lips and into my mouth. They taste salty, with a hint of the meal we shared. He strokes the short barbs on my tongue, and the pads of his fingers rougher than I expected.

The feel of him inside my mouth is foreign, but I like it, like the taste of him and the pressure against my tongue. My lips close around his fingers, sucking on them, and he lets out a small whimper, his hips thrusting against my hand to bring my attention to his hard cock.

"You'll need to open wide," he groans, nudging my mouth back open. His finger skims along the top of my teeth. "And try not to use your teeth. Take your time."

The way he trembles increases my excitement, and I undo the top button on his pants before dragging his zipper down. His blue boxer briefs pop out of the opening, the front already damp with pre-cum.

A heady scent of musk makes my mouth water, and I lean forward to press my nose against him, dragging in a deep breath. "You smell so good."

His hand tangles in my hair as he groans. "You're going to kill me."

Tipping my head back, I stare up the length of his body. He stares down at me, his lips parted on fast breaths, his face flushed, and his eyes glassy. Yes, that's the expression I want to see, and pleasure courses through me that I put that look on his face.

Eyes still on him, I slowly pull his boxers down, then lean forward to nuzzle against his hot, bare cock. He feels so soft against me, his skin like warm velvet over hard steel. Something damp coats my lips, and I lick instinctively, tasting salt and Shig.

He reaches down, touching himself on the underside of his cock. "I'm especially sensitive here." He traces the thick vein that runs up his center, then pauses at the base of his head. "And here. Use your tongue to get me wet. It will make it easier."

Bending, I do as he instructs, licking up his hot shaft, then sucking on that spot under the tapered head of his cock. When he groans and grips my shoulders, I repeat the motion, experimenting until his breath hitches and his legs tremble.

Excited to have discovered this new pleasure, I do it again, flattening my tongue and pressing hard as I slick up his cock before sucking hard just under his head. Pre-cum dribbles from his slit, and I move higher, licking away the salty drops.

Shig's breath catches again, and he nudges my mouth open wider, then gently urges me forward.

The head of his cock settles heavy against my tongue, and I wrap my lips around him, sucking on just the tip before I open once more and take him deeper. My hold on him shifts, one hand on his hip while I grasp the base of his cock with the other. I can already tell I won't be able to take all of him into my mouth without choking, at least not on my first try, so I fist what won't fit and experiment with using my mouth and hand to stroke the entire length of him.

His hands in my hair offer silent instruction, telling me when to slow and when to speed up, and when I press my tongue to the underside of his cock and pull back, he moans and clutches me harder.

"Juro," he gasps. "I don't think I can keep standing."

Reluctant, I pull off of him, then help him onto the bed, tugging his pants off in the process. He lands in the center of the mattress, his legs open and his cock wet and glistening. The sight makes my breath catch, and I crawl between his legs, taking that long, slender cock back into my mouth.

This new position gives me more room to experiment with angles and depth, and I push his cock a little farther in until I feel him at the back of my throat.

Looking up the length of his body, I find Shig watching me, his eyes half-veiled by his lashes as he pants.

He reaches down, his fingers skimming along my stretched lips. "God, seeing you do this is so sexy."

Pleasure rushes through me, and I put my

tongue and lips to good use, milking the moans from him as I suck his cock.

When the tugs on my hair become more frantic, and his hips start thrusting on their own, I ease back, fisting his base once more and stroking him.

"Juro, I'm going to..." He tries to pull me off him, but I reach up and grab his hand, pressing it to the mattress as I drive back down on him.

I feel the first pulse against my tongue as he stiffens, then hot cum fills my mouth, hitting the back of my throat. I swallow around him, drinking every last drop of his pleasure before I release him from my mouth.

Boneless and gasping, he slumps on the mattress.

I crawl up his body to grin down at him. "Good for my first time?"

A satiated smile spreads across his face. "Excellent for your first time. Did you enjoy yourself?"

"Very much." I rub my jaw, only now realizing it aches. "Might have to practice, though. Build up my stamina."

He laughs and knocks me to one side before curling against me. "You don't need more stamina. You have the perfect stamina."

Warm and fuzzy from the wine and what we just did, I gather him close as Senichi's question from earlier rings in my ear. Could we be mates? Do I want to know? Does Shig?

The time we've spent together has felt more natural and better than anything else in my life. But dare we tempt Fate by seeing if we're destined for each other?

UNICORN PANCAKES & PARK DATES

I wake up with my head achy and feeling like it's stuffed with cotton balls.

Groaning, I hug the warm body beneath me tighter.

"Are you finally awake?" Shig murmurs, his voice a low rumble under my cheek.

"No," I groan. "Remind me never to drink cheap wine again."

He strokes my hair. "How's your head feeling?"

"Heavy." I press it against his chest. "See?"

"Yeah, super heavy," he agrees with a grunt. "Did you have fun last night?"

"I fell asleep *way* too early on our movie date." Shifting, I ease my weight off him and snuggle against his side instead. "Did I sleep on top of you all night?"

"Most of it, yeah." He gives a full-body stretch. "It was cozy."

"And heavy." I slip my arm over his waist. "Sorry I passed out."

"I like that you felt comfortable enough to let go." He tugs my head back to his shoulder. "When was the last time you did that?"

"First year of transition school?" I peek up at his face in the shadows. "Alcohol and I obviously don't mix well."

"I don't know, I kind of liked you and alcohol," he teases.

A blush heats my cheeks as I remember the second half of our night, but it makes me happy, too, knowing how much he enjoyed himself. "I kind of liked that part, too."

He shifts against me. "Oh, yeah?"

"Yeah." My hand drops lower on his waist, and I encounter soft fleece pajama pants. "When did you put these on?"

"After you fell asleep." His stomach muscles flex under my hand. "You'll notice we're also *under* the covers now."

"I appreciate that." I dip a finger under his waistband. "Maybe I should return your kind—"

Behind me, the door creaks open, flooding the bedroom with light from the hall and soft giggles.

I freeze in horror, my fingers still inside Shig's pajama pants.

"Hey, I told you to leave them alone," Senichi hisses loudly.

I roll away from Shig, and we both sit up as the bedroom door crashes open, spilling Deka and Rin into the room.

"Daddy, it's time to get up!" Rin announces as the kids crawl up onto the bed.

They still wear their pajamas with matching green and yellow nightshirts, though Rin seems to have lost the bottoms to their pajamas.

"Sorry, guys, I tried to distract them," Senichi says from the doorway.

"It's fine, we were awake," Shig says.

"Where are your pants?" I growl playfully as I reach for Rin.

"No pants!" Rin giggles, rolling around at the bottom of the bed.

"ShiShi, we made you breakfast!" Deka announces.

"Oh?" He glances at Senichi. "With supervision, I hope?"

Deka stands on the bed and points an imperious finger at their brother. "Sen, bring the breakfast!"

"Breakfast in bed!" Rin scrambles up to sit in my lap.

Senichi vanishes from the doorway, then returns a moment later carrying two plates of pancakes. As he passes them out, I notice colored dots fill the batter in a rainbow kaleidoscope.

Shig examines his plate. "What do we have here?"

"Unicorn pancakes!" Deka announces proudly.

"There's an entire bottle of sprinkles in there," Senichi warns. "Also, the house is completely wrecked, so have fun with that. I gotta run. Sasha's picking me up soon."

"Hey!" Shig calls after him.

"This is what happens when you leave the kids alone!" Senichi yells, his voice growing distant.

"We left them with you!" Shig protests.

Laughter fills Senichi's voice. "I'm one of the kids!"

The front door opens and closes with a bang.

Rin grabs one of the pancakes and holds it out to me. "Try it! It's yummy!"

Apprehensive, I take it from their little hand. "Have *you* tried it?"

"We ate the first batch," Deka informs us.

Dutifully, I take a bite, and sugar crystals crunch between my teeth. "Mmm, super yummy."

The kids clap and giggle.

"Okay, go brush your teeth and get dressed." Shig rolls Deka toward the edge of the bed. "We're going to the park, then grocery shopping."

Rin crawls off my lap, their chubby knee digging into my thigh. I wince but hold back the grunt of pain as Rin somersaults off the bed, dimpled legs flying. "Make sure to put on some pants!"

"Never!" They scream and bolt from the room, Deka close behind.

Their feet stampede down the hall, followed by the slam of their bedroom door.

I drop my pancake back to the plate. "What are the chances we can pretend we ate these and they won't know the difference?"

"If we hurry while they're distracted..." Shig scoots out of his side of the bed, his full plate held aloft. "Think Sen took pity on us and made coffee?"

"Depends on how he felt about being left alone with the kids all night." I crawl out of my side of the bed and jam my feet into my slippers.

Shig hurries out of the bedroom, his tail wafting as he peers down the hallway toward the kids' room. "Cost is clear."

Together, we tiptoe out into the main part of the house.

"Oh, my," Shig says as we enter the dining room.

Senichi wasn't lying when he said the house was a wreck. Glitter, paper pieces, pipe cleaners, and glue litter the dining room table, and the kitchen looks like a tornado hit it.

But the smell of fresh coffee makes up for it as we hide our pancakes under the empty bag of flour in the trash bin.

Shig and I sit on the metal park bench, our shoulders pressed together as we huddle around our coffees. We decided to leave the disaster of the house for later and prepped our hot beverages to go.

Now, Deka and Rin run around the snow-covered park, playing with the other kids brave enough to face the cold.

"Think they'll run off all that sugar?" Shig asks as Deka and Rin bolt past.

"We can hope." I bring my coffee to my face, hoping the steam will help thaw my nose.

Shig presses his thigh against mine. "I talked to my mom."

My head lifts. "And?"

"She thinks you have a solid case, and she filed the paperwork to put a halt to Karen's visits." He glances at me. "I hope you're okay with her going forward with it before I spoke to you."

"No, I appreciate it." I bite my lip as Rin runs past again. "But, what does it mean?"

"Karen will have to pay child support for any documented times that she skipped taking care of Rin, and she can't see them unsupervised while the court evaluates her fitness to be a parent." Shig presses a little closer to me. "We can argue for child abandonment, but I'm not sure she's missed enough visits to make that case stick. The hope is that Karen will sign over full custody to avoid having to pay the child support, but it's all up for negotiation."

Unease and worry roll through me. "I don't want to take Rin away from Karen, but I also don't want our child to be used as a weapon against me, anymore."

"I understand that, and if Karen is willing to sit down and talk, you can come to an agreement that allows her visitation rights. *If* she wants to continue to see Rin, which may not be the case once she can't get money out of you anymore." He pauses for a moment before taking a deep breath. "You should have the paternity test done, though, in case this goes to court. Based on what you've said, I don't think Karen will want the expense or hassle once she realizes she can't push you anymore, but..."

"It's better to be prepared." I watch as Rin clambers up the ladder to the tube slide. "How did it come to this?"

Shig's hand settles on my knee. "We'll get through it."

We sit in silence for a bit, before I finally ask, "How do we do the test?"

"It's an easy cheek swab. I have one of the kits back at home. My mom's contacts can have the results in a couple days." He squeezes my fingers. "You don't have to look at them, if you don't want to. Not unless we actually go to court."

I nod. "I should find a way to thank your mom. I really appreciate all this."

Shig's shoulder presses against mine "My parents *did* ask me to bring you and Rin over for dinner sometime soon."

"Oh, God." I lean my head back. "The dreaded meet-the-parents."

He pats my knee. "I told them they'd have to wait. Doing the family thing over the holidays is expecting a bit much."

Shifting my coffee to one hand, I cover his with my free one. "How much family are we talking about?"

He drops his head to my shoulder. "My parents, my grandparents on both sides, two uncles, a handful of cousins…"

I wince. "Next year?"

He turns his face against my shoulders, but can't hide his happiness. "Deal. What about you?"

"My parents retired to warmer regions. I usually go see them over summer break. My grandparents on my mother's side live in a retirement home now. They're the ones who left me the house." My throat tightens for a moment as grief surges through me, but Shig, pressed against my side, helps hold me together. "My dad's parents were already old when they had him, and they passed before Rin was born. No siblings, and no cousins near enough to be close to."

"Do you and your parents get along?" he asks.

Not wanting to jostle him, I restrain the urge to

shrug. "They were strict and had pretty specific ideas about things."

His voice comes out muffled against my jacket. "Like marrying Karen as soon as she got pregnant?"

My stomach twists. "Yeah, like that. And figuring out how to support my new family, finding a place for us to live..."

He stays quiet, keeping his opinions to himself, though he needn't have bothered. I've had years to play the what-if game, but thoughts like that don't change what happened. And I wouldn't trade Rin for the chance to go to university and continue to be a child a little longer.

Shig straightens and drapes his arm behind me, his focus on the kids as they run past again. "So, do I want to know why Sen has new bruises and his lip is busted open again?"

I laugh quietly. "Should've known you'd notice."

"I figured you already saw it, and if it was bad, you would have told me." He sips his coffee. "Do I need to worry?"

"You need to talk to Senichi." I turn my head to study his profile. "He said he's not seeking out the fights, and I believe him."

"I believe him, too, which worries me more." He huffs out a breath that fogs in the cold air. "If he was seeking out the fights, it would mean he could stop. But if fights are seeking him out..."

I tap my fingers against the side of my coffee cup. "Maybe a car would help?"

"Are you offering to teach him to drive?" Shig teases.

"If you want," I answer seriously.

Shig turns his head to stare at me in shock. "Really?"

His expression makes me laugh. "Yeah, really. Though we'll be using my SUV." I shake my head at him. "Your sports car is..."

He arches his brows. "Sexy?"

"A stick shift." I purse my lips for a moment. "And worth more than I make in a year."

"I need a dad-mobile, don't I?" Now, it's his turn to groan. "Can I at least keep the sports car for fun?"

I keep my face serious. "That depends on how well you do cleaning out the garage."

"You're really determined to put it in the garage, aren't you?" he says.

"It seems only fair." I shake my head. "Poor thing didn't *choose* to be owned by someone who isn't concerned about treating it right."

"Oh, I'm feeling challenged now." Standing, he yells for the kids.

I rise to my feet more slowly, warmth chasing away the winter chill as Rin and Deka bound over. The two kids throw themselves at Shig, latching onto his legs and laughing when he tries to walk to the car with them still attached. I love seeing Rin open up to Shig and how Deka treats Rin like another sibling.

This feels good, like this is the family that was always meant for us.

A REAL FAMILY

"It's too early for manual labor," Sasha groans as he takes down a box and opens it to inspect what t holds. "Can't we do this at a decent hour?"

"It's two in the afternoon," Senichi responds as he tosses items into the donate bin. "Quit your whining."

"This is why you're always too prickly," Sasha counters. "Not enough beauty sleep."

"This is why I'm always taking your morning shifts at the cafe." Senichi grabs another box and looks around. "Deka, this one is yours!"

Deka appears in the doorway, bundled up in their winter coat. "Bring it inside!"

"No, you haven't brought back the last two."

Senichi sets the box on a low table. "Go through it out here. And I want to see what you decide to keep."

"Rin!" Deka shrieks. "Come out to the garage."

"Never!" Rin yells back, but they appear next to Deka a moment later, round as a ball with all the layers they wear. "Is it a good one?"

I exchange a smile with Shig as we keep working through his set of boxes.

We started the garage clean out yesterday and made enough progress to make room for a couple tables to be set up to make the sorting easier.

This morning, we picked up where we left off as soon as we cleared the breakfast dishes off the table, and Senichi's friend arrived at noon to help out. Today, instead of the punk look he sports at school, he wears untorn, clean jeans and a shirt buttoned up to his chin. A clip holds back his long bangs, and what looks like hand-knitted, fingerless gloves cover his hands and forearms. No earrings or eyeliner in sight.

If I didn't know he was Sasha, I would have mistaken him for someone else altogether.

Senichi takes the change in stride, though, which makes me think this is normal behavior, jumping from punk to fashionista.

Senichi, too, left his earrings out today, and he wears a worn pair of jeans and a light sweater. While not drastically different from his usual attire, it's enough to take notice and makes me wonder if he plays up the punk look at school to fit in with the rough crowd he runs with.

Should I suggest dressing less punk as a way to make the gangs lose interest? Or would that just make him appear weak and make everything worse?

I really want to talk to Ryuu about it, but it smacks of abusing my position at the school.

"Oh, tell me this is yours!" Sasha holds aloft a round, rainbow bunny as big as a beach ball.

Senichi slaps it back into the box, his head whipping toward Deka and Rin. "Don't let them see that."

"OMG, it *is* yours," Sasha giggles.

"Yeah, and I'd like to keep it that way," Senichi hisses. "So, leave it in the box and take it to my room."

"That's a horrible hiding place," Shig says as he rewraps a set of plates and puts them back in their box. "They'll find it right away."

"Basement." Senichi points to the door. "Now."

"Slave driver." Sasha lifts the box and carries it to

the stairs that lead to the lower level. "How much longer are we going to be doing this?"

"Until it's done," Senichi grunts.

"That's going to take *days*," Sasha whines as he disappears from view.

"Why don't you call more friends over?" Shig asks, his voice filled with innocence. "Maybe Aye and Yuki?"

Senichi's back stiffens. "I told you we're not friends anymore."

Sadness fills Shig's face. "But you guys used to be inseparable."

"Things change." Senichi grabs the box in front of himself. "I'm going to take this one to the basement, too."

Shig's shoulders slump as he vanishes into the basement. "I don't know what happened. They used to hang out all the time before they moved. I thought, when the kids came back, that at least Senichi would have them to lean on, but every time I bring them up, it's a sore subject."

"Are they tailed?" Sometimes transitioning into different groups breaks friends apart.

"Yuki is, but Aye is horned." Shig moves his box to the donation pile. "They're in the same class this year. I was hoping that would rekindle their friendship, but apparently not."

"Oh." Realization dawns, and I studiously stare at the open box in front of me to avoid Shig's too perceptive gaze.

No luck, though. I'm a horrible actor as Shig proves when he leans across the table. "You know something."

I lift out a handful of notebooks. "Do you want to go through these?"

"Juro." At his stern tone, sweat breaks out over my body.

That voice is why Shig's such a good lawyer. It has to be. It makes me want to immediately confess everything I know.

But while I don't think Shig would care who his nephew has a crush on, it's not my secret to tell.

I peek up through my lashes. "Maybe don't keep pushing about Yuki and Aye?"

He cups my cheeks, his hands warm against my chilly skin. "You'll tell me if it's something I *need* to know, right?"

I reach up to cover his hands. "Of course."

"I trust you." His eyes drop to my mouth, and my heart trips.

Shig hasn't tried to kiss me since that first

disaster, and while part of me appreciates him letting me take my time with what I'm comfortable with, another part of me wants to try that kiss again, to see if it will stir me in ways it didn't the first time.

Leaning forward, I whisper, "You can—"

"I'm sorry!" Sasha yells, his footsteps loud on the wooden steps, and Shig and I pull apart. Sasha appears in the doorway, his phone pressed to his ear. "Yeah, I'll go. Just calm down." He hangs up on the angry voice on the other end of the line, then peers over his shoulder. "I gotta go, but I'll come back later."

Senichi's voice drifts up from behind him. "Take care of what you need to."

Sasha nods at us before jogging into the house. A moment later, the front door opens and closes.

Shig raises his brows at Senichi. "Everything okay?"

"Yeah, his mom just wants him to go check on his brother-in-law." Senichi shrugs. "He's a widower, and they send him food, but he didn't answer the door for the delivery today, so she's worried but can't leave the cafe."

"That's nice of him to help look after him." Shig droops dramatically. "If only I had a loving nephew who took care of me."

Senichi snorts. "That's what you have Juro for."

"You're right." Shig grins and comes around the table, his tail a soft pressure against my leg. He tips his head back. "Juro, spoil me."

Startled, I wrap my arms around his waist. With his winter coat on, I can't feel the slender muscles I know are there. My arms don't reach as far around him, but he still fits snuggly in my embrace. "How should I spoil you?"

Senichi makes gagging noises. "You guys are too sweet."

"You should go check on the kids, then," Shig teases. "We're about to get even sweeter."

Shig laughs as his nephew flees the garage, and I rub my cheek against his soft hair. "That's one way to *not* clean out the garage."

He turns in my arms, looping his around my neck. "I think we're making good progress. Once the donation van picks up what we have, we'll be able to fit half a car in here."

I tug him closer. "Isn't the goal a *whole* car?"

"Baby steps, Juro." Shig leans forward, and for one heart-pounding second, I think he'll pick up from before we were interrupted. But he just leans his head on my shoulder, his breath a light flutter on my neck. "Should we take a coffee break?"

I rub my hands over his back. "Are you cold or tired?"

"Yes." He nuzzles his frozen nose under my ear. "I'm hungry."

"Pizza?" I suggest, even though we just had that on Friday. "With extra pepperoni?"

He sighs with pleasure. "You're so good at this spoiling thing."

Without letting him go, I walk us toward the open door to the house. "Well, I need to make sure I keep you happy."

"I *am* happy," he breathes. "I don't know what I was before I met you."

My chest tightens. I feel the same way. I was just going through the functions of life before I met Shig, putting all of my focus on Rin to make sure they were happy and asking nothing for myself. I didn't realize we could *both* have our happiness.

This feels like love. The urge to say it pushes at my lips, but I hold them back. It's too soon for that, right? Throwing out the L-word now might just scare Shig away.

Or, it might make him want to test for a mate bond, and I'm not ready to know yet if we're *meant* to be together. I like what we have, and it feels like an unnecessary risk to bring things like Fate into it.

Now, I'm suddenly thankful for our interruption earlier. I don't know if Shig wears a palate protector or not. I haven't seen one, but I haven't been looking, either. He could keep the cleaning tabs in the bathroom medicine cabinet, where I feel like too much of a snoop to look. And we get ready for bed at night separately.

I want to ask him, to know before making the decision to kiss. But that feels like it adds pressure to actually follow through with said kiss, and now that the moment passed, I'm not sure how to handle the situation.

How do people who are dating do this? Does it just naturally come up in conversation? Or is it always weird to bring up how much protection is being used?

They should teach this stuff in school. Really dive deep instead of skimming over it in the first year after students transition. I remember that class. The horned and tailed took it separately, and it was all about aggression and how to approach our tailed counterparts. There were pamphlets about palate guards and condoms, but that was it. And what teenager reads pamphlets?

"Hey, are you okay?" Shig asks, disrupting my thoughts.

I look at his concerned face, and not wanting to worry him, I smile. "Yeah, just thinking."

Misunderstanding the cause for my concern, his gaze shifts to the living room, where Deka and Rin have items from their boxes spread out. "It will be okay. Whatever the result, it doesn't change how you feel."

We took the DNA samples as soon as we got home from the park, yesterday, and Shig overnighted the package to his mother's contact, who promised to have the result by the end of the week. I don't even want to know how much that cost to have them process the test so quickly with Yule coming up next week and most places already closed for the holiday.

"Thank you." I rub my cheek against his before letting him go. "Let's get you your coffee and order that pizza."

Proving they have selective hearing, Deka and Rin pop up over the top of the couch. "Pizza?"

Senichi appears from the kitchen. "I want sausage."

"Cheese!" Rin shouts, and Deka nods in agreement.

"Sen, can you make the call?" Shig asks. "You can put it on my card."

Senichi grabs the cordless phone and heads for the dining table. "I'm getting cookies, too."

"Cookies!" the kids shout in unison.

Shig shakes his head in resignation and beelines for the kitchen to get his coffee.

I join the kids in the living room, taking in the disaster. "Okay, let's get this picked up before food arrives. What's staying, and what's going?"

Deka points to a box on the coffee table. "That's for babies, so it should go to babies."

Rin nods in agreement.

Curious, I walk over to inspect the contents. Sure enough, it's filled with bottles, cloth diapers, and onesies. Reaching in, I pull out a pair of baby shoes, and a lump forms in my throat. I had a box like this for Rin. It contained all their firsts. First outfit they wore home from the hospital, first pair of shoes, first haircut.

That's all gone, now. Burned away in the fire.

My eyes prickle, and my hands tremble as I drop the shoes back into the box and close the lid. They're just things. What matters is that Rin is safe.

"Daddy, are you crying?" Rin tugs on my pant leg. "We can keep the baby stuff if it makes you sad."

"No, I'm not sad." Bending, I lift Rin and hug

their soft body, made even softer by all the layers they wear.

Rin wiggles, chubby legs kicking. "Daddy! You're crushing me!"

"Oh?" I squeeze tighter. "Crushing, you say?"

They giggle and wiggle to escape. "No! Don't crush me!"

"Me! Crush me!" Deka demands, tugging on the hem of my jacket.

Since I can't lift both kids at the same time, I crouch, open my arm, and pull Deka into the hug, crushing them together.

They shriek in protest, trying to escape but not seriously, because as soon as I loosen my arms, they demand to be crushed again.

Senichi leans over the back of the couch. "You're never going to escape that now."

"Oh, yeah?" Grinning at him, I whisper to the kids, "Senichi wants to play Yip Yip."

His dark eyes widen in horror. "No."

Deka and Rin zero in on him with laser focus. "Yip Yip!"

"Not happening!" Senichi shouts and bolts for his room, the kids chasing after him.

"I love that," Shig says as he presses up against my side, bringing with him the warm smell of coffee.

"They didn't laugh this much before you guys moved in."

"Neither did Rin." I loop my arm around him. "And, thank you. You're right. It doesn't matter what the result is. It won't change this."

And I mean it. Both for my parental love for Rin and how I feel about Shig.

Fated mates or not, it won't change this feeling of warmth, contentedness, and happiness I have every time I'm with him.

It's worth it to explore this feeling.

FIRST FIGHT

"No!" Rin's shriek fills the house. "Stop it! I hate you!"

Shig and I drop the boxes we were sorting in the garage and head for the house, Senichi a step behind.

Over the last week, we made good progress in organizing the garage, and the dump and donation piles now take up more space than the boxes destined for storage.

Senichi had been a real trooper, which spoke volumes about his determination to get his own space. He even started drawing up plans with the construction company who came to evaluate the space, making sure his room was on the opposite end of the floorplan from the home office.

Deka and Rin, though, lost interest before the end of the first day, and without the distraction of school or the park to burn off energy, they became progressively crankier.

We find the kids in Deka's room, where Rin hugs their large, purple hippo, their body half turned to hide it in the space near the closet. Face red, Deka stands in the middle of the room, and fat tears roll down their cheeks as they clutch one round, purple ear.

Oh, no. In a glance, I know what happened. I can practically see the tug-of-war before the maiming.

As soon as Rin sees me, they run over and smash against my legs, wailing, "Deka's mean! I want to go home!"

"I just wanted to play!" Deka sobs, raising the torn ear. "I didn't mean to hurt Hip-Hip!"

"I want to go home!" Rin shrieks, their voice hitting that special octave right before full tantrum sets in. "Take me home. I want my own room!"

Helpless, I exchange looks with Shig as he kneels next to Deka, gathering them into his arms. "Shh, it's okay. We know you didn't mean it."

I crouch and reach out for the stuffed animal. "Here, let me see."

"Hip-Hip's broken!" Rin wails, tears forming in

their eyes. "Deka broke Hip-Hip. Deka's not my friend anymore!"

"Hush, now," I say as Deka sobs harder. "You don't mean that."

"I do!" Rin stamps one small foot. "I hate Deka!"

Sighing, I gather Rin up and pass Senichi in the doorway as I walk out. Nothing's going to stop this until the kids wear themselves out.

In the living room, I sit on the couch, Rin in my lap. I rock back and forth, my arms around their small, round body as they cry.

This part never gets easier, even after doing it for six years. The sound of my child crying will always hurt, even when I know it's over something small like this. It's not small in Rin's world, and while they might not care about the stuffed animal in a few more months, it's important now, which is all that matters.

When Rin eventually quiets to gasping hiccups, I lean back and wipe the wetness from their face. "Can I see Hip-Hip now?"

Nodding, Rin holds the hippo up. Sure enough, one of its ears is missing, and white stuffing pokes out of the hole.

"That looks pretty dire," I say seriously. "Do you think Hip-Hip needs an operation?"

Rin sniffles and studies the studded animal. "They'll never hear right again."

"Then, you'll just have to whisper all your secrets into the other ear." I tweak the one still attached, turning the pink underside toward Rin. "I bet this one still hears just fine."

Feet shuffle in the hallway, and Deka comes into view, Shig walking behind with one hand on their shoulder. They still clutch the hippo's ear, but at least, Deka stopped crying.

Shig nudges Deka forward. "Don't you have something to say to Rin?"

Deka looks up at their uncle before stumbling forward and holding out the ear. "I'm sorry I pulled on Hip-Hip's ear. I didn't mean for it to come off."

I wince at that. It's probably more a result of me being cheap than any strength Deka put into the tug-of-war.

Rin sniffles and reaches out to take the ear.

I nudge them. "Don't you have something to say to Deka?"

"I'm sorry I said I hate you," Rin mumbles without looking up.

Senichi appears wearing a white apron—probably from his shifts at the cafe—and holds up hands covered in the hippo oven mitts. "Did I hear there's a patient in the house?"

Rin's lower lip juts out. For a moment, I think the tears will return, but then Rin slides off my lap and hesitantly walks over to present Hip-Hip and the missing ear to Senichi.

Shig nudges Deka. "You should go help fix what you helped break."

Sniffling, Deka shuffles over to the dining table, where Senichi lays Hip-Hip on a placemat and the torn-off ear on a second placemat, treating them like hospital beds.

I stand and walk over to Shig, my body feeling heavier than it has in a long time.

Without asking, he opens his arms, and I step into them, dropping my head to his shoulder. "How am I going to tell them our house burned down?"

I knew this conversation would need to be brought up at some point, but I was also secretly hoping Rin would just forget we ever lived anywhere but here. We were lucky up until now that the kids got along so well and didn't mind the extended sleepover. But the bubble has officially burst, and there's no way to avoid it now.

Shig rubs my back. "How about I take Sen and

Deka out to get ice cream, and you can talk to Rin without us around to be a distraction?"

I lift my head. "I don't want to kick you out of your house."

"I want this to be *our* house, Juro," he confesses softly, his moss-green eyes shimmering. "I know it's too early, that we haven't been dating very long and everything's happened so fast, but I don't want you or Rin to leave. I want this to be your home every bit as much as it's mine."

Throat tight, I nod. I had hoped he felt the same way I did and thought his eagerness to move forward on the renovation was a good sign. But hearing the words out loud eases a disquiet inside I didn't realize bothered me until it vanishes.

His smile holds hesitant hope. "Yeah?"

"Yeah." I rest my forehead against his. "But…"

He gives me puppy dog eyes. "But?"

"If this is *our* house, then I get to help pay for the renovation." When he opens his mouth to protest, I hush him with a finger over his lips. "Let me help, Shig. I have the money from the insurance check coming in, and even if I put a portion of it aside for Rin's future, I still have enough to contribute here. Let me help make this house a place that works for all of us."

"You're sure?" he asks. "Because, once you invest, I'm going to want to put your name on the house, then I'm going to want more and more from you."

Feeling sure of myself for the first time in a while, I pull him close. "Do that. I want to meet all your expectations."

"Shared chores," he warns.

"Done."

His eyes narrow. "Making house rules and supporting each other when the kids get mad."

I smile. "Done."

"I'm super cranky when I get sick. You *will* want to leave, but you're not allowed."

"I want all of this," I tell him. "The good and the bad."

His tail wafts back and forth. "You say that now, but not even my mom could handle me when I was sick."

"I won't run," I promise.

He searches my face. "It's so hard not to draw up a contract and make you sign it just so I can have it to pull out when you're ready to run."

I laugh at that. "You can't be that bad."

"You have no idea." He gives me a wolfish smile. "But you will. And you'll have no one to blame but yourself."

"I've already resigned myself to giving you all my pepperoni in the future," I tell him. "That's way more of a sacrifice than caring for you when you're sick."

His smile widens. "*All* the pepperoni?"

"All of it." I cross my heart.

He sighs in appreciation. "Now, I'm really never letting you go."

"Good," I tell him. "I don't want to be let go."

Rin takes the news about our house as best as I could have expected.

There are tears and screaming about the toys lost to the fire, but when I tell them we're officially going to be staying with Deka, Senichi, and Shig, Rin calms down enough to ask questions, like, does this mean they don't have to visit with Karen and her mate anymore? Is Shig their dad now, too? When do Senichi and Deka become their siblings? Will their nanny, Hana come back when school starts up again? And, the most important one, when will we be going to Yipiland to celebrate?

By the time Shig and the kids return from getting ice cream, Rin is already planning out our trip, which will happen no later than summer vacation.

Shig has Deka sit at the dining table with Rin, then Senichi makes a big show of presenting each kid with a fancy, upside-down ice cream cone decorated to look like a clown.

Rin's eyes grow huge, and they look at me as if to make sure it's okay to really eat the ice cream.

I nod in encouragement. It's exactly the type of cone Rin always wants and Karen always refused to buy back when we were still together. It's even bubblegum flavored, Rin's favorite.

Shig comes out of the kitchen with two mugs of coffee and passes one to me. "Everything work out?"

"Yeah." I take one of the mugs and warm my fingers around it. "Did you tell Deka and Senichi?"

Pink stains his cheeks. "I told Sen a few days ago. I wanted to make sure he was really okay with it before talking to you about this becoming permanent."

That makes me love Shig all the more, that he took his nephew's feelings into consideration first. If I didn't already know what a caring man he was before, I'd know now.

How did I go so many years, trying to make a bad relationship work with Karen? It feels like so long ago, now, that I thought we'd be together at least until Rin graduated from high school. I almost want to thank her for cheating on me, because I never would have broken it off myself. My family raised me to believe that divorce meant quitting, and when they heard about my separation from Karen, they put the blame on me for not trying harder. It hurt, especially since I knew they never liked Karen.

Only my grandparents seemed to understand. But they were true mates, and they always subscribed to different beliefs than what my parents pushed. Too bad I didn't listen to them back in high school. My life would have been so different. But then, I might not have met Shig, and I wouldn't change that for the world.

Shig catches my free hand. "What are you thinking?"

Not ready to talk about what's on my mind, I take a sip of coffee to calm my racing heart. "That the kids will be be hyped-up on sugar all night and cranky when we wake them early tomorrow."

We have our big trip into the mountains to hunt down a Yule log planned for tomorrow, and the train leaves early. It's a three-hour trip up to the mountains, and I was already worried the younger kids would get antsy before we arrived. Add no sleep, and they're going to be nightmares.

"They're too excited for the train ride to have

slept tonight anyway," he points out. "We'll just ply them with hot chocolate and cookies. If we're lucky, they'll pass out from exhaustion on the ride back down the mountain."

"Fingers crossed." I watch Rin happily diving into their ice cream, frosting all over their plump cheeks while Deka uses a spoon. Senichi watches over them, a small cup of ice cream in his hands. "But if not... That's what big brothers are for, right?"

Shig laughs quietly. "Exactly right."

MOONING

As expected, the younger kids don't want to get out of bed and dress in the morning, so we bundle them up in their pajamas and stuff them into the back of my SUV. We have a small bag packed with a couple changes of clothes and some healthy snacks to offset the sugar they'll get from the meal service provided.

Shig and Senichi follow us to the train station in Shig's car, highlighting the fact we really do need a dad-mobile. It doesn't have to be the horror Shig imagines, though. Some of the bigger SUVs have third-row seating while still looking stylish. Maybe I can buy one with some of the insurance money that doesn't go into savings or into the remodel.

Excited happiness rolls through me. I've never

once thought I'd be in a position where I could consider a car as a gift. But, really, it's less a gift than a household expense, right? One that just happens to put Shig on the insurance? If I do that, then I can teach Senichi to drive my current SUV, and Shig won't have to give up his sports car.

The idea makes me grin. I can't wait to see Shig's reaction.

In its holder on my dash, my cell phone buzzes with an incoming call. I turned it to silent so it wouldn't wake the kids, and I glance at it now, expecting Shig's name to be on the screen.

Instead, Karen's name pops up, and the sight brings instant dread.

Reaching out, I silence the vibration. Whatever she wants will have to wait until tomorrow. Today is about family bonding time, and I won't let her ruin that.

Eventually, the call goes to voicemail, and an alert pops up. I ignore that, too. Hearing her voice, listening to her demands for money and threats to take Rin away... I just can't handle that right now.

At the train station, dozens of cars fill the parking lot, and I find an area near the back that has two spots side-by-side.

I climb out and wave as I head to the back

passenger door and open it, letting in a cold breeze. Neither of the kids moves.

Shig pulls in right next to me, and Senichi hops out as soon as the car parks to immediately stride to Deka's door and free them from the car seat.

"I can take them," Shig offers, holding out his arms. "Can you grab the bag with our tickets in it?"

Senichi hesitates before passing his younger sibling over. The care he shows to them breaks my heart. After losing both their parents, he probably fears losing them as well.

Deka grumbles at the transfer, then immediately falls back asleep on Shig's shoulder. At this rate, the kids might sleep all the way up to the mountain.

Rin fusses when I put gloves on their chubby hands and a hat over their brown curls. Once I have them out of the car, they snuggle against my neck and still.

Senichi grabs our backpack of supplies from the back of the SUV before double-checking it's locked up. Satisfied, he shoulders the bag, and we head to the train station.

The train already waits at the loading platform, and we show our tickets to be let on.

Excited conversation fills the first box we enter, and we pick our way down the aisle until we find a group of seats together. It's not like any train I've ever been on, and my pulse quickens with excitement.

Instead of bench seats all facing the same direction, they're set up two benches face each other, with a table between them, like a dining booth. We get two right across the aisle from each other, and I settle Rin on the padded seat next to me. Senichi claims the table across from us and tosses the bag into the empty seat on the other side of his table, making it clear he expects Shig to take the open space across from me.

Shig smiles at his nephew before he carefully sets Deka down, then slides in to block access to the aisle.

"Look, there are menus." Senichi grabs one from a clear plastic holder against the wall and opens it. "Is this all included in the ride?"

"One meal there and back, and unlimited beverages," Shig tells him. "If you want more snacks, we have the veggies we brought."

Curious, I grab a menu and flip it open. They have a three-course meal option that I'm happy to see isn't all sugar. The first course offers a selection of meats and crackers, the second course a selection of dried fruits and nuts, and the last course a choice between chocolate dipping, cookie decorating, or a selection of small cakes, with the usual caraway cake as well as a couple more kid-friendly options. At the bottom are a list of drinks: hot chocolate, cider, eggnog, and juice.

On the opposite page are sandwiches, curry, and chili, as well as soda options. At the bottom are more adult beverage choices, such as mulled wine, though those are marked at an additional cost.

The back of the menu lists the itinerary for the trip, and I spot storytime in car A and crafts in car C. According to the schedule, we'll arrive at the Holly King Fields in just under three hours.

Senichi leans across the aisle, his dark eyes bright with interest. "Can I get mulled wine?"

Shig frowns at him. "You're still a minor."

"Old enough to mate should be old enough to drink," he argues, and I can't fault his logic there.

Shig's frown deepens. "Is that something you're considering? Are you and Sasha—"

Senichi shakes his head vehemently. "I was just saying that the drinking age is a little skewed. Don't worry, I'm not racing out to find myself a tailed mate."

I wince at his wording, knowing he has no interest in tailed at all.

"The drinking age is set at twenty so you have

time to gain control of your aggression before you start adding behavior-altering substances to your body." Shig gives him a significant look. "When you stop coming home with bruises, I'll reconsider."

Senichi slumps in his seat, his enthusiasm deflating.

Shig glances at me, a worried frown on his lips.

I shrug in response. My parents always gave me a small glass of mulled wine at Yule as part of the tradition, so it never felt exciting or special. I switched to grape juice after Karen got pregnant in a show of solidarity when she couldn't have alcohol and haven't felt the lack. But if Shig wants Senichi to wait until it's legal, I'll back him on it. We're partners, after all.

Shig purses his lips, his eyes jumping back to his nephew, before he whispers, "But it wouldn't hurt for you to have a taste. We can buy some better stuff to have at home. But only a *small* taste." He holds up his fingers, pinching them an inch apart to show exactly how small he means.

Senichi smirks and darts a glance at me. "Is uncle Juro getting the same amount?"

Groaning, I drop my head into my hands while my face catches on fire. "No, no mulled wine for me."

"Don't worry." Shig's feet nudge against mine

under the table. "We can get some cheap stuff that you'll like."

I laugh and kick him back before Senichi's words finally register, and I flush harder. Did he just call me uncle? Is that his way of letting me know he welcomes me to the family?

"Why's your face all red?" Shig teases, and I cover my cheeks to hide the glow.

Thankfully, the train blares its horn, announcing we'll be departing soon.

Rin lurches upright to stare around in blurry confusion. "Are we there?"

"Not yet." I pull the hat from their head. "Do you want to sleep more?"

Rin shakes their head, curls bobbing, and gets up on their knees to stare out the large window. We got the side that faces away from the station, so the view isn't that exciting, yet. But once we leave the city limits and head into the mountains, that will change.

"Daddy!" Reaching back, Rin tugs on the sleeve of my jacket. "It's snowing!"

I lean over them to look outside. "Well, look at that."

Small white flakes swirl down from the cloudy sky. Not enough to worry about right now, but if it gets worse, we might have a problem getting home tonight.

Rin bounces in place with excitement. "I want to play in the snow!"

"There will be plenty of that in the mountains." Shig encourages Deka to sit up, but they just blink a couple of times before slouching against his side and falling back asleep.

I guess the fight yesterday really tired them out. Senichi had stitched up Hip-Hip like a pro, but tension still ran deep. Between that and learning about our new living arrangements, the kids spent the night doing separate things, and Rin ended up sleeping with us last night, while Deka crawled in with their brother.

Hopefully, the excitement of today helps the kids move past their first big fight. If things work out between Shig and me, which I think they will, then there will be many fights in their future that they'll have to get over. Because that's what family does, and I sincerely want us all to be a family.

My phone buzzes in my pocket, but I reach inside to silence it, then decide to just turn it off. Everyone I want to talk to right now is here with me. Anything else can wait until later.

The train lurches into motion, bringing a cheer

of excitement from our fellow passengers, and the train slowly rolls out of the station. Soft music fills the car, not loud enough to discourage conversation while providing white noise that makes it easy not to focus on what other families are doing.

As we leave the city, two tailed women enter the car pushing and pulling a large cart filled with drink selections and the first course of food.

I look down at Rin, who still stares out the window with wide eyes. "What do you want to eat first? Fruit and nuts, or crackers with meat and cheese?"

"Pancakes!" they announce.

I smile. "They don't have that here, but we can have pancakes for breakfast tomorrow. How does that sound?"

Rin brightens. "Unicorn pancakes?"

I fight the urge to cringe. "If you like."

"Meat and cheese," Rin decides after a long minute as the cart rolls toward us.

"I'll get Deka the fruit and nuts, then." Shig strokes their hair affectionately, then looks at Senichi. "What are you going to get?"

He double-checks his menu. "Ham sandwich." Then, he frowns. "I kind of want the curry, too, though."

"I can get the curry, and we can share," I offer, wanting to show him how good of an uncle I'll be.

Shig pouts. "What about me?"

Smiling, I hook my feet around one of his. "I'll share with you on the way back."

He grins. "What if I want the cheese and crackers?"

I squeeze his foot tighter. "Then they'll go great with my chili."

"I'll hold you to that," he warns as he hooks his free foot around mine.

"Ugh, you guys are so sappy." Senichi pulls his earbuds out and pops them into his ears. "Let me know when you're done mooning over each other."

Rin giggles, while Shig and I share a smile.

Mooning over each other while we take a train ride up into the mountains sounds just about perfect.

HUNTING THE YULE LOG

"Is this Wonderland?" Rin breathes as we disembark from the train, and I have to agree with the sentiment.

The company really went all out here, filling the gift store with everything that could possibly be needed to celebrate Yule. Colorful decorations fill the place, along with gifts geared toward kids.

It reminds me of the time I went to Yipiland with my classmates for our pre-graduation trip.

Cloth ropes line the path off the train, directing us away from the gift store, though strategic gaps along the way offer immediate access for those too impatient to go through the entire process of hunting their Yule logs.

Even Senichi looks excited, his earbuds firmly stashed away in his pocket as he holds Deka's hand.

"Welcome to Holly King Fields," a woman greets us. She wears a black knit sweater and a plaid skirt over thick, black leggings, and a heater blasts from overhead. She gives us a bright smile. "Is this your first visit?"

"Yes," Shig answers.

"Fantastic," she says with the same enthusiasm I'm sure she directs to people who come every year. She holds out folded papers to all of us. "Here are your maps. Cocoa stations are marked along the way. You can find baskets to transport your Yule log right outside the door. The lost and found is in the gift shop." She smiles down at the kids. "And, don't worry, we're in a gated area, so there's no chance anyone will wander off and get hurt. Departure back to town is at four o'clock, but if you find you want to stay longer, we do have a lodge on site. Have a happy visit!"

We take our maps and file out onto a stone patio swept free of snow. Tables rest under more outdoor heaters, and an exterior cocoa stand waits off to the right, next to the gift shop entrance. While the tables are empty now, I'm sure they'll fill up fast with exhausted parents once the first hour passes.

Senichi grabs two baskets from a pile next to the door, passing one to me, and opens his map. "There's a maze that has presents hidden along the way. Or there's the forest where the Yule logs are."

"Presents!" Rin screams, and I wince at the noise.

They had woken up with a vengeance on the train, and the cookie decorating only added sugar highs to the fire. By the time we're done with the day, the kids are going to be cranky and exhausted, but too hopped up on sugar to go to bed easily.

It will be worth it, though, to be able to give Rin this memory of their childhood.

Senichi looks down at Deka. "Do you want to do the maze, too? Or do you want to go to the forest?"

"The maze," they say quietly, then peer at Rin as if unsure that's okay.

I nudge Rin and receive an eye roll for my efforts before they stomp over to Deka and grab their hand. "I'll let you open the first present we find."

Deka brightens, and tension eases from my shoulders at the knowledge they'll be okay.

Senichi glances at us. "Do you want to do the maze, too? Or go get the Yule logs?"

Shig checks his watch. We have a few hours before the train will leave to take us back home, but a maze can take a while. If we miss the forest area, we can always buy Yule logs in town, but it feels like a waste not to get one here, since they're included in the pass Shig bought.

I reach out for Shig's hand. "If you're fine with the kids, we'll go to the forest. We can always go again when you're done with the maze."

"Sounds good." He squints at the stream of people heading down the path toward the maze. "We'll likely have a line to wait in. It says they only let small groups in at a time."

Probably to restock the presents after each group. "We'll buy some hot chocolates, then, to keep you warm."

"Cider for me, please." Senichi reaches out and grabs the back of Rin's coat when they start to scamper toward the steps off the patio.

"Got it." Releasing Shig, I hurry over to the cocoa window and dig out my wallet before Shig can offer to pay. He already spent so much on this trip, the least I can do is buy the treats.

But when I try to pay, the barista tells me they're free, and I put my money away. I'll just have to find another way to spoil Shig the way he's spoiling us.

Once the drinks are ready, I thank the barista, thread the handle of the log basket over my arm, and carry the tray back to my waiting family.

Senichi takes the tray and puts it in his basket to disperse later before he lets the kids drag him down the decorated path after everyone else.

"I bet we'll be the first back with our Yule logs," Shig says, rubbing his glove-covered hands together with childish excitement.

Grinning at his enthusiasm, I reach out to adjust his knit hat. "Oh, you think so?"

"If we're fast, we can get a couple of presents bought before the kids return." He grabs my hand. "Let's go!"

"Why am I starting to feel like we're here for you more than the kids?" I laugh as I let him pull me down the stairs.

At the bottom, snow crunches under my feet, but not enough to cover more than the top of my boots. The owners of the place keep everything nice and tidy, and more heaters offer places to pause along the path. A wooden sign at the beginning of the path directs people left for the maze and right for the forest.

We head right and immediately pass another cocoa station. There's no way anyone is freezing while being up here, despite the chill. The snow flurries that started when we left town stopped before we even made it to the base of the mountains, and only clear blue fills the sky, wiping away my worry about having to dig out our cars when we get home.

As we enter the forest area, which is cordoned off with more cloth-covered rope, Shig releases my hand to open his map. "It's just a big, open forest, so we can pick whichever direction we want to go."

I glance around the trees. "What kind of log are you hoping for?"

"Oak," Shig says instantly, "and birch."

Oak for healing, strength, and wisdom, birch for new beginnings. My eyes sting at the consideration he put into something so simple, and I nod. "Yeah, those sound perfect." I sniffle and stare some more at the trees until the burn in my eyes fades. "I think I see some oak trees off to the left."

"Perfect." Grabbing my hand once more, he marches forward as if he knows exactly where we're going.

I love that about him. How confident he is with everything he does. He probably learned that early on while growing up. Coming from a family of lawyers, they would have taught him confidence wins half the case.

It lets me feel like I can lean on him more, that no matter what happens, Shig will take it in stride and come up with a solution. The comfort that brings makes my chest tight, and the urge to tell him I love him pushes for release.

How could I *not* love this man? It feels like it was destined to happen from the very moment our eyes first met at the parent-teacher meeting. With our kids already best friends, and with Hana getting sick, this all feels like too much for coincidence.

Where we are right now, tromping through the snow, with our kids happily playing together, is Fate. It has to be, and the desire to kiss Shig, to know he's mine, almost overwhelms me.

My steps slow, and Shig glances over his shoulder, one brow lifted in question. "You're not pooping out already, are you? I know you have more stamina than that."

I shake myself and give his hand a squeeze. "No, not pooping out at all. I'm here for the long haul."

Reading more into my words than I say, his lips part on a fast breath before he nods. "Good. Now, get your butt moving, or we won't have first dibs."

"Yes, ShiShi." Quickening my steps, I walk alongside him into the forest, eyes out for any oak trees.

Here and there, I spot little yellow flags poking out of the snow, indicating an available log, but we bypass those without checking. Despite his words, Shig doesn't seem in a hurry to complete our log hunting.

Happiness flushes his cheeks pink, and his green eyes shine as we walk together.

At last, Shig stops. "That's the one."

I stare up at the giant oak, its bare branches spread wide and heavy with snow, its sturdy trunk so wide that Shig and I together couldn't reach around it. "How old do you think it is?"

"It had to have been here before Holly King Fields set up shop." Shig's gaze sweeps the snow-covered ground at its base. "There! I see one!"

Sure enough, a little yellow flag sticks up from the base of the trunk. I spot closer ones littered around the path up to the tree, but I focus on the one Shig wants. We need all the healing, strength, and wisdom burning this log can impart on our new family.

"Watch your step," Shig cautions as his feet slide in the snow.

"Maybe we shouldn't hold han—" my words cut off as my feet slide on an icy patch hidden by the snow, and I pitch backward.

I try to let go of Shig, try to not take him down with me, but his hand stays tight in mine.

We tumble to the ground together, but luckily, our thick coats and the snow keep us from injury as we land flat on our backs. Snow rains down from the branches overhead, dusting us in cold crystals.

Shig laughs and rolls toward me. "I'm so glad Sen wasn't here to see this."

"He'd never let us live it down," I agree.

"Look at you." Shig pulls off a glove to wipe the snow from my face. "You're going to get a cold if we don't warm you up."

I catch his hand. "You're not any better." I breathe on his cold fingers. "Put your glove back on before you lose some digits."

He smirks down at me. "That only works on Rin."

My eyes drop to his full lips. The first time he kissed me, I was too shocked to register anything but soft and warm. Will it be the same if I kiss him now? Or will it be different, now that I'm in love with him?

"If you keep looking at me like that, I'm going to kiss you," Shig says gruffly.

"You can." I lift my eyes to meet his. "If you wan—"

Shig swoops down before the words fully leave my mouth, his lips claiming mine.

As far as kisses go, he keeps it chaste, but the

feeling behind it is anything but pure. His desire burns against my skin and finds an answering need buried deep inside of me the demands *more*. But he's careful not to push my boundaries, to take more than I'm ready for.

When he pulls back, the pink in his cheeks has deepened to red, and his breathing comes in fast pants.

We stare at each other from inches apart, and he searches my face. "How was it?"

"Again?" I beg and grip his lapels, frustrated that I can't feel his body through our winter coats. "I want more."

"I'll give you everything you want," he promises.

"Mamma!" a child's voice calls. "I found one!"

Shig cringes and lifts up high enough to peer down the path. "We have company."

I groan. Things were just progressing between us, and I don't want to stop.

"Later." He drops a quick kiss on the tip of my nose. "When we have a closed door between us and the world."

Body on fire, I nod in agreement.

Later can't come soon enough.

PERFECT FIT

Senichi hangs the last of the strings of decorated pine cones as I come back from putting the kids to bed.

They had shocked everyone when they insisted on decorating their Yule logs as soon as we got home, and the Yule logs now sit in the hearth, waiting to be burned. Paper snowflakes and strings of popcorn and pinecones hang from every wall, lending to the festive feel, and it makes my chest tight.

We never did this. Not at my parent's house when I was growing up or after Karen and I moved in together. To her, Yule had been about how expensive my gift was, and it always came up short. She didn't want any spare money going to seasonal decorations when it could go toward making her present better.

Rin only discovered what they were missing out on once they started at the daycare, when part of the activity plan was creating decorations for every holiday imaginable. Rin and Karen got into a lot of fights around those times, which usually ended in tears, slammed doors, and accusations of favoritism from Karen when I told her she was being too harsh.

But here, warmth fills the home, no doors were slammed, and despite the fight the kids had, no more tears were shed.

Senichi drops the tape, and I hurry over. "Here, let me help."

I bend to grab the tape, then rip off a piece so he can tack the end of the string to the wall.

"Thanks." He dusts his hands together in a vain attempt to wipe away the glitter that clings to everything in the house. "We're going to be finding this stuff three months from now."

"It's here to stay," I agree happily, knowing Shig won't throw a fit about the glitter invasion.

Senichi doesn't seem bothered by it, either, but that could be because he hasn't seen the pink and green flecks that decorate his cheekbones and wink in his dark hair. Then again, I don't think it will bother him even after he sees he's almost as decorated as the pine cones.

I glance around. "Where's your uncle?"

"Bathroom," Senichi points to the hall.

"I'll finish cleaning up if you want to head to bed." I check the time and wince. We let the younger kids stay up way too late, but there was no way they were going to bed until they passed out at the table, glue bottles still in hand.

Senichi eyes the mess still on the table and edges toward his own room. "If you're sure?"

I flap my hand, telling him to go, before I dig out the cleaning supplies and get to work scraping the decorating remnants off the table. I throw empty bottles of glitter into the trash and stop at the shopping list next to the phone to make a note to buy more. As far as I'm concerned, there can never be too much glitter.

By the time Shig comes out, warm and pink from the shower, I have everything mostly picked up.

"I just need to set the coffee pot," I say as I put the trash near the door to take out in the morning.

"Go wash up. I can do that." Without waiting for a response, he disappears into the kitchen.

Loving that we have a routine, I hurry into the master bathroom, quickly wash off as much glitter as

I can, then brush my teeth. Nervous flutters fill my stomach at the promise we made on the mountain, but I try not to get my hopes up. It's after midnight, and we've had a long day.

When I step out, the lights in the main part of the house are off, and Shig stands at our doorway, stretched on his tiptoes as he tries to take down a sprig of mistletoe taped above our door.

He glances over at the sound of the bathroom door opening, and his face turns red with embarrassment. "I'm sorry, Sen probably put it here to tease us. I'll take it down—"

Lengthening my stride, I catch Shig around the waist, turning him far enough to slide my mouth over his.

He lets out a surprised sound of pleasure and releases the mistletoe to wrap his arms around my neck, his body warm and flush against mine.

After a breathless moment, I pull back far enough to ask, "Is this okay?"

"More than okay." He sways forward to nibble on my bottom lip. "Take me to bed."

He doesn't have to ask twice. Bending, I scoop him up, and a surprised laugh escapes him before he slaps a hand over his mouth and casts a worried glance toward the hall.

"You better be quiet, or you'll wake the kids back up," I tease as I bump the door closed with my hip.

"The room is soundproof," he whispers from between his fingers as I lay him on the bed. Then, he pulls me down on top of him, hooking one leg around my hips. "Kiss me again."

He doesn't have to tell me twice. The first kiss wasn't nearly enough to satisfy the hunger that woke in me on the mountain. Bending, I slide my mouth back across his, open and hungry for the heat of his tongue slipping past my lips. He kisses with confidence, deep and searching, then playful, ratcheting my desire to new heights.

Soon, I'm gasping against his lips, desperate for something I don't fully understand but need.

Shig pulls back, and I open my eyes, staring down into his blown pupils. "I'm not wearing a protector, but I have one, if you want me to put it in."

My eyes drop to his glistening, swollen lips, then rise to meet his gaze. "I don't... If you're okay with this, then I want..."

"It's okay, Juro," he soothes, lifting his hands to stroke my horns. "I want this. I want you."

My breath catches, my eyes dropping to his mouth once more, and I lick my sensitive lips.

"It's okay," he says more softly, his hands in my

hair urging me back down. "No matter what, I want you."

Groaning, I crush his mouth beneath mine, my tongue thrusting into his mouth. He groans with approval, the leg around my hips pulling me tighter until I feel the hard press of his cock against mine and pleasure zings through me from head to foot.

His tongue twines with mine, urging me to explore the secrets of his sweet mouth, before he licks along the underside of my tongue, encouraging me to find that last, most intimate part of him.

Shaking with need, I stroke my tongue against the grooves of his palette, and he bucks beneath me, his moan loud and vibrating down my throat. Then, the barbs on my tongue find the perfect fit, locking us together. It feels like the world stops—everything stops—and it's just us, floating together, our souls entwining, merging, before they separate, taking pieces of each other with them.

I crash back into my body with a cry, my hands frantic on his body, pulling at his pants, needing them out of the way, needing access to that other sweet part of his body.

In turn, he tugs the elastic waistband of my sweats down, freeing my aching cock as he lifts his knees. His tail brushes against my balls as he pulls me forward, murmurs of encouragement spilling from his lips as he positions me at his entrance, where he's already soft and slippery.

Grabbing his hip in one hand, I surge forward, meeting resistance before his body gives beneath me, and I slide past his tight ring of muscles. He feels amazingly hot as his body hugs mine, and I push deeper, hips rocking as I make room for myself inside of him.

My hips buck frantically, apologies raining between kisses, as I thrust into his heat. I know there's no finesse or skill to my actions, that I should slow down and pay more attention, but I can't stop. The need to claim this man, to paint his insides with my cum, drives me on.

He tenses and shudders beneath me, moans rising from his chest a moment before his body squeezes around me. Hot cum hits my stomach as he finds his release.

Groaning, I rock into him harder as a tingle starts in my balls, and my stomach tightens. Then, my orgasm crashes over me, and I thrust as deep as his body will allow as my cock pulses, my release filling him.

Reason returns as the crazed rush to join fades,

and I lift onto my elbows to take my weight from him.

Embarrassed, I look down at his daze expression. "I'm so, so sorry, Shig. I can do better—"

"Hush." He lifts a shaky hand to cover my mouth. "That was perfect."

"I could have hurt you," I protest as I realize I didn't even consider prepping him. I felt his heat against the tip of my cock and dove right in.

"You didn't, though." His legs drop back to rest loosely around my hips, and my cock slides free of his warm embrace. "I prepped, just in case."

"I want to prep you next time." I drop my head to rest on his chest which I realize is still covered by his sleeping shirt.

Belatedly, I notice I'm still fully dressed, my pants shoved down below my ass, and his pants still hang off one leg.

"Oh, God, I swear I can do better than this." Reaching down, I finish pulling his pants off. "I'll do better, take my time..." Unwillingly, my eyes slide to the clock on the nightstand, which shows that barely any time passed, and I groan again. "Oh, God..."

"Hey, I came first, remember?" He rises up to kiss my jawline. "We have time to do anything and everything you want."

I want more, I realize, even though I just spent myself inside him.

Turning my head, I kiss his swollen lips, then his chin and throat. I push up his shirt to expose his chest and dip lower to swipe my rough tongue over his nipple. He groans, his back arching, and I slip my hands beneath him, lifting him higher.

He gasps and whimpers, his body shifting restlessly. "Juro, you don't have to—"

He cuts off as I catch his taught nipple between my teeth, then lick away the sting. His heart pounds against my lips as I press kisses across his chest, then move down his center. Smears of cum cover his stomach where it seeped through his shirt, and I lick it away, the taste salty and good as I swallow it down.

He groans again and spreads his legs without prompting, his spent dick twitching at half-mast.

Bending, I take it into my mouth, enjoying the weight of it against my tongue, the way it jumps and thickens.

"Juro." He tugs fitfully on my hair. "I'm not sure I can—"

His words cut off on a sharp cry as I suck hard, pulling out every last trace of cum. His hips buck beneath me, and I slip my hand beneath him, finding his slick entrance and thrusting my finger into him. As if I've done this a dozen times, I find the rough bundle of nerves inside and rub against them.

His cock thickens in my mouth, pushing deeper into the back of my throat, and I hum my approval.

The vibration pulls a whimper from him, and he tugs on my hair harder. His hips move in short bursts of motion, his ass riding my fingers as he thrusts into my mouth.

I want him to cum down my throat, to mark me the same way I marked him, and I push down on his next thrust, taking him in deeper.

His moans fill the room, music to my ears as he finds his pleasure, then he stiffens beneath me, his hand shoving my head down as his hip thrust up, nearly choking me as he pulses and comes inside my mouth.

I wait for him to relax before licking him clean once more.

"Come up here," he says roughly, pulling on me to move back up his body.

I go eagerly, then raise my arms as he tugs on my shirt, pulling it over my head. I help him to take his off, too, so our sweat-slick chests press together.

He lifts his lips to mine. "Kiss me."

I do without hesitation, sliding my tongue into his mouth so he can taste the flavor of our passion.

My barbs stroke across his palette, finding those special notches once more, and he shudders beneath me.

His slender thighs wrap high around my waist, pulling me forward, and I drive into his heat once more, moving more slowly this time, making sure the sounds he makes come from passion and not pain.

I wrap him in my arms, marveling at all the ways we fit together. When his dick thickens once more and taps against my lower stomach in a lazy bounce, I pick up speed, thrusting harder as I gauge how much he can take. Heat flushes his body, turning his skin a beautiful pink.

He gasps and throws one arm over his head to press his hand flat against the headboard. "Harder."

Gripping his waist, I rise onto my knees and lift his hips.

"Yes," he groans as I slam into him, rocking his entire body. "Yes, just like that. Oh, I love you. I love you so much."

I shiver and thrust into him again. "Say it again."

His eyes open to hooded slits, and he stares at me. "I love you."

Head bowing, I gasp and shudder as I move

inside my mate, his body clenching around my cock, his moans and gasps filling the room.

I feel the first shiver that rolls through him, feel his thighs tightening around my hips, and shift him, thrusting more shallowly, hitting that spot inside him.

His eyes fly open, his back arching as he shoves down onto me, taking my cock to the hilt. He shivers and shakes with orgasm, but nothing comes out of his cock.

I grind into him, and he moans and shivers harder, his entire body tense.

Unable to hold back any more, I let my own release take me, filling him once more.

He cries out, clenching around me like he just came again, then he sags, his breaths coming in desperate gasps.

Slowly, I pull from his body, and he gives me a lazy, contented smile. "Okay, you proved you can do better."

I glance at his cock, now soft and nestled in the tights curls between his thighs. "But, you didn't…"

"It's called a dry orgasm." He lifts shaky arms. "Now, come here so I can hold you."

I fall into his arms, my head on his chest as I listen to his racing heart slow to an even pace.

Tracing a path over his chest, I look up at him. "I love you."

Warmth fills his green eyes. "I love you, too, mate."

Mate. The word burrows into me, finding all the wounds created by my failed past and filling them in.

I hug Shig, nestling into his embrace. My mate.

At this moment, my life feels perfect.

MASSAGES & MESSAGES

A soft hand strokes my cheek, pulling me from sleep. "Juro, wake up, love."

Stirring, I groan and nuzzle against Shig's throat. "Not yet."

A quiet chuckle vibrates beneath me. "I hear the kids in the hall. We need to put on pants before they barge in here."

With another groan, I lift up onto my elbows to stare down at him sleepily. "We need a lock on the door."

"I'm seriously considering it." He reaches up to stroke my face. "Good morning."

Still half asleep, I smile and bend to kiss him, my tongue slipping past his parted lips to rub against his palette, reconfirming that, yes, this man is my mate.

He shivers and whimpers beneath me, his arms winding around my waist as one knee lifts to press against my hip.

Pulling back, I rub my nose against his. "Morning."

Now, it's his turn to groan. "I'm going to the hardware store today."

Reaching between us, I grasp his hardening cock. "We can tell Senichi to take them to the park."

"Yes." Eyes closing, he thrusts into my hand. "Do that." I move to let go, and his hand locks around mine, his eyes opening in a glare. "Don't you dare stop now."

Obliging, I tighten my hold on him, and a soft moan drifts from his parted lips. "If I don't stop, how will I tell Sen to take the kids out of the house?"

He turns his head toward my nightstand. "Text him. You only need one hand for that."

Laughing, I lean to the side, stretching until my fingertips find my cell phone, and I drag it close enough to grab. When I power it back on, dozens of texts and messages ding to life, mostly from Karen, but a couple from my old neighbor, Mrs. Thomas.

The ones from Mrs. Thomas worry me the most. I gave her my number for emergencies, and the last time she used it, my house was on fire. What could she possibly be calling for now?

"What's wrong?" Shig pushes up onto his elbows to see my phone.

"I'm not sure." I release his softening cock with an apologetic peck on his cheek, the mood ruined.

As he rolls out of bed to grab our clothes, I skip through the messages from Karen and press play on the one from Mrs. Thomas, putting it on speaker.

Her worried whisper fills the room, as if she doesn't want someone else to hear her. "Juro, dear, Karen is here with *that man*, demanding to know where you are. She said she came to spend Yule with you and sweet little Rin and seemed shocked to find your house gone. She said you weren't picking up your phone. I hope everything is okay. I gave her your new address. Give me a ring to let me know you and Rin are safe. And come by for tea soon, I have a present for Rin."

Panic shoots through me, and I check the time on the message. She called ten minutes ago. Damn me for forgetting to turn my phone back on after we got back from Holly King Field.

"Shit. Shit, shit, shit." I scramble out of bed and grab the pants Shig holds out. "Karen's going to be here any minute."

"You didn't tell her about the fire?" Shig asks.

"I was going to tell her after the holiday. I didn't want to deal with it before then." I hop on one foot, then the other as I pull on my pants, then catch the t-shirt Shig throws at me. "This isn't her year to have Rin. We argued about it, and I didn't want to rehash what was already decided. But she came anyway. She wants more money."

Shig's expression turns cold. "She would have received the restraining order by now. It was sent certified mail."

I scrub my hands over my face. "This isn't good."

"It will be okay." Shig strides for the door. "Sen can still take the kids to the park so they're not here when she arrives."

Relieved he's keeping a level head, I nod and follow him out of the room.

We find Senichi on the couch in the living room, snuggled up under a blanket with the kids. Cartoons play quietly on the TV, and a bowl of half-eaten dry cereal rests in his lap.

He looks up as we enter, a smirk on his lips. "Sleep well last night?"

I can't even be embarrassed that he knows what happened. We weren't quiet, and despite Shig's assurances that the room has good soundproofing, the gap under the door lets noise drift out.

My heart races as I pick Rin up off the couch and give them a push toward their bedroom. "Go get dressed. Senichi's taking you to the park."

"I am?" he asks in surprise and glances down at his pajama shirt and bowl of cereal. "Right now?"

"Yes." Shig lifts Deka over the back of the couch and sets them on their feet. "Go get ready."

Frowning, Senichi sets his bowl on the coffee table and frowns. "What's wrong? What's going on?"

Shig casts a wary glance toward the hall, waiting to make sure the kids are out of earshot. "Juro's ex is coming by, and it's not going to be pretty."

"Got it." Instead of heading to his room, Senichi goes to the entryway, pulling a heavy winter coat over his pajamas and cramming his feet into his boots. He grabs the kids' jackets and mittens, then yells, "If you're not out here in one minute, I'm going by myself!"

Squeals of protest come from their room, followed by pounding feet. Rin and Deka reappear, wearing their yellow school jumpers and sweatpants. That will have to do. I kneel and help Rin into their shoes while Senichi takes care of Deka.

Rin pats my bowed head. "Why aren't you dressed, Daddy?"

I force a tense smile. "I'm staying here to make pancakes for when you get back."

Rin grins. "Unicorn pancakes?"

My chest tightens with unease, but I push it down, not wanting to worry Rin. "Sure, whatever you want."

Their eyes widen with greed. "Whipped cream."

"Okay, sure." Standing, I grab the jacket Senichi holds out and help Rin into it before I look at Senichi. "Can you take the long way to the park?"

I don't want to risk Karen seeing Rin as they drive up.

"No problem." He crams a hat over Deka's head and opens the door. "Let's go. First one to the swings gets extra big pushies."

Excited, Deka and Rin race out the door, but then Rin freezes on the porch. "Mommy?" They turn back to look at me, the happiness dimming from their face. "Mommy's here. Why is mommy here? I don't want to go to Scott's house. I want to stay here."

Senichi's shoulders slump. "Sorry, guys."

"It's okay." Shivering, I step out onto the porch in my bare feet as I hear car doors slamming. "I appreciate the effort."

"Why don't you guys play in the backyard, instead?" Shig suggests. "Juro, come back in before you catch a cold."

I want to, but my feet feel frozen to the porch as Karen stomp up the walkway, her face set in an expression I've come to dread over the years. She's here for a fight and nothing less than getting her way will stop what's coming.

"Juro!" she snaps as soon as she spots me. "How *dare* you not tell me about the house fire! I told you to get that porch light fixed. And what is this about restricted visiting rights? You can't take my child from me!"

"Come on, guys," Senichi whispers, herding the kids back into the house. "Let's go out back. We'll play Yip Yip."

Eyes wide with fear, Deka goes back inside, but Rin ducks under Senichi's hand and runs forward to wrap their arms around my leg. Their small body trembles, and when I glance down, I see tears filling their eyes.

My chest squeezes painfully, and I stroke the top of Rin's head. "Rin, go inside with Deka and Senichi. Don't worry, you're not going anywhere."

"You don't get to make that decision." Karen bounds up the porch steps and reaches for Rin.

"Come on. You're leaving with me and Daddy Scott."

"He's not my daddy!" Rin's hold on me tightens, their entire body shaking. "He takes my toys and yells at me. I don't want to go!"

Heart breaking, I gently disentangle them and step back far enough to set them inside the house. "Go on. Go find the others."

"You can't keep me from my child!' Karen yells, then twists to glare at her mate, who stands at the bottom of the stairs, looking like he'd rather be anywhere else. "Scott, *do* something!"

Scott squares his shoulders and puts a foot on the steps. "Now, see here, Juro, Rin deserves a family that's whole. And with your house now gone—"

"Rin could have died if you'd been home!" Karen shrieks, cutting him off. "And you didn't even see fit to tell me? I expect my share of that insurance money, too. Don't think you can keep it all for yourself. I have rights!"

"No, you don't," Shig says coolly as he steps out onto the porch. "Your name was nowhere on the deed, which means you don't have any claim on the insurance money."

Karen whips toward him, her eyes raking over his pajamas. "And who's this? You're shacking up with some man, now? At least, you found someone who can do all the work in bed while you just lay there like a dead fish."

Anger burns in my cheeks.

My mouth opens, but Shig's hand on my shoulder stops me. "I'm Shig Akutsu, Juro's mate, and I'll ask you not to speak of him like that again."

Her lip curls with disgust. "I wouldn't be walking around bragging about that. He's a loser and always has been. But maybe you like doormats."

I flinch at that, though she's called me worse.

Shig's fingers twitch on my shoulder as he takes another step forward, putting himself partially in front of me. "I'm *also* Juro's lawyer, and I've reviewed your divorce paperwork. You have no legal right to be here right now, and you're scaring my family. Please leave."

Karen's chin juts out. "I'm not going anywhere without *my* child." Her sharp gaze cuts to me. "And don't think you're scaring me with this stupid, restricted access bullshit. You know you can't keep Rin unless I let you." She raises her voice. "Rin, pack your bag! We're leaving!"

"Karen," Scott says, taking a cautious step up onto the porch as he reaches for his mate. "Maybe now's not the best time…"

She jerks away from his hold. "Don't be a coward, Scott." She turns a mean glare on me. "Juro knows what he needs to do if he wants to keep Rin."

Shaking with anger and fear, I pull back my shoulders. "I'm not giving you more money. I wasn't legally required to before, and I'm done now. No more."

Karen's tail snaps as she stalks forward. "Then, you don't get *my* child."

Shig steps fully between us, his tone calm and collected. "We'll let the courts decide that. Expect a summons to arrive soon."

Karen ignores him, her eyes fixed on me. "Rin's not even yours," she hisses. "You were just a means to an end. We'll go to court, and you'll lose. Biology trumps whatever feelings you have toward Rin."

A sharp gasp comes from behind me, and I spin to find Rin peeking around the open door.

Their wide eyes meet mine, and their bottom lip trembles. "Daddy?"

"No, baby, she didn't mean that." I rush to kneel in front of Rin. "We're just fighting. But you're mine, I promise." Tears cloud my vision as I pull Rin into my arms and stand, walking back into the house. "It's okay, Daddy's here."

"Leave before I call the police," Shig commands, cold fury in his voice.

A moment later, the front door slams shut, and Shig's hand touches my back. "Juro…"

I bury my face in Rin's hair, taking a shaky breath of their shampoo. "Just…promise me it will be okay."

His arms wrap around both of us. "We'll do everything we can."

While not a promise, it's the best I can hope for right now.

ZOOM, OFF TO THE SKY

The rest of the morning passes in a daze.

Rin clings to me, crying and refusing to let me out of their reach. And no matter how much I reassure Rin, uncertainty and fear fill their eyes every time they look at me.

Shig vanishes into the garage, his phone to his ear as he calls his parents for advice.

At noon, Rin finally falls asleep, exhausted from crying.

I put them to sleep in Deka's room, making sure to tuck Hip-Hip in with them.

Quiet fills the house. Senichi had taken Deka to the park for their promised play-date. He apologized more than once for not making sure Rin was out of hearing range of the fight, but I reassured him I wasn't mad.

No, all my anger goes toward Karen. How did I stay with such a nasty person for so long? Why didn't I stand up to her sooner?

I slump onto the couch, staring at the half-empty bowl of cereal still on the coffee table. I should make lunch or those promised, sprinkle-filled pancakes for when Rin wakes back up, but I can't find the energy to move.

The garage door opens and closes, then Shig slips onto the cushion next to me. Without a word, he pulls me down until my head rests on his thighs, and he gently strokes my horns, offering comfort and the quiet I need to sort my thoughts.

I had wanted to avoid going to court because I was too afraid of finding out I'm really not Rin's father, afraid of losing them altogether. But if I was braver, pushed the matter sooner, maybe all of this could have been avoided. Now, it seems inevitable that we're in for a fight. Cut off from my money, Karen will want to make this as painful as possible. And as expensive as possible. It doesn't matter that she doesn't want Rin; she wants to punish me for failing to be the perfect husband she wanted me to be.

Shig's touch moves to my arm. "Do you want to know? Before we have to go to court?"

I don't ask what he means. I saw the envelope when it arrived in the mail late on Thursday. I pretended not to see Shig slip it into his briefcase, not wanting it to spoil our night. I don't actually want to know. I love Rin as my own child, whether or not we're blood-related. But it would be stupid to go to court blind to a potential outcome.

Reluctantly, I force myself to sit up. "Will you look at it?"

"Of course." He stands, his fluffy tail drooping, and pads into the dining room where he keeps his briefcase.

I flinch at the sound of the latches opening and hold my breath as I listen to him break the seal. As papers rustle, I pull my knees up to my chest and wrap my arms around them.

His feet shush across the floor as he comes back and sits beside me, the papers folded in his hand.

I give them a wary glance. "The verdict?"

Silent, he opens them to the last page, and I read the word *Positive Match*.

The air sticks in my lungs, and I choke on a sob of relief. God, I really didn't think, not in the secret parts of my heart, that I was Rin's father. Not with how much I struggled with intimacy with Karen. Not with her little digs that made me question.

My hand trembles as I take the papers, and tears spill down my cheeks. "Thank God for bad booze making me horny."

"Come here." Shig pulls me back into his arms as I read over the papers. "Everything's going to be fine, okay? We'll get through this."

"It's going to be expensive." A laugh escapes me. "Thank God for the house fire. Otherwise, I'd never be able to afford it."

"Don't forget, my mom's working your case pro bono." Shig squeezes me tighter. "Rin's not going anywhere."

"Yeah." Nodding, I lean back against his chest. "Thank you. Thank you so much."

He kisses the top of my head. "That's what mates are for."

When Senichi returns with Deka, we have cocoa waiting to warm them up and lunch on the table. Not knowing when everyone would be ready, we opted for sandwiches and chips.

Senichi and Deka grab plates and dig in. We eat in silence for a bit, everyone's mood subdued.

Cheesy puff in hand, Deka peers worriedly toward the hallway. "Rin?"

"Just taking a nap." Shig pats their head. "We're going to be extra quiet, okay? Rin's had a hard day."

Deka nods but still looks worried as they stuff the chip into their mouth.

"Did you have fun at the park?" Shig asks as he sips on coffee.

"The place was empty, so we had the swings all to ourselves." Senichi rubs his young sibling's hair affectionately. "Deka almost went over the top of the bar."

Deka giggles, cheese dust all over their face. "No, I didn't."

"I thought you were going to fly right off," Senichi insists. He shoots his hand into the air. "Just zoom off into the sky."

Deka giggles harder and smacks him, leaving behind a cheesy handprint on his dark shirt.

"Ugh, you're so messy!" he complains dramatically, making Deka giggle some more. "Go wash your face and hands, cheese monster."

Still laughing, Deka slides off the chair and sprints for the hall bathroom.

As the sound of running water follows, Senichi looks at us. "How's Rin doing?"

"Confused and scared." I pick at my untouched sandwich. "It's going to be tough for a bit."

Senichi scowls. "No offense, but your ex is a real bitch."

"Sen," Shig warns, but I wave it away.

"He's not wrong." I take a shaky breath. "But, once I have full custody, she won't have as much power as she does now."

Senichi snorts. "That man of hers is a total waste of space, too. She's probably regretting divorcing you, now, but it's her loss. You're too good for her."

Flattered, I smile at him. "Thank you. That means a lot."

"I'm just speaking the truth." He shrugs, uncomfortable with the attention. "So, are you guys mates?"

Now, it's my turn to be uncomfortable, but I can't help but smile. "Yeah, we are."

"That's good." He peeks at me from the corner of his eye. "Do I get to call you uncle Juro at school now? What kind of benefits are we talking about here?"

"Stop it," Shig says, his tone firm but amusement twinkling in his eyes.

Running footsteps come from the hall, and I look over to see Deka dragging Hip-Hip by the ear.

I'm on my feet in an instant, dread pooling in my gut.

Senichi stands, too. "You didn't wake Rin, did you? We don't need another fight over that hippo."

Deka shakes their head, hair whipping back and forth. "Rin's not in our room. I can't find them."

MISSING

Dread continues to build as we search the house, opening every cupboard and checking every hidey-hole for Rin. Senichi even pulls down the ladder to the attic space and checks the eaves on the off-chance Rin somehow made it up there.

But as time passes, the certainty grows that Rin isn't in the house.

I rake my hands through my hair as I stare around at the overturned house. "How did they get out?"

Shig returns from the backyard, his expression grim. "The gate was open. Rin probably went out the window."

Senichi dashes for the front door. "I'll check the park. Maybe they went there to play on the swings."

"I'll take my car and drive around the block." Shig grabs his keys. "They can't have gone far."

"I'll go with you." I grab my coat, then grab the kids' coats, too, and lift Deka before I follow Shig outside. "I'll call the police as we search. In this weather, it's not safe for Rin to be outside."

But we don't find Rin, and Senichi calls to let us know the park is empty.

I call Mrs. Thomas, too, on the off-chance Rin somehow made it back to our old house. They might have tried to go there. The turret was their safe place, and after today, they were probably feeling insecure.

Mrs. Thomas assures me she'll have her grandson go over and check the house, and Shig and I turn back toward home.

We meet the police in the driveway, and they perform another sweep of the house.

"The lock on the window looks forced," a young deputy announces as he comes out of the kids' room. "Would anyone want to kidnap your child?"

My gut tightens. Bile surges up my throat, but I choke it down. "My ex. We fought this morning about custody. But she would never..."

My voice trails off because Karen *would* take Rin. She must know she'll lose the case if this goes to court, but she never really wanted Rin, so why would she take them...

I sway, and Shig grabs my arms for support. "She knew about the fire."

Shig pats my back. "Yes, Mrs. Thomas—"

"No," I cut him off, the fight from the porch replaying in my mind. "She knew the specifics. Where it started. That we weren't home. Scott and her messed with the light on the porch a few days earlier. And the insurance company asked about suspicious wiring. They set the fire for the money. Now that she knows she won't get it—"

Hand over my mouth, I rush for the bathroom, making it barely in time as my stomach heaves up the meager food I managed to eat today.

When I stumble back into the main room, I find Shig there, giving the police the make and model of Scott's car, as well as a description of both Karen and Scott. Thank goodness he can keep a level head right now, because panic pushes me to go back out to the street, to search until I find Rin.

Senichi returns with Deka as one of the deputies leaves to call in the information.

Without being asked, he takes his sibling to his room to distract them.

Shig makes coffee and passes it out, while I collapse into one of the dining chairs.

An older, tailed man, Detective Hara, sits in the chair beside me. "Have you tried calling your ex?"

I stare at him blankly before shaking my head. I pat my pockets, digging out my phone. The dozens of messages from Karen still sit unread, and my stomach rolls with a fresh wave of nausea. My hand trembles, my fingers clumsy on the buttons, and the phone clatters onto the table.

"Do you mind?" Detective Hara asks as he takes my phone.

I shake my head, glad to have someone else take control because I obviously can't right now.

"You have a number of unread messages," he comments. "Do you mind if I check them?"

I shake my head again, beyond caring if a stranger sees the kind of nasty things Karen sends me. I'm done trying to pretend she's a good person for Rin's sake. Not when she's kidnapped my child with plans to do God knows what.

Detective Hara's brows pinch as he skims through the messages, and his lips thin. "Do you get stuff like this often?"

"It's usually about money or what a failure I am," I say tiredly.

He looks at me, his expression serious. "You're filing for full custody?"

I nod. "She's been promising to sign the paperwork for a while, but she always put it off and was using it to leverage more out of me. It escalated, though, once I got a lawyer."

Looking grim, he opens my contacts and pulls up Karen's number, but hesitates before hitting the call button. "I want you to try to stay calm, okay? If she answers, try to get a location from her. Tell her you've changed your mind and want to give her a check in any amount she wants. Try not to antagonize her."

"I'll try." I glance around for Shig, needing his support.

He stands in the living room, talking to another of the officers, but when he catches me searching, he strides over to stand behind me, his hands on my shoulders.

"Ready?" the detective asks, and when I nod, he presses the call button and puts it on speaker.

The phone rings three times, and I stare at it, willing Karen to pick up.

Right before it switches to voicemail, the line clicks over, and quiet sobs fill the room.

I lurch forward, but Shig's hold on me keeps me grounded. "Karen?" I demand. "Is that Rin crying? Are they okay?"

"Always about the kid with you, isn't it?" Bitterness fills her voice. "I shouldn't be surprised, though. Rin's the only reason you married me to begin with."

My mouth opens and closes, unsure what she wants to hear. Of course, Rin's the only reason we got married. Until that party, I never talked to Karen outside of school. And without her pregnancy, we would have continued our separate ways, well outside of each other's orbits.

"I guess I have your attention now." Her voice grows muffled as if she covered the speaker. "Shut up! How much longer are you going to keep throwing a tantrum?"

"How much do you want?" I demand, desperate to pull her attention back to me. "You want the insurance check, right? Bring Rin back, and I'll sign it over to you."

Her voice returns, filled with satisfaction. "I knew you'd give in once you saw how serious I am.

You shouldn't try to grow a spine this late in the game, Juro. I know you better than that."

"Where are you?" I ask. "Can I speak to Rin? They sound scared."

"Rin's fine," she snaps. "And I'm not telling you where I am. Do you think I'm stupid? You'll meet me with the money."

"And you'll bring Rin?" I press.

"Yeah, I'll bring them." The speaker grows muffled once more. "Take the next exit. We're turning back."

"I don't like this, babe," Scott says. "What if he doesn't show? I don't want to raise this kid."

"Don't worry, baby, I'm taking care of us like I said I would." Her voice comes back loud and clear. "Meet me at the high school. I'll let you see Rin."

Fear rushes through me. "You mean you'll let me take Rin home, right?"

"I don't know." Gloating fills her voice. "You've been pretty rude to me lately. I don't think the insurance money is enough to earn Rin back."

Detective Hara makes a rolling motion with his hand, telling me to keep going.

Throat tight, I ask, "What do you want?"

"You've worked with the school district for a while now. You must have a nice retirement saved up," she muses. "I want you to cash it out. Once I have that, I'll give you Rin. I'll even sign that stupid paperwork you keep harping on about."

"That will take time," I protest. "At least a couple of weeks."

"Then, you'll have a couple of weeks to reflect on your actions," she snaps.

"Babe, that wasn't the plan," Scott protests in the background.

"Shut up and keep driving," she hisses.

"When do you want to meet?" I cut in.

"Thirty minutes, and leave that mate of yours at home. I don't like the way he talked to me."

The line goes dead, and Detective Hara sets my phone down. "You did well. Thirty minutes means they didn't go far. We'll set up patrol cars on the highway and catch them before they even get to the school."

I reach up to clutch Shig's hand. "What if she hurts Rin?"

"She won't do that," Detective Hara reassures me. "It doesn't sound like that was the plan. She's greedy, so she won't hurt Rin. It's the only leverage she has right now."

Shig squeezes my shoulders. "It doesn't sound

like her mate's thrilled with her plan, either. That means he's a weak point."

Uncertain, I look at Detective Hara, who nods in encouragement.

"Should we go to the school anyway?" I ask hesitantly. "Just in case?"

"We're not that far away from there. If we don't hear from the patrol cars in the next twenty minutes, we'll head over." He stands and picks up my phone. "We'll keep this in case she calls back, but after Rin is returned, we'll need it for evidence. She made some threats in the messages. It will help with the conviction."

I stare at my phone, feeling queasy. If only I checked last night, maybe this could have been stopped before it even happened.

He must see the guilt on my face because he reaches out to pat my hand. "You did nothing wrong here. People like this… They're just broken in the head. But that's not your fault, and we'll get your child back, you hear me?"

Throat too tight to speak, I nod, and he walks away to speak to his officers.

"Do you want anything?" Shig asks as he slides into the detective's abandoned seat. "You're shaky. Food might help."

"No." I press a hand over my stomach, trying to shove down the nausea. "I can't, not while Rin is—"

My words choke off, and Shig scoots his chair closer so he can wrap his arms around me. "It will be okay. We'll have Rin back soon."

The minutes tick by, each one taking an eternity while we wait for news that they found Rin, but when the minute hand hits twenty with no news, my stomach sinks.

"I'm going with you," Shig says as he stands.

I shake my head. "She said not to bring you. I don't want to make her angry."

He lifts his chin stubbornly. "I'll wait in the car, but you're not going alone."

I don't argue. Selfishly, I need him there with me.

Detective Hara gives me instructions as we head out to my car and climb inside, and I trust Shig to remember what he says because my mind refuses to focus. It's probably not good for me to drive, but if Karen arrives ahead of us, I don't want her to spot Shig behind the wheel.

Two unmarked cars follow us to the school, and I drive around the empty parking lot. It feels weird to be here at night during the holiday, with no lights on at the school. It's hard to imagine it alive and active with students at a time like this.

The police cars pull around to the side of the school, cutting their headlights to blend in with the darkness.

When I park near the entrance, Shig slides low in his seat, his hand clutching mine, and we wait. I spot dark shapes clinging to the shadows as a couple of officers scurry across the parking lot, taking up position behind the bushes.

My heart pounds out the minutes, the clock on the dash telling me we're past the promised thirty-minute mark.

What if she changes her mind? What if they don't come?

When headlights turn into the parking lot, I squeeze Shig's hand so tight it feels like his bones bend, but he doesn't protest.

"Be careful," he whispers as I push open the driver's side door.

Nodding, I let him go, feeling bereft as I leave the car alone.

I know the police are nearby, that Karen won't get out of here with Rin, but my pulse races with fear, worried about all the things that can go wrong.

When Scott's car pulls up next to me, I know immediately that something *has* gone wrong because he's alone, with no sign of Karen or Rin.

THE ARRANGEMENT

Scott pulls up next to me, stops, and rolls down his window. "Give me the money."

"Where's Rin?" I demand. "Karen promised I would be able to see Rin."

His lips twist into a bitter smile. "Karen promises a lot of things. You'll get a video call once I'm out of here." He sticks his arm out the window. "The check."

"Police!" shouts fill the air, and Scott's eyes widen in surprise. "Put your hands where we can see them, or we'll shoot!"

Slowly, Scott lifts his hands into the air. "This wasn't my idea!"

An officer rushes up to the car, another one on

the other side, both with guns trained on Scott. "Where's the kid?"

"I dropped them off at the Happy Palace down the street," he says quickly. "They're in the play center."

Turning, I dash back to my car and leap behind the wheel, tires squealing as I slam on the gas.

Shig grabs the handle above the window. "What's going on?"

"She sent Scott alone." I grip the steering wheel so hard my knuckles ache. "They're at Happy Palace."

"We should wait for the police," he cautions, but I ignore him.

Rin needs me, and the police will be close behind.

I don't slow down until I take the turn into the parking lot in front of Happy Palace and park out of sight of the play center.

When I fling open my door, Shig follows, and I don't try to argue for him to stay in the car. Sirens sound off in the distance, coming on fast, but I refuse to wait for them to arrive. They might spook Karen into running, though she won't get far without a car.

The warm smell of fried potatoes and grease wafts out on a warm breeze as I yank open the door and stride past the checkout counter, my eyes sweeping the fast-food restaurant. An elderly couple sits in a booth off to the right, and teenagers fill the booth in the corner, but no Karen.

Heart in my throat, I hurry to the back, to the place where Shig and I shared our first meal together.

A wall of windows offers a view of the play center with its colorful jungle gym and tube slides, and I spot Rin peering out of one of the round, fishbowl windows near the top. Karen stands below, hands on her hips, and even through the glass, I hear her shouts for Rin to come down.

Wrenching open the glass door, I storm inside.

"Daddy!"

Rin's shrill voice cuts through Karen's angry shouts, and my ex whips around, her eyes narrowing on me. "I should have known better than to trust Scott to get things right. He's almost as incompetent as you."

"It's over, Karen." I walk past her to the slide nearest Rin. "Come on, baby, we're going home."

Rin scrambles down the tube to the slide, coming down headfirst in their eagerness to leave.

"What about Scott?" Karen demands. "Is he out in the parking lot?"

"No, he's with the police." Shig leans out the door to the play center and calls, "We're back here! Rin is safe!"

Karen tosses her hair, her tail snapping with annoyance. "You called the police? They can't arrest me for spending time with my own child."

"Yes, they can," Shig tells her as I catch Rin and lift them into my arms. "You're going to jail for kidnapping."

"You can't do that," she scoffs, then backs away as police flood into the play center. Turning, she stares at me. "You can't press charges. I'm Rin's mother."

"I *am* pressing charges," I tell her as I cuddle Rin close. "You went too far this time. You and your mate are going away to prison. And once the insurance investigators link those wires on the porch to Scott, you'll be facing arson charges, too."

"You can't do this!" she shrieks and lunges toward me.

I take a step back, but the police catch her before she gets far.

"You can't do this to me, Juro!" she yells as she fights their restraint.

Looking away, I press Rin's head to my shoulder and cover their ear to block the sounds of Karen's arrest.

Yule arrives with a flurry of snow that blankets the city in silence, and we spend the morning opening presents and eating cake, much to Deka's and Rin's delight.

We had spent the last two days in and out of the police station, filing reports and making sure Karen didn't somehow wiggle out of her arrest. Unsurprisingly, Scott turned against her for a reduced sentence, making sure she went away for a long time.

Every moment I was home, Rin clung to me and even slept between Shig and me at night. Shig didn't protest, knowing I needed the closeness every bit as much as Rin.

Shig hired a repairman to fix the lock on the window and added a security system that dings every time a window or door is opened. It gives me peace of mind while aggravating Senichi and his early morning escapes from the house. But he doesn't complain beyond a grumble, and I catch him checking the security panel more than once to make sure it's on.

Presents, though, seem to be the prod Rin needs

to leave my side, and they rip into them alongside Deka.

I smile at their excitement over the toys Shig and I picked out at Holly King Field and laugh when Senichi presents Rin with a bucket filled with mittens to replace all the ones they keep losing.

When Shig pulls out a large, rectangle box and hands it to Senichi, his eyes widen in surprise before he rips into it with the kids' help.

"Seriously?" he looks from the new stereo system to us. "This must have cost a fortune."

While not quite that much, it wasn't cheap, but Shig and I agreed he deserved it after all the help he's provided in looking after the kids.

"There's a bass, too, but you don't get that until you move downstairs," Shig tells him.

Senichi strokes the box, though he doesn't open it. He probably doesn't want to risk one of the kids damaging it.

"There's one more." I lean forward to hand him an envelope.

His brows pinch together as he carefully sets the box behind him—out of reach of the kids—and tears the envelope open. A flush creeps up my cheeks as I watch him pull out the piece of paper. I feel way too old to be giving someone a handwritten coupon as a gift, but Shig said Senichi would like it.

Senichi stares at the white rectangle, his eyes wide in disbelief, before his head snaps up, and he stares at me. "Really? You're going to teach me to drive?"

"If you wan—"

I break off as Senichi flings himself across the wrapping paper-littered floor to hug me.

Then, he jerks back, pink staining his cheeks and his ears red as he looks away. "I mean, that's cool. Thanks." He glances at his uncle. "Do I get to drive the sports car?"

"We'll see." Shig gives him a stern frown. "But if you want your own car, you'll have to cover the insurance and gas."

"I will." Senichi stares down at the coupon once more. "When do we start? Can we go now?"

He half rises, but Shig plants his foot on Senichi's knee, keeping him down. "Tomorrow will be soon enough. We have dinner to make, candles to light, and a couple of Yule logs to burn."

"Right." Senichi catches Deka trying to open his stereo box and rolls his sibling away. "I'll be right back."

Grabbing the box and clutching the coupon, he stands and scurries toward his room.

"Daddy." Rin pats my knees, eyes wide and shining. "Are there more presents?"

"Haven't you opened enough?" Bending, I grab them and smack kisses all over their soft cheeks while they giggle and squirm. "There's a present!" Kiss, kiss. "And there's a present!"

"Stop!" Rin shoves at my face.

"Why don't you guys change into snow clothes, and we can go out to build snowmen?" Shig suggests.

I release Rin, who scampers off to change, but Deka stops in front of me and stares with wide eyes.

"What do you need, honey?" I ask.

With a quick glance at Shig, Deka presents their cheek. "I want kisses, too."

Chest tight with happiness, I bend forward and plant a big kiss on their cheek.

Deka beams and runs toward their bedroom. "Rin, I got kisses, too!"

"They like you," Shig murmurs.

The happiness that fills me feels too much for my body to contain.

"What about me?" Shig prods, and when I turn to him, he presents his cheek. "I want kisses, too."

Laughing, I pull him in and plant a sloppy one on him. "There you go."

He gives me a considering look, then offers his other cheek, and I dutifully kiss that one as well.

Sighing with contentment, he leans against me. "This is the best present I could have asked for to welcome in the new year."

I hug him close, loving the way he fits against my body. "Me, too."

Shig is the best gift I could have received, and it fills me with so much love and happiness that he didn't give up at my initial rejection, that he stuck it out and helped me realize what I needed and wanted from a partner.

The fact we're mates is just the bow on top of this gift, and I can't wait to cherish him for the rest of our lives together.

EPILOGUE

"Are you ready to go back to school tomorrow?" Shig asks as he walks out of the master bathroom after getting ready for bed.

"Not at all." I glance at him in the mirror over the dresser as he rubs his hair dry, a towel slung low around his waist. After we mated, he stopped using the hall bath and getting dressed in there, and I didn't realize before then that he was taking my comfort into consideration.

We've grown closer over the last few days, more comfortable as we learn how we fit together. This relationship happened so fast, so unexpectedly, but now, it feels like we've always been here, existing in each other's space.

Rin finally returned to their own bed tonight, and while I still have moments of panic that they'll disappear again, I'm glad to have the room back to just us. It's the one place in the house where we can be together without the watchful eyes of the kids.

Shig joins me at the dresser, leaning past to grab the brush he keeps on top, and holds it out to me. "Brush my tail?"

"With pleasure." I take the brush from him, and he lies down on the bed, his arms pillowed beneath his head.

This has become one of my favorite parts of our evening ritual, and I settle on the bed next to his hip, running the brush down his fluffy black tail.

He sighs, his whole body relaxing as I work out the knots left by his shower.

"Are you sure Hana is okay with picking up both kids?" he frets.

My nanny overcame her cold, caught up on her schoolwork, and asked when she could return to work. I was happy to have her back, even if I hope to not need her as much soon.

I stroke the brush over Shig's tail. "She's happy for the raise, and Rin and Deka entertain each other. She'll be fine."

"When does your teaching assistant start work?" he mumbles drowsily.

"Not until next week." I lift his tail to get the underside, and his hips shift restlessly. "Long nights until then, but once they're trained, I'll be able to start leaving after the final bell."

"I'm hiring a paralegal," he announces. "I should have done it a while ago, but I wanted to prove myself first."

"Isn't winning all those cases proof enough?" I tease. "Or did you buy this house by losing?"

A smile fills his voice. "Hush, you. I wanted people to know I wasn't just winning because my parents gave me a good helper."

I move the brush toward the base of his tail. "Does hiring a paralegal mean you'll be bringing less work home at night?"

"Mmm." He shifts again, the towel loosening around his waist. "Hopefully, but there will still be nights where I'm prepping until late."

"I'll have to come visit you in your new office, then." Setting the brush aside, I hook a finger into the edge of his towel. "All the way down in the basement."

Construction officially started the day after Yule, despite not having the garage fully cleared out, and walls were already up. Soon, Senichi will be moving down there, Rin will get their own room, and Shig will have a dedicated place to lock up his files.

His hips lift, letting the towel slip out from under him. "It's such a long trek. I'll have to reward you for your efforts."

"Oh?" I smooth a hand over one perfectly round ass cheek. "What kind of reward?"

He lifts into my touch, his tail swishing out of the way. "What do you want?"

Bending over him, I breathe in his freshly showered scent. "Open your legs."

Shig's legs part in an instant, and I murmur my appreciation. Thanks to him, I'm more confident now in asking for what I desire, and his openness to letting me explore leaves me humbled. He never demands sex, and never gets angry when I don't want him to pleasure me, which makes my desire to touch him burn all the hotter.

He's proven time and again that he accepts me exactly as I am, giving me the confidence to do what I want, which is to please him in every way possible.

Shifting, I move between his legs, spreading his cheeks to expose his sweet entrance. Head dipping, I lick the delicate ring of muscles, and his hips twitch before he stills. Gentle and slow, I lick and suck until he loses hold of his self-control and moans into the mattress, pressing himself back against me.

I wiggle the tip of my tongue at his center, pushing past the tight clench of his body.

He gasps sharply at the invasion, and I lick deeper, tasting the deepest part of him.

His tail caresses the side of my face, then curls around my shoulders as I take my time, working him until he's soft and slippery before I breach him with my fingers, seeking out the tight bundle of nerves that make him cry out and buck beneath me.

He rocks against my fingers as he mumbles unintelligibly into the mattress, and I reach between his legs, past the soft weight of his balls, to find his cock hard and weeping.

I stroke him from both sides, reveling in his moans and the way he unabashedly gives in to his pleasure. Watching him makes me hard, but it's a distant desire, and one I don't feel the need to take care of, not with Shig moaning and coming undone in my hands.

Shig's tail quivers, his muscles going taut, and I sweep my thumb over his leaking cock while rubbing his prostate to push him over the edge.

He cries out, shaking beneath me as he tightens

around my fingers and warm cum pumps into my hand.

Sagging back to the mattress, he gasps to catch his breath, and his voice shakes. "You're officially banned from my office, or I'll never get any work done."

I smile and nip his ass cheek. "You sure about that?"

His tail knocks me upside the head in reproach. "Only on Fridays."

I crawl up the bed to lie beside him. "And Mondays."

He slits his eyes open, but the glare falls short with his face still pink from his release. "You're getting far too comfortable with manhandling me."

I grin. "You like me manhandling you."

With a heavy sigh, he lifts himself sideways to sprawl boneless across my chest. "I do, but I'm going to plead the fifth."

"I don't think that works when you've already answered," I whisper against the top of his head.

He lifts a limp hand to cover my mouth. "Shush. I'm the lawyer here, not you."

I smile against his fingertips. "Thank you, Shig."

He lifts his head to pop his chin on my chest. "For what?"

"For everything." My eyes skim over his beautiful face. "I didn't realize how lonely I was until you swept into my life."

"Then, you should be thanking Sen for being a problem student," he teases. "Otherwise, we may never have met."

I cup his face. "I'm being serious."

"I know." He turns his head to kiss my palm. "I'm thankful, too. You weren't the only one lonely. It was Fate that brought us together at just the moment we both needed each other the most."

Sitting up, I kiss him, reconfirming our mate bond. I'll never get tired of that moment when we fit together perfectly, or the sweet gasp Shig gives every time, as if he's struck with the same amazement I am that, out of everyone in the world, we found each other.

Today, tomorrow, through hard times and good, we'll be together, and that knowledge makes everything worth it.

ABOUT THE AUTHOR

Sophie O'Dare is the alter ego of paranormal and sci-fi author Lyn Forester.

She loves writing stories about guys falling in love with each other and all the shenanigans that go along with romance!

www.SophieODare.com

REVIEWS

"This is an amazing coming of age story. There are authors that you know you can depend on to fill certain reading desires you may have. You know who to go to if you want a strong heroine or an action-packed story, sexy times or teenage angst. When you pick up a book by Lyn Forester you know that you are going to be transported into another world."

— Amazon Reviewer for *You to Me*

"I loved this novella. A sorta enemies to lovers story with lots of miscommunications and surprises. I'm not sure how Warren turned out to be such a nice guy coming from his terrible family but it was easy to see the damage inflicted on him. He couldn't see his own value and trust was nonexistent. Roman was pure Alpha but truly awful in the romance department. Together they are a hot delight!"

— Amazon Reviewer for *Bad With Love*

"WARNING: DON'T START BEFORE BED!!! I stayed up way too late to finish this book. I love how Lyn's characters are multi-dimensional and the world building is unique and complex. She doesn't disappoint with this next installment in the Tails x Horns series. If you love romance, give this book a try...even if you have never done MM romance before. It was absolutely stunning."

— Amazon Reviewer for *Just Not You*

Printed by Libri Plureos GmbH in Hamburg, Germany